TWO TURTLE DOVES

A Christmas Anthology

Sarah-Jane Fraser

To Lisa, Alex, Karen and Holly.

CONTENTS

A PARTRIDGE IN A PEAR TREE

A Christmas Novel

'Oh to be a pear tree - any tree in bloom!
With kissing bees singing of the
beginning of the world!'

- ZORA NEALE HURSTON

THEIR EYES WERE WATCHING GOD, 1937

CHAPTER 1

A waft of cinnamon and spice drifts over, distracting me from stuffing some golden envelopes. Seeking the source of the delectable scent, I peer around a pile of leafy garlands and through a cluster of twiggy trees covered in twinkly lights. Amber is back from the coffee run.

'You're just in time for the weekly team briefing. Apparently, there's an update on the Christmas gala dinner.'

As she searches for a clear spot to deposit the stack of cardboard drinks trays, I whip some boxes of lights out of the way. I'm halfway through getting the old decorations checked over for the annual Winter Wonderland fund-raising gala dinner and the inventory has spilled *everywhere* causing the events office to host a forest even Narnia would be envious of.

'Holly, you should have seen the place.' Amber untwirls a huge scarf. 'The café had all the new seasonal flavours in so I decided to go off-piste. I thought it'd help get us in the mood.'

'I love this time of year when it gets all festive

everywhere.' Pushing back on my wheelie chair with a flourish, my blonde curls flick over my shoulder. 'I'll help you carry them through to the board room.'

Sweeping up my Christmas themed notebook and half of the drinks, I smile. I'm armed with an event planner's two most vital weapons, stationery and coffee. *Look out world. I'm coming.*

Passing along the labyrinth of corridors, suddenly I'm forced to flatten against a wall. A couple of my colleagues from the R and D team bowl out of the director's office and stalk past me, distracted and huddled together muttering, their faces blotchy and red. They don't register my presence and miss my commiserating expression.

Deborah, the managing director, *dictator more like*, has clearly been up to her usual trick of upsetting people; all in the name of upholding the company's values. Not wanting to interfere, lest I ire Deborah any further, I carry on my journey through the maze of corridors. The precious coffee hasn't spilt, perhaps that's a good omen.

It's not.

Amber pushes open the boardroom door with her bottom. Other than the company logo, a huge monogrammed 'MYT', fixed to the wall, the room is dull and bare, with only a wall-mounted screen and a square of tables surrounded by chairs. I miss my grotto of Christmas joy. When I started here three years ago I'd expected more pizazz from one of the leading software firms in the country; this place is severely lacking in beanbag chairs, let alone the indoor slides that might be found in Silicon Valley.

I place the cups on the table and look over to Amber. 'You didn't swap Deborah's drink for a festive special, did you? I mean, she's hard enough work even when she has got her extra hot, double shot, skinny latte.'

Amber juts out her jaw. 'I thought she'd like the change.'

'She won't. She likes things just-so. Did you really not get her one?'

Amber shakes her head and her cheeks flush pink, a shade which clashes with her auburn tresses.

Crap. 'You'd better go and try to make one before she gets here. Put it in one of these cups or she'll notice.'

It's too late. Deborah sweeps into the office and scowls at the large table. 'Where are the printed agendas?' Her sharp nose and cruel beady eyes give her the appearance of a vulture, which her pointy manicure does nothing to diminish. Sometimes I imagine her swallowing the bones of employees whole.

'I thought I'd ping it up on to the big screen, save the trees...' Amber's voice peters out under Deborah's withering glare.

'I don't pay you to think, I pay you to do as I ask. Go and print them off.'

Amber scuttles away as a knot tightens in my chest. Amber started an internship with us after she left college this summer and much to my regret, we hardly pay her a bean. And no one deserves Deborah's wrath, no matter how much they earn.

Deborah eyes the cups steaming on the table. When it comes to the Christmas gala, she's always even more irascible than usual. Trying to appease her in the run up to it is a complete bloody nightmare. In order to protect the peppy intern, I have to intervene. 'We got you a festive coffee but I can ask Amber to make you a proper one with those organic Hawaiian beans if you'd prefer.'

Deborah purses her lips. 'She'll probably get it wrong. I'll take my chances with one of these.' Her spikey nails capture a cup and place it at the head of the table.

The agendas are still warm from the photocopier as Amber lays them out by each of the chairs.

'I thought this was supposed to be a tech firm?' She mutters to me, rolling her eyes at the abundance of paper Deborah insists we use.

As she places Deborah's copy down by her cup, Amber's hand falters. There's some garish red lipstick smeared along the rim. 'Everything alright with the coffee?' There's a hint of hesitation in her voice.

'It'll do.'

A small smile twitches at the corners of Amber's mouth as she finishes preparing the meeting room. The tension seeps away from my shoulders; at least one minor crisis has been averted.

Once a representative from each department is present, Deborah stands by the screen with her arms crossed, clutching the remote control, her knuckles blanching. 'The Christmas gala dinner is only twenty days away and Montague wants an overhaul.'

A low rumble goes around the room. My heart thunders into overdrive. *What the actual-?* This is the first year I've been allowed to lead on the event and now, suddenly, there's going to be a change, worse than that, an *overhaul*. And just when I've almost finished with the confirmation details too, dammit.

Deborah continues, 'His granddaughter's studying art at college and in a move to make the company more family-focused, he's decided to showcase her class's talents at the event. So, our annual fundraiser will no longer be a glamorous, sumptuous, quality, festive extravaganza, the crowning glory of our events calendar and most anticipated evening of the whole year but instead, will be a glorified parents' evening.'

Amber starts to say something but Deborah glowers and she shuts her mouth. Very wise.

With a click of the remote, a presentation springs up on the screen. 'The Twelve Days of

Christmas,' announces Deborah. 'Each student will be artistically interpreting a day and it's our job to make it look not shit.' Deborah pauses. 'Actually, it's your job.' She fixes me with another trademark steely glare and continues.

My coffee sits untouched, going cold in front of me while I studiously scribble notes for the rest of the meeting.

'Why the change? I hear you ask.' Deborah's eyes travel the room, flashing. 'Montague's vision is to move in line with STARS, his chosen charity.'

Montague Young set up MYTechnology from scratch about forty years ago. Nearly always seen in a cardigan patched at the elbows, his brain is incredible and he's refreshingly kind for such a successful business man. He's an adorable geek really, but sadly I don't answer to him. To everyone's lasting regret he employed shrewd and intimidating Deborah to be director. She's viciously competitive and completely intolerant of disobedience.

Scanning her notes, Deborah reads them out in a monotone. 'Nurturing talent and celebrating the individual from a grass roots level.' She tosses her paperwork to the side. 'And he said something about valuing families and relationships to build a brighter future, or some other bull. Hence the granddaughter. Anyway, Holly, your first job is to reprint the confirmation details to reflect the new theme.' Holding up a finger to the Finance Department's representative, she adds, 'The Winter Wonderland decorations already in store can be incorporated into the new scheme so our losses will be minimal. The budget must stay on track. Any questions? No? Good. Jump to it then.'

Deborah sweeps from the room. My colleagues filter out while I read over my notes. My huge workload has become monumental.

'I'll get the minutes typed up straight away.' Amber bounces out of the room.

'Good idea.' I get up and walk slowly back to my office. 'I love this time of year,' I repeat quietly, bracing myself for the impending chaos.

CHAPTER 2

Back in our office, I glance at the detailed working schedule I'd made for the gala; an almost minute by minute plan for the event. It had been painstakingly created over the last few weeks but with this sudden change of scope I need to start again. Stopping myself from plunging it in the shredder, in case I can borrow some specifics, I place it to one side with a sigh. Today's target was to get all the confirmation details sent out to the guests but, adorned with the old theme, they're now obsolete.

I call over to Amber, 'I'm going to need your help please.'

Amber doesn't strictly answer to me, but Deborah never organises much for her to do, so I'm trying to take her under my wing. She's brimming with talent, it's such a waste. Deborah just thinks of her as a bit of cheap labour. To give us both a bit more credibility, I started calling her my assistant, but now I feel even more responsible for her.

'I'm all yours, Deborah hasn't assigned me much yet.'

'She will. You'll get there.' I give my most encouraging smile.

'I've been here five months and I'm still just the general factotum on coffee and minutes duty. I can do so much more than that.'

'We all have to start somewhere and once you've got Deborah's trust you'll be flying.'

'But I've got all these ideas-'

I hold up a hand. 'I know, but there's no rush. A softly-softly approach will get you onside much better.' I should know, I've been biding my time for the last three years.

When I applied to work at MYTechnology, I knew hard work would be on the cards. However, I hadn't fully realised that it would mean the death of my social life, let alone my love life, and that even then my sacrifices wouldn't guarantee my aspirations.

I've spent my adult life so far working towards being a successful events manager and have several years of experience in the field before coming here. Now I'm events co-ordinator in title alone. The trust of the company director still eludes me. The trouble is Deborah started out in events too, and wants to retain managerial control. Basically, she is trying to do two full-time jobs at the same time. Trying to extricate the department from her clutches is nigh on impossible. At least this year she told me I'm leading the organisation of her hallowed Christmas extravaganza. Not that you can tell by the amount of autonomy she actually gives me, seemingly everything still needs to be run by her.

'I don't think she likes me,' sighs Amber.

'She doesn't like anyone, but it doesn't matter. She's our boss, she's not here to like us. Now, please help me destroy this set of joining instructions. I've got to create new ones that reflect the new theme and they can't get mixed up.'

'Why are they called *joining instructions* anyway, surely people don't need to be instructed to join a party, a simple "show up at this time" would probably suffice. I could just ping them an email saying *yo, party over heeere!*' Amber gives a little dance in her chair.

I rub my temple. I'm not sure what's harder, working for the most highly-strung director in the country, or stopping the Tigger-like intern from self-destructing through naivety and enthusiasm.

'Joining Instructions. It's just what they're called. Everyone in the trade uses the term.'

'And, why are we destroying these?'

'It would look unprofessional if we sent out the old design. We're inviting our most important clients.'

'But these are lovely.' Amber fingers the luxurious embossed card.

'Thanks, but they've got to go. Can you carry on with getting rid of them while I sort the new ones?'

My background in graphic design always

comes in handy whenever we have marketing or events paraphernalia to produce. The Christmas gala dinner is something I started working on in the summer but this last-minute change of theme has wreaked havoc on my meticulous designs. Zoning out from Amber's chattering about upcycling the invites into hamper stuffing, I mock-up a couple of new options. At least all the pertinent details can remain the same. After an hour of tinkering with them, I send the drafts over to Deborah with apprehension, hoping the new concept passes muster.

Of course Deborah insists on muscling in on the design process. I know my boss isn't going to pass the gala organising baton without some compromise or sharing on both sides but I didn't anticipate it would be so hard to dislodge her vice-like grip. I've got this funny notion though, that if I can show her what a bloody good job I can do of it all, she'll finally back off.

While I wait to hear back on the design I fire off some emails regarding a launch event for some new software in the spring. There's always something to keep me busy, always some other plates to keep spinning.

After Deborah makes some negligible tweaks she forwards the designs on to Montague, who has ultimate say over the finished product, and by the end of the morning, the new version is finessed.

Interlocking my fingers, I raise my arms over

my head, and loosen my neck, stretching it from side to side. Not allowing any more time for a break, I pluck up my phone and dial the printer. While pinching the bridge of my nose, I explain the situation, breathing a sigh of relief when he tells me they can reprint them today.

'Thanks, Mark. I'll send the file over now and if you can print and get them couriered over by four then I'll still make the evening post.'

'You'll owe me one, Holly.'

Dryly, I reply, 'Yes, that's two I owe you now. I'm keeping a tally. I'll make sure you get a deluxe hamper this year.'

'If it gets to three you'll have to go out for a drink with me to say thanks.'

'There's more chance you'll get invited to the charity gala!'

'I'll hold you to that.'

With another thanks, I hang up the phone.

From behind a stack of boxes, Amber peeks over with great interest. 'All sorted?'

'Yes. The printer's happy to rush our order through as a priority today, so we should make the deadline.'

'That's very generous of him.' Amber sings out, teasing.

'We put a lot of business his way, *and* we are paying him.' I realise there's a defensive shrill to my voice.

'But still, sounds like he does you a lot of favours...'

Balling up some scrap paper, I throw it at Amber. 'It's a completely professional relationship.' I try to set my features to stern but laughing ruins the effect.

A buzz cuts through the fun and I grab at the phone. Deborah's voice snarls down the line. 'Holly, we need a face to face. My office. Now.'

'I'll be there right away,' I say.

In one move I gather up my notebook, a pen and the Christmas gala file. 'Got to dash, can you send the email for me?'

'To the printers?'

'Yep, attach the document entitled "Twelve Days", and mark it as urgent. Thanks.' I run from the room without a backward glance.

The sound of Deborah's simpering voice oozes through her partially shut door and, not wanting to interrupt the phone call, I loiter outside catching some of the conversation.

'That's such a shame, Mr Perdreau... I shall see to it personally... I look forward to working with him. Have a wonderful trip...'

As the receiver clicks back into the cradle, I enter the room.

'That was the owner of Cherrywell Manor. He's going away for some winter sun and has left his son in charge of all matters relating to the gala.'

'What's his name? I should meet with him to get him up to speed about our plans so far.'

'Mr Perdreau has asked that *I* speak with Lawrence. He wants to be sure the event is in safe hands.'

My heart starts to skitter. *But surely it's my job?* My big chance to prove myself is withering away. *Be assertive and professional, Holly, you can do this.* 'Wouldn't it be better if he discusses things with me?'

Deborah remains stony quiet. Despite my resolve, I start to witter, 'You do want me to lead on the event still, don't you?'

'Of course, you can't shirk the responsibility now.'

'I wasn't trying to...' I stop myself from prattling. 'Could we discuss the workforce for the event. I've been looking at the running schedule and I think we need a team of-'

'A team? You've got Amber, haven't you?'

'Yes, but it's a pretty big undertaking so I thought if we had a team of assistants for the set up-'

'I've never needed a *team*. I managed perfectly well with just you last year. Besides, it's simply not in the budget. Are you sure you're up to this?'

'Yes. I didn't mean-'

Raising a finger, Deborah interrupts again. 'Next you need to sort out the abomination of a menu that this *reimagining* of the theme has caused. Now, don't just stand there, make some notes-'

'Did you send the email okay?' I ask Amber as I

return to my desk.

'Yeah, he replied saying it was received.' Amber's sitting by the shredder emptying the last golden envelopes. 'What was the panic about?'

'Urgh, menu change. Deborah was freaking out. Apparently, we can't serve chicken when part of the theme is three French hens.'

Amber tilts her head to the side. 'I'd change it to an all vegan menu.'

'We're going for lamb shank in a cranberry jus.'

'But vegan's good for everyone.'

'I know but Deborah barely concedes to a vegetarian option, she's not going to entertain the idea of vegan.'

'But what about accommodating people's dietary requirements? Surely-'

'Deborah's answer would be that they could just not eat. She doesn't eat, she doesn't really understand why other people need to.'

'But how does she keep going?'

I sigh. 'A healthy diet of coffee and bitterness. Now, let's crack on before we give her anything else to be bitter about.'

CHAPTER 3

'The reprinted joining thingys are here.' Amber bounds into the office with a box.

Glancing at my watch, I say, 'Okay, we have exactly eighty-four minutes to stuff two hundred of them into those gold envelopes, or we'll miss the post.'

'Easy.' Amber shrugs.

Wrenching the cardboard tab emits a zipping sound. As I lift up the flaps of the box the smell of freshly printed paper seeps out and a shimmer reflects from within. My hands tremble as they reach inside.

'What the...'

'They look good,' Amber says eagerly, peeking over the side.

'Krampus!' I exclaim it like a swear word. I'm thinking Shit-The-Bed but I'm saying Krampus, but that's just me, part of my professional façade means no swearing at work.

'What?'

'It's the wrong design. Deborah wanted black and silver but Montague wanted gold. Which file did you send?'

'The one you said, Twelve Days-'

I knuckle my forehead. 'I must have told you the wrong one. Deborah's trusting me on this and I'm blowing it before it's even begun.' Moving to my computer I start to search the sent box. 'Here it is.' I click to open the document.

'Wait,' says Amber. 'It's my fault. There were two files. One was called "Twelve Days" and the other was called "Twelve Days - use this one". I didn't know which one you meant so I chose that one.' Her voice starts to falter. 'It said *use this one*. I knew there was a deadline and I didn't want to have to keep asking you stuff all the time.'

Count to five. Breathe. I've definitely read somewhere breathing helps with stress. I exhale steadily through my nose. 'It's okay, you weren't to know. They were shared files, Deborah was editing too and she changed the name. That was her favourite design so she changed the title to "use this one", trying for some less than subliminal control I guess, but Montague got the final say and he plumped for the gold version.'

'Which was just called "Twelve Days" like you said?'

Bobbing my head, I try not to let Amber sense my exasperation.

'I'm sorry. What are we going to do?'

Straightening my shoulders, I proclaim, 'I'm calling in that third favour.'

Curling and uncurling an errant piece of sparkly ribbon around my fingers, I wait for the man at the printers to pick up.

'Hi, Mark, it's Holly again.'

'Did everything arrive okay?'

'Oh yes, thanks. But there's been a slight problem, more a problemette.'

'How can I help?'

How do I put this? I suck in my breath through my teeth, as I try to find the least embarrassing words. 'The wrong file was sent. I need you to print them again please. Urgently.'

'I can do it right now, but you're not going to make the post, you know. I can't get them to you for you to process them in time.'

I can't miss the deadline. Think...think... 'Would it be okay if I come over to you? I could put them in the envelopes as they come off the line and then I can post them from there.'

Mark's inhale is audible. 'It's a bit...'

'I know it's unconventional, but I'm desperate here. Deborah will go through the roof if I miss the post today. Please.'

'I was going to say it's a bit of a mess here but you're welcome. There's a post office with a late collection around the corner.'

'You're a lifesaver, thank you. I'll send the document now.' My finger hit send as I spoke.

'That's four favours. So, you owe me two drinks now.'

'See you soon, Mark.' Hanging up, I rise from

my desk. 'Come on, Amber, let's go!'

Amber doesn't need to be asked twice. She's already slinging her scarf around her neck. We each grab a box of empty envelopes and hightail it out of the office.

The MYTechnology headquarters takes up several floors of a large concrete office block, which is surrounded by other similar towering monstrosities all hailing from the sixties. The road below is a typical city street; buzzing with people and vehicles rushing around. The sight of the bleak boxy greyness usually erodes my soul but I don't have time to reflect on the depressing construction right now. Instead, I focus on hailing a cab and soon we're speeding through the streets to the printer's headquarters in an older part of the city.

'I think that Mark guy likes you.' Amber looks mischievous.

'I expect he's just being friendly.'

'Maybe, but maybe not! When did you last go on a date?'

When was that? 'It's been a while but I've been busy with work.'

'Tell me about it! I haven't been on a date for months. This job has virtually killed my social life.'

'Exactly, and there's so much to do. I really can't get side-tracked now.'

'What about when it's all sorted, after the

gala? You deserve a little love in your life, Holly.'

'Maybe. I can't risk all my hard work by getting distracted by some guy.' *That would be ridiculous. Wouldn't it?* In an attempt to change the subject, I say, 'We're here.'

We draw up to the top of a road banked by a raised railway, a paradigm of fine Victorian architecture. Nestled in the arches underneath the train track is a throng of small, independent businesses. The waft of hops from a nearby craft brewery snakes through the air as we walk along searching for Repro365, our printers.

'Here it is,' calls out Amber, bounding up to the entrance.

A blond-haired man in his late twenties opens the door. 'Let me help you with that,' he insists as he unburdens Amber from her cargo.

Catching the door with my shoulder, I push my way in behind. We fill the small space, mainly with the sheer volume of mustard yellow scarf Amber's unwrapping. There's a gentle humming mechanical sound as the printing machinery purrs away in the background.

'You must be Mark,' says Amber.

He grins back at her. 'Guilty. And you're Holly?'

'Nope that's me,' I speak up from behind the curtain of scarf that Amber's unwinding.

'Oh, hi.' Mark glances uncertainly between us. 'Nice to put a face to a name.'

'This is Amber, my assistant. Thanks so much

for bailing us out.'

'You're welcome. MYTechnology was one of my earliest customers when I was just a start up. They'll always have a special place in my heart.'

'Finding you was one of the first things I accomplished when I started.' I can't help but smile at the memory. It was the very first time I was able to assert a little bit of myself into the role. Not quite first and last, but almost.

'Can I get you a drink?'

As Amber replies with an 'I'd love a coffee, please,' I give a firm, 'No, thank you. We're on a tight deadline here.'

'I've cleared you a space at the back, you can process the invites from there.' Mark moves to the rear and indicates to a table.

'They aren't invitations they're *joining instructions*.' Amber makes air quotes and giggles.

Mark's eyes twinkle. 'Joining instructions? What's a joi-'

'Can we just call them the confirmation details and move on please?' Exhaling through my nose, I pretend to glower at Amber who returns a dazzling smile.

Mark smirks as he follows our exchange, before heading out of a door in the back wall.

'He seems nice,' says Amber with a suggestive tone.

I raise my eyebrows. 'Let's crack on, we aren't here to socialise.'

Just as I finish setting up a processing production line, Mark comes back. After passing a steaming mug of coffee to Amber, he turns to me. 'Anything else I can do for you?' His intense blue eyes look between Amber and I.

'We're already making a huge imposition, I'd hate to ask anything else.'

'Try me.'

'You wouldn't mind sticking on the stamps, would you?'

With a chuckle Mark settles himself at the end of the line.

'I think the tally's now up to five favours. That's got to be worth at least a meal, if not dinner, then lunch,' pipes up Amber.

Flicking my foot out to nudge Amber's ankle, I have to swallow a wince as I catch my shin on the table leg. Amber's eyes dance with mirth but she's sensible enough not to continue on that tack.

'Your charity event is in support of STARS?' Mark holds up one of the cards.

'Yep, we do it every year. They're a small charity who-'

'No need to tell me.' Mark says kindly. 'I'm very familiar with their work.'

'Really? How come?' *Amber!* Such a nosy parker.

'I wouldn't be here without them. They helped me get my qualifications.'

While Amber grills him further, my brain starts whirring, like the printing press juddering in the background.

CHAPTER 4

Working as a team, it doesn't take long to process the new batch of confirmation details and soon we have two boxes full of them.

'The nearest post office is just in the next road, isn't it?' I examine a map on my phone.

'Yep.' Mark squints at the clock. 'You've got fifteen minutes until they shut.'

'Why don't we post these and then go for a celebratory beverage?' suggests Amber, starting to wind her scarf on once more.

'I'd love to but we need to get back to the office,' I reply. *God, I sound boring. When did I become so dull?*

'The craft brewery next door is excellent, they have a little bar area at the front. Why don't I go and get a round in while you post them?' Mark looks like an eager puppy dog.

Amber is vigorously nodding her head. Maybe we don't *need* to get back.

'It'd be a shame for you to miss out on the best beer in the county,' encourages Mark.

'Okay. But just a half for me, thanks. See you in

a bit.'

It's starting to get dark outside and the Christmas lights reflect in the puddles left by a recent shower. Amber is almost squealing with delight as we scurry along the damp pavement, producing a constant stream of babble about how lovely Mark is. 'He seems scrummy. You should ask him out.'

'You know I've not got time for all that. Besides, I'm not sure he's right for me. And anyway, Deborah's got that rule about not mixing business with pleasure. I imagine it'd be frowned upon in the very least.'

'Really?'

'Yep, no intra-office relationships.' My mind flicks back to the couple in the corridor that morning and a pang of sadness creases my heart. Imagine having to choose between love and a career. Perhaps it's lucky I haven't got any love in my life, I try and console myself. At least I haven't had that dilemma.

'That's so... dated.'

'Deborah is old fashioned. I expect it's so that she's respected in a largely male world.'

'Surely no one has rules like that anymore? She needs to move with the times, or she'll find herself left behind.'

'Deborah will probably still be working for MYTechnology at the end of time. And she still won't have changed the rules about fraternising with co-workers.'

'But if you can't meet someone through work and you're at work *all* the time, how are you going to meet someone?'

'I'm not, apparently. Look, her rules have worked for her so far, she's not going to change them now.'

'Are you defending her?'

'It sounds like it, doesn't it?' My voice is flat.

Not wanting to confirm quite how on the nose Amber is with her questions about finding a guy, I try to end the subject. 'Here's the post office.'

A bell tinkles as we go in. Without a hiccup we drop off the envelopes ready for the last post of the day and then head back towards the craft brewery.

'Joining instructions- check!' sings Amber.

'At least we've hit one of Deborah's arbitrary non-negotiable deadlines.'

'Definitely time to celebrate.'

'Don't breathe a word of this at work.'

'I'm not stupid.' Amber rolls her eyes, 'Although Dastardly Debs could really do with letting her hair down, a beer might help...'

'Oh god, don't call her Debs. She'd fire you on the spot and that's before she found out about this detour. We'd better work late this evening to make sure we're up to speed.'

Amber huffs. 'Fair enough. But let's not talk about work while we're here, otherwise it still counts as working.'

When we arrive at the craft brewery we find

Mark chatting animatedly with the barman, his drink already a good way down the glass. Two half pints are waiting next to him.

'Mission accomplished?' he asks as we join him.

'Oh yes. Cheers!' Amber lifts up one of the beers and takes a swig.

After clinking glasses, I take a sip and the smooth citrusy taste rolls over my tongue.

I needed that.

Bemoaning that she's hot, Amber peels off the scarf again, scuffing my head as it flicks by. 'Oops, sorry!' Amber chuckles.

Mark's eyes sparkle as he watches her.

After setting my locks in order, I stand back a little, Amber's comments about dating ringing in my ears. *Maybe I should get back on the dating horse?* But Mark isn't the right guy to saddle up with. He's nice but I'm not feeling *it*. But it's been so long, maybe I wouldn't recognise *it* if it hit me in the face.

As Amber and Mark natter away about his ethical solutions for printing and some recently discovered environmental inks, I find myself smiling on the side-lines. Even if I'm not sure about myself, I can definitely recognise *it* for other people. A wicked plan brews in my head.

Checking that no one is watching, I reach over and knock Amber's scarf off the bar. It slithers to the floor. The barman catches my eye, looking curious. I give a wink and twitch my head in my colleague's direction. He replies with a nod and goes back to polishing a glass.

Noticing our drinks are empty, Mark offers, 'Another one?'

I look at my phone to check the time. 'Oh no, Deborah's been trying to get in touch. We've got to dash.'

Grabbing Amber by the elbow I usher her out of the brewery, shouting byes and thank yous as I go. We jump into a passing taxi and whizz up the street.

Filling the cab with a cloud of breath freshener and perfume, we try to disguise any lingering brewery scent.

'It's just here on the left,' I direct as we draw close to our building. I twist towards Amber. 'Let's go in and pretend that never happened. No mention of celebrating, or the brewery. Don't even talk about the re-prints. Everything has gone to plan and we're just returning from dropping the envelopes off perfectly in time for the post.'

Amber agrees, 'Nothing to see here.'

'Exactly.'

'Disapproving Debs doesn't need to know a thing!'

'Do you like living dangerously?' I laugh.

After paying, we exit the cab and I flick my expression to serious professional. I've worked hard to get where I am. And now I'm being trusted to take the reins on the most prestigious event of the year, I'm not going to risk every-thing by upsetting Deborah with one silly after-noon of larking around.

The shrill ring of the telephone on my desk echoes down the corridor. I know who that is. It somehow has a sharper pitch when it's Deborah on the other end.

'Hello.'

'What took you so long?'

'Hi Deborah, I'm just back from the post office. Everything's right on schedule.'

'I should hope so.'

Scrunching up my nose, I force myself to smile down the receiver in an attempt not to swear at my boss. That was as near a compliment as I could ever expect from the ice queen.

Glancing at the calendar on my desk, a big red circle shows there are only three weeks left until the winter gala, afterwards my boss's scrutiny might scale back a bit. Then the Met Office might declassify Storm Deborah to snowy showers ra-ther than full scale blizzard.

Picking my words carefully, I ask, 'Was there something we can do for you?' Somehow, I man-age not to laugh as Amber silently struts around the office impersonating Deborah in the back-ground. Scribbling in my jotter, I make some notes, feeling more and more like I'm Deborah's secretary. I *need* to assert myself in this process more. *Come on, Holly.*

As she pauses for breath, I pluck up the courage to say. 'I've had an idea for the gala.'

'I've left clear guidelines with you for what is required. This is an important event, you know.'

'It ties in with Montague's new brief.'

'Go on then, tell me.'

'I thought it would be good to have a short speech from someone who's benefited from STARS in the past. Give some insight into the amazing work they do. It might help make more donations on the night.'

'It's too late to find someone appropriate now. We wouldn't want some commoner whose only accolade is that they've scraped through some exams.'

God, she's a bitch. 'I don't think that's fair.'

'We'd need to get someone PR worthy. You know, in line with our company and values etcetera.'

'The person I was thinking of is one of our suppliers.'

'Send me the details. I'll think about it. And make sure you run any other ideas you have past me first. I need to make sure this is done right.' The phone line clicks off as Deborah hangs up.

I do a little victory shimmy in my seat. *I will break her down!*

CHAPTER 5

My insides feel all swirly like a shaken snow globe but that isn't stopping my determination to take control of the gala – *my gala*. I'm going to prove to Deborah that I'm more than capable. If I can finally wrestle the mantle from her, show her I can do a good job, then maybe she'll allow me more autonomy in the future. She must.

Nicola, Deborah's PA, gives me an encouraging smile as I approach the door.

Something on her computer screen is causing Deborah to frown and she doesn't look up when I enter.

Assuming a confidence and assertiveness that's entirely fabricated, I announce, 'I'm going to liaise with Lawrence Perdreau regarding the new theme this afternoon. I presume you're too busy to attend the meeting as well.' I'm getting antsy about how everything will pull together after the last-minute change of plan.

'Haven't you done that yet? Goodness, what have you been doing?' Deborah taps loudly on her keyboard.

SARAH-JANE FRASER

Err, what? The last time we spoke about it you implied you would make contact.

I pick my words carefully. 'Well, I-'

'No, don't answer that. Perhaps I should inform Cherrywell of the amendments after all. I have so much on my plate at the moment but we want to make sure it's done right.'

'I can do it. I want to do it.'

'Are you sure? Don't you have something else to be doing? Here in the office?' Deborah's attention is now wandering to the pages of an organiser she's whipping through.

'I just-'

'Goodness girl, stop milling around and do something. You're almost as useless as that temp.'

The demeaning comments sting like a slap.

'She's an intern.'

'What?' Deborah raises her head finally, searing me with her beady eyes.

'Nothing.' I swallow. If I can just survive this event then surely Deborah's tight grip of control would loosen. 'I'll set up a meeting and report back the outcome.'

'Well, of course,' replies Deborah, back to scrutinising her computer screen.

Nicola buzzes the intercom. 'Call for you.'

With a primp of her hair, Deborah reaches for the phone. 'Put them through.' With her hand hovering over the handset she turns to me and hisses, 'If you're so keen to shirk your duties you can go to that bloody college and see what abominations we're supposed to showcase. There's a meeting with the art teacher tomorrow. Nicola can give you the details.'

'Consider it done.' I start backing away, before Deborah can change her mind.

'I expect a full debrief Thursday morning.' Deborah's features crack into a smile and she reclines into her chair, putting the receiver to her ear. 'You're through to Deborah...'

'Absolutely,' I whisper as I spin on my heel. A shot of excitement skitters through me. Finally, I'm getting a chance to show what I'm made of.

After speaking with Nicola, I head straight to my desk. Firing off a quick email to Cherrywell Manor to confirm our meeting this afternoon, I then gather up my things.

Today, Amber's sequestered with the pay roll team so I make the journey by myself. Leaving the busyness of the city, I can feel the knots in my shoulders relax. As the horizon emerges and expands before me it feels like I'm escaping; like I'm uncurling from being cramped in a tight cage. While the countryside opens up around me, my gaze can finally stretch, my lungs expand, my spirits soar.

Cherrywell Manor is nestled in a patch of forest about an hour from the city centre. A sweeping gravel drive takes me to the front of the mansion. I kill the engine of my car and crane my neck up to take in the façade. The huge expanse of Georgian sash windows glint in the winter sun, while two large columns tower each side of the gargantuan wooden front door. I vaguely remember it from previous years but I'm usually so completely stressed by Deborah I've never really paused to appreciate it before. The property inspires a calm reverence.

Taking my time, I move up to the door and give it a firm knock before standing back off the step to wait.

The chilly breeze catches a loose tendril of my hair, playing with it while I wait. Gathering the unruly strands behind an ear, I climb the step again and clunk the heavy knocker. Nothing.

Hammering on the door with my fist I bellow out a, 'Hello?'

There's a crunch of feet on the gravel and I turn. The wind takes the opportunity to whip my hair out of any sort of control. Through my dancing locks, a man materialises with a faded cap pulled low over his face. I flash him a smile and swipe at my hair, trying to tame it.

'Can I help?' He looks perplexed.

I trail my eyes down his wax jacket, over dirty jeans to his wellies and then back up to his face, finally settling on some fresh stubble prickling his chin. Mmmm, the rugged type; this day is getting better and better.

'Yes please, I'm here from MYTechnology. I have a meeting with Mr Perdreau.'

'Have you been waiting long?'

'Not long.' Scanning the huge building again, I whisper, 'Am I using the right door?'

There's a warmth in his chuckle as he replies, 'Yes. I'm not sure where everyone is. Let's try the side entrance.'

'Thanks. I'm Holly by the way.'

'I'm Rory.' His face rumples into a nervous grin.

'Are you the gardener?'

'Something like that.' Rory pauses. It seems as if he's about to say something else but then changes his mind. 'Let me get Barnes for you.'

Rory leads me along the west side of the building and up to some French doors. He grasps an ornate metal handle which opens directly into the ballroom.

'It's warmer in here.' He holds the door for me. I squeeze past him, through the narrow space he's left, noting his earthy fragrance.

Stepping in to the grand room I look up, taking in the gilded duck egg blue panels on the towering walls, all the way up to the three chandeliers suspended from the ceiling. The sparkling glass hangs like a thousand icicles on a frosty morning.

'Absolutely stunning.'

'I'd say so.' Rory's reply comes from behind me.

He's still outside when I turn back to him.

'Wait in here, I'll be back soon.' He lifts up

a wellingtoned foot as if in explanation before closing the door and heading off.

My footsteps echo off the parquet as I move around surveying the beautiful decor.

'Uch-hum.' A deep cough resonates from an inner doorway and I twirl in surprise.

A tall man stands on the threshold, his chest puffs out filling his waistcoat, and his arms are clasped behind him. 'Can I ask what your business here is?'

After I explain everything to him, he gives me a kind smile and dips his head, revealing a shiny spot amongst his white pelt.

'I had not realised *Rory* had shown you in. That's not how it should be done. I can only apologise I did not greet you at the door when you called. I am Mr Barnes, the house manager, or butler, if you will.'

'Nice to meet you, Mr Barnes. Am I too early for my meeting with Mr Perdreau?'

'There has been a slight change of plan, did you not get the message?'

'No.'

'Mr Perdreau is indisposed and I have been instructed to represent him today.'

'Okay.' I tap my notebook. 'There's been a few changes to the original plan so I just wanted to pass these on. Ensure everyone's on board so it all goes smoothly.'

'Very good. Shall we start in here?'

Mr Barnes is extremely knowledgeable about the history of Cherrywell and is enthusiastic about the new plans. However, despite his warm manner, he moves at a glacial pace. There seems to be the occasional muffled wince but I can't be sure. He's so incredibly formal.

Having had a tour to review the new requirements, we move in to the entrance hall where Rory suddenly bursts through from a small door off the side. 'Ah, Barnes! I was starting to get worried about you.'

'*Rory*?' There's a funny edge to his voice, sounding a little uncertain.

'I was just looking for you to tell you that, Miss- er, that Holly was here and-'

Mr Barnes holds up a steady, calming hand. 'Everything is under control. Thank you.'

Rory straightens up. 'Of course, yes. Well, if you need me to do a tour of the grounds or anything, please let me know.' He seemed flustered, awkward. *Has he been searching for Mr Barnes the whole time? That's adorable.*

Confusion flashes across Mr Barnes's face but he's quick to compose himself.

'If it would please you, Miss Holly, then...' Mr Barnes doesn't finish his sentence, instead he wafts his hand towards Rory as if in resignation.

'That sounds great actually, yes please.'

'I think we have finished in the house, so Rory can take over from here. If there is anything else I can do to assist you then please let me know.' He gives a small, funny bow and stiffly moves off.

Intrigued, I look to Rory. He opens his mouth as if to say something but then shuts it again.

The silence has gone on a beat too long. 'So, the grounds?' I prompt.

His face breaks into a wide beam. 'Yes. Shall we?' He gestures to the front door and then marches off with long strides.

CHAPTER 6

R ory comes alive outside, showing me around the various terraces and gardens close to the house. His eyes spark with passion, his enthusiasm is infectious. I can't explain the instant affinity I feel towards the house and the grounds, there's an intuitive connection. Fresh ideas seem to leap into my mind and snuggle down, working so perfectly as if they were always meant to be.

'This would be ideal for the fireworks.' I survey a formal terrace. I flick through my notes to check a detail. 'It's not what Deborah had in mind though,' I mutter to myself.

Rory gives a knowing laugh. 'I'd forgotten you'd know *Deborah*.'

'She's my boss. I didn't realise you'd know her.'

'She's been coming here since Montague first started using the place for the gala. Used to liaise with the owner and now he's left it to his son to sort out while he gallivants in the Caribbean, so she's started harrying him instead.'

A smirk creeps across my face as I listen to Rory talk so candidly about our respective bosses.

'Don't hold back on my account, say what you really think,' I joke.

Rory gives me a coy smile. 'The owner's in The Bahamas as we speak - he's not going to hear me.'

'His son might.'

'He won't mind. Especially now Deborah's delegated the organisation to one of her colleagues.'

'That's me. She's working on a different project and has finally given me the chance to get stuck into organising the event this year.'

'That's lucky. For his son, that is.' Rory holds my gaze and then glances away, suddenly seeming shy.

My heart thuds. *Is he flirting?* I roll my lips together, savouring the unexpected sensation. He doesn't see me flushing.

Rory moves over to a large urn shaped planter, and pulls at a weed. I inhale steadily, I hadn't anticipated this routine site visit to be quite so... rousing. I take in the stunning grounds rolling out in front of me, exhaling as my eyes roam up and up, to find the distant horizon.

'This place is so amazing. You must love your job.'

'It has its ups and downs,' replies Rory, his voice sounds solemn.

He suddenly seems to have the weight of the world on his shoulders. I'm resisting the tug inside, pulling me to comfort him. That would be weird.

There's a tiredness in his eyes. He smiles but it's strained. How do I get flirty Rory back? I turn and look back out over the estate. 'I guess it's a lot of garden to take care of.'

'Yes. It's a lot of work.' He gives a heavy sigh.

Bail out, bail out. Somehow, I'm making this worse. 'Speaking of which, I should probably leave you to it. You've been so generous with your time.'

'Oh, I didn't mean to... you don't have to go...'

'I don't want to get in the way and I have a long drive to get back...'

'Just one last thing before you go. Please. Let me show you the kitchen garden, it's my favourite place.' Rory's eyes are twinkling again. 'It's on the way to your car.'

'Okay, you've twisted my arm.' I'm pleased to have an excuse to stay a little longer. We chat amiably as we walk in a different direction, round to the rear of the house, Rory's burdens apparently forgotten.

Part way along an ancient red brick wall, there's a doorway, partially obscured by ivy and covered with flaking green paint. The wrought iron hinges are a work of art in themselves, swirling over the wood and squeaking as they open. Rory leads us through it and down some rocky steps into a sunken walled garden, sprawling with herbs.

Grabbing a terracotta pot from a stack he

swipes some soil into it, then producing some shears from his jacket he cuts a sprig of rosemary from a large shrub. After a few tidying snips, plunges it into the soil, pressing the compost firmly around the stalk. His hands are working the earth so masterfully, it's distracting. He pushes the pot into my hands, leaving a smudge of dirt and a trail of fire on my skin.

'Keep it covered until you see some new growth and then it's good to go.'

Stunned, I manage to say, 'Thanks.'

'Rosemary for remembrance,' says Rory as if in explanation. 'You've got a lot going on with organising the gala. It'll help you remember everything.'

'Thank you,' I repeat, still mostly speechless.

'If you leave through that gate there-' he points to the opposite wall. 'You'll find yourself back round the front where you parked.'

'Okay.' I look between Rory, the gate and the pot and then back to Rory. He's picked up a garden fork and has started digging while my brain scrambles to compute the gift, with the Hamlet reference, with the scorched feeling on my skin. My mind wanders. I wouldn't say no to those muddy hands finding some other places. *Oh, pull yourself together, Holly!*

I start to retreat towards the exit. 'Right, thank you.'

His lips curl into an exquisite smile. 'You're welcome.'

'This is lovely and thank you. For everything. Thanks.' I turn and hightail it off, putting an end to my nervous bumbling.

With the terracotta pot belted in to the passenger's seat, I drive away. The smear of mud stands out on the back of my hand as I hold the steering wheel. It's hard to concentrate, it keeps pulling my gaze from the road and reminding me of Rory. *What happened back there?*

Giving myself a firm talking to, I give myself permission to crush on the gardener for exactly half of the journey, then it's back to Work Mode. It's not as though I'm likely to see him again and I really can't afford to get distracted now.

CHAPTER 7

The warmth from the steamy café hits me as I walk in for my regular early morning coffee fix. A little treat to start the day well. The barista fills my travel mug with my usual and I turn to leave, preoccupied with thoughts of Rory. I'm almost at the entrance to our office block when I realise Mark has been trying to get my attention.

'Holly, wait up!' He's scurrying, trying not to spill his drink as he dashes after me.

'Sorry! I was in a world of my own. Have you been following me from the café?'

'Yes, I'm glad I spotted you. I'm hoping you'll help me bump into Amber. I have her scarf; she left it behind the other day.'

I smother a small smile, satisfied with my cunning. 'That's kind of you. I've been meaning to get hold of you, actually. I have a proposition, perhaps I can fill you in while you wait for her?'

'That'd be great, thanks.'

Signing Mark in at the front desk, I lead him to the lifts. The door glides shut and we start our ascent with a judder.

Mark takes a sip of his coffee. 'What did you want to ask me about?'

'How do you feel about public speaking?'

'I've never done any.' He hesitates. 'Why?'

'Would you be up for giving a short speech at the Charity gala? The one that we're holding to raise funds for STARS?'

'Me?'

'Yes, you.'

'I'd love to help them out but I'm not sure I'd be any good.'

The lift chimes as it arrives at my floor and I guide Mark to my office, indicating a free chair by my desk. He sits down, placing his coffee on the side.

Perching opposite him, I give a reassuring look. 'Of course you can decline, but I think you'd be the perfect person for the job. It doesn't have to be for long, just talk a bit about your business and your experience with STARS. Rave about how wonderful they are. Plus, you'd get to come to the gala-'

'Morning!' sings Amber as she comes into the office. She does a double take as she sees Mark. 'Oh hi,' she beams at him.

I nod at him with encouragement and he flashes me an awkward grin before standing and walking over to her. He holds out a bag.

'Hi. You left this behind the other day. I thought you might need it.'

Feeling like a third wheel, I reach under my

desk to switch on my computer. Their voices filter over to me as I busy myself, trying not to listen in on their chat.

'Perhaps we could go for another drink sometime...' Mark murmurs in the background.

Pretending to find something very interesting in my bag, I delve into it, rummaging, trying to disappear.

'So, this gala, is there a dress code?'

Glancing up, I find Mark's now looking at me, a twitch of a smile his face.

'Are you coming to the gala?' Amber interrupts. Her face alight.

'Hopefully,' I reply. 'For the guests it's black tie and cocktail dresses, but as long as you're formal, it'll be okay. You don't need to rent a tux unless you really want to.'

He rubs his chin. 'Okay. I'd love to help out STARS. Will you email me the details?'

'Absolutely! The finer points need to be ironed out, but as you're on board with the idea, I can get stuck in to organising it.'

Mark nods and turns to Amber. 'I'm looking forward to it.' Then to both of us he says, 'I'd better leave you to your morning and get back to work myself.'

'I'm so pleased you popped by.' I check my watch. 'Is that the time? I've got a meeting soon.' I look to Amber with an eyebrow raised. 'Amber, do you mind helping Mark find his way out?'

She nods and conveys a look that says I have

all the subtlety of a pantomime horse.

'Thanks, see you soon.' I wave as they leave and then sink down into my chair feeling a little smug that my master plan seems to be working.

On her return, Amber says, 'Did you really have a meeting?'

'No, but I'm not going to tell Mark that. How did it go?'

'He found the exit okay, if that's what you mean?' Amber bites her lip and giggles.

'You know it's not. You don't have to tell me.'

'Of course I'm going to tell you! He's asked me on a date tomorrow night.'

'Fantastic! Perhaps if things don't work out in events I could go into matchmaking?'

'So, you don't mind?' Nerves tighten her face.

'Why would I mind? I thought you two looked cute together.'

'But I was trying to encourage you to go for it with him and I've stolen him.'

'Don't be silly. I'm more than happy for you. In fact, I hoped this would happen.'

'And it's okay that he's one of our suppliers?'

'Doesn't bother me and Deborah doesn't need to know.'

'Phew! I think this calls for some celebratory chocolate.' Amber reaches into her drawer and pulls out a family-size sharing pouch.

'It's not even nine o'clock yet,' I exclaim.

'I know! Even more reason to celebrate.'

After checking and answering my emails, I pull up the STARS official website on my internet browser. I'm rather proud of my idea to have a special address from someone that STARS has worked with in the past. Everyone loves a good news story and it will help personalise the charity and hopefully raise them more money. However, before subjecting Mark to the scrutiny of Deborah, I figure I'd better discuss it with the STARS head office first, if they're not on board then the whole idea is a bust anyway.

They seem like a friendly organisation; the website has a banner across the top that says, 'Just pop in!'

'Amber, I'm going out for an early lunch to try and find the STARS headquarters.'

'I was researching them earlier. They're in a dodgy part of town. Wouldn't you prefer to call?'

'I like speaking to people face to face. Plus, it's the middle of the day; I'll be brave.'

'Good luck!' she calls out as I sling my coat on.

CHAPTER 8

As I stride down a littered street I decide Amber was wrong, it wasn't so much dodgy as rundown. Scanning the numbers, I soon find myself outside a tired, gloomy building that is in desperate need of some renovation. It seems the home of STARS is in an old tower block which is shared by multiple organisations, all listed on a faded slip of paper by the door. Nothing happens when I press the buzzer. *Should I call them?* I hold my finger on the button again and a teenager bowls out of the door.

'That's knackered,' they call over their shoulder as they walk off.

Sticking a foot out, I catch the door before it shuts, letting myself in.

The lobby has an abandoned feel to it with the lift also seeming in need of repair, so I take the stairs up to the third floor.

A Perspex plaque tells me the right door and I give a knock and enter. The draught from the opening door causes a notice board of 'thank yous' to flutter. A couple of chairs stand below it, one revealing some yellowing foam spilling from inside. There's no one behind the welcome desk.

'Hello?' Perhaps I shouldn't have popped by quite so unannounced.

'Oh hello, dear.' A lady in her fifties potters out. Frizzy curls form a helmet around her head and her glasses are secured by a chain around her neck. She has the look of a kindly mother hen; I warm to her immediately.

'Hi, I'm Holly. I work for MYTechnology. Sorry to drop by unexpectedly.'

'It's wonderful to meet you, my dear. I'm Barbara Bridges. I think we've spoken on the phone before.'

'Yes, we have.'

'I apologise for this place being in such a disarray.' Barbara straightens a couple of old magazines, edges curled with use. 'We're outgrowing our digs but rent's astronomical in the city. I'm not sure what to do.' She systematically goes around, tidying the foyer. Picking up a discarded canoe oar, she glances around but with a loss of where to put it, stashes it behind the desk. 'Now, how can I help you?'

'I wondered if we could have a quick chat about an idea for the Christmas gala dinner?'

Barbara clasps her hand to her chest. 'Such an exciting event. And very much needed, I can assure you. What do you need?'

'Could we ask one of your previous clients to speak at the event? Would you mind?'

'That's a wonderful idea. It would give the benefactors a clue about what we really do.' She lowers her voice. 'I'm not sure if they know.'

'Why do you think that?'

'No one from STARS has ever been before. We could be an astrological charity for all they know.' Barbara giggles. 'Still, we're always so very grateful for the donations.'

This is outrageous. 'You've never been?'

Barbara shakes her head.

'Not ever?'

'Oh no, dear. Fancy galas aren't really for the likes of us.'

I'm betting that's what Deborah would have them believe. 'Well it is this year. Please come and bring a guest too.'

Barbara's eyes light up. 'I could bring my assistant, he'd love it. But I'm not sure if MY-Technology would want us there.' She drops her voice. 'We might lower the tone.'

'Don't be silly. And I'm sure Montague would love to have you. He's made the gala very different this year, more intimate and more about family and going back to our roots.'

'It sounds splendid. If you're sure, I'd be delighted to come. Now, do you have someone in mind for the talk?'

'Do you remember Mark Gutenberg? He runs Repro365.'

'Do I? I remember them all like they're my own kiddies.' Barbara bats her hand. 'Of course, I shouldn't call him a kid, he's a grown man now. But they're all like my children to me. Would you like a cuppa, dear?'

'Yes, please.' Stepping over some rolled up sleeping bags and a pile of raincoats, I follow Barbara through to her office.

'Don't mind the mess through here, we've just come back from an enrichment night away and I've yet to work out how to store all the equipment. My assistant, Luke, usually sorts it out. Getting it out of the way again is like trying to store toys inside a Jack-in-the-box.'

As the kettle boils, Barbara potters about, trying to tidy some more, but is actually just moving the piles around to new places. 'Sorry about all this. Often the kids don't have anything so I like to keep a stock of things they can borrow.'

'Please don't apologise. The work you do is amazing, I'm not surprised it causes a bit of chaos.'

'That's right dear, you can't make omelettes without breaking eggs. Sadly though, we need a bigger frying pan.'

Barbara bumps her hips into a cupboard to try and wedge it shut and then serves the tea.

After a lovely chat with Barbara, discussing the finer points of the arrangements, I head back to work with the winter sun warming my back. My heart feels light. Arranging for STARS to be more involved is exactly the right thing to do. They should have been more involved from the start.

A cracked cement planter housing a shrub and a host of hopeful weeds catches my eye and my mind drifts to Rory and the beautiful Cherrywell Manor. The rest of the walk passes in a blur and soon my office block materialises ahead. I try to banish thoughts of him and get back to Work Mode.

The soaring buildings cast me into a shadow and a sense of foreboding creeps over me. *Did I get carried away inviting Barbara? Surely Deborah won't mind? It's only right that she's there. Isn't it?*

CHAPTER 9

Back at my desk I type out an email to Barbara, confirming the details we'd discussed.

Amber scooches over to me on her wheelie chair. 'I've been meaning to ask…'

'Yeah?'

'Are you trying to suffocate a miniature Christmas tree?' Her gaze has settled on the cutting from Rory. I've fastened a sandwich bag over it, securing it to the pot with an elastic band.

'Oh no, it's a cutting. It needs to be covered until it roots. I thought I could keep an eye on it better at work.'

'Well, I figured, if it *was* a miniature Christmas tree then it would need some teeny-tiny decorations.' She holds out a string of paper clips.

I chuckle. 'That's super cute, thank you. Deborah got you twiddling your thumbs again?'

'Counting paper clips, literally,' replies Amber before wheeling back over to her desk.

I wind the garland around the cutting with care, enjoying the scent as it drifts up. Rosemary for remembrance, Rory had said. Which is prophetic as he is proving particularly difficult to forget. *Uh, that smile... those hands...* My phone rings. Back to work.

'Holly, I want Amber to update some databases. I'm sending her an email with the files and details.' Deborah hangs up before I can reply. The horror of a data entry task. Poor Amber.

I fill her in on her next assignment and then, after double checking my calendar, grab my coat once more.

'Are you off somewhere?' asks Amber.

'Trip to the college. Meeting with the art teacher.' I sling my bag over my shoulder.

Amber leaps up, holding a notepad, the furry llama on the front has a Santa hat on. 'Can I come this time?'

'I really need to deal with this on my own.'

'It's just that I-'

'Please just carry on with the task Deborah has set you.' It's an effort to keep the exasperation out of my voice.

Amber slumps down into her chair and stares at the monitor without blinking.

'See you later,' I call out. Amber waves weakly in response.

Perhaps I shouldn't have left her out? Is it selfish that I just want to get on with this myself? Amber's just keen to help and to get away from the godawful busy-work that Deborah finds her. Guilt steers my feet to one of my most favourite places. The stationery shop. This new theme

surely demands new notebooks? Purely to ensure everything stays neat and well organised, of
course. This has nothing to do with my insati-
able stationery habit.

The air is permeated with scented pens and
I instantly feel calmer. Aromatherapy for the
event planner. Making a beeline for the notebook section, I select a matching pair for Amber
and I, and go straight to pay without allowing
myself to browse. I could lose hours in a place
like this. A check of the time confirms that I need
to hightail it to my meeting with the art teacher.

The college is housed in a huge red brick building, converted from an all-boys school in the
eighties. The entrance is up a set of wide flagstone steps. After studying a map just inside the
door, I head in the direction of the art studio
where the meeting's been arranged.

A woman is bending and stretching, sloshing
a huge canvas with cobalt blue paint, her back
to the door. Her top knot of dreadlocks pokes
through a vividly coloured headwrap of reds and
pinks. I watch with awe as a naked form starts to
take shape.

Without glancing up, the lady says, 'It's not
ready to see yet.' Her voice is deep and melodic.

'It's amazing.'

In surprise, she turns quickly. 'I thought you
were a student. Hello, I'm Malika Jones.' She
places the brush down and wipes her hand on

her dress before holding it out.

'I'm Holly. That looks fantastic.' I shake her hand with as much authority as I can muster.

'It's supposed to symbolise women's plight of overburden as we strive to be all things. She needs to be laden with some symbolic red next.'

'That sounds... wow...'

Malika moves over to a table and starts pouring out a large quantity of pillar box red paint into a tray.

'I've come about the project for MYTechnology that your students are getting involved with.'

'Oh yes, I thought someone called Deborah was coming.' Malika surveys me sceptically.

'I'm leading the event so it's best if I come to discuss the brief.' I try to sound as assertive as possible.

'The students are very excited for their work to be displayed to the public.' Peering past my shoulder, she says, 'Ah, here's Lottie, now.'

A petite teenager walks in, the large portfolio slung across her shoulders dwarfs her.

Malika beams at the student. 'We have you to thank for this wonderful opportunity for the class.'

'The Christmas exhibition? Well, it's Grandpops, really.' Lottie says, bouncing up and down on her toes. 'Have you come to talk about it?'

'Yes, I'm Holly. I'm organising the event-'

'I'm so pleased it's not that awful Debbie

woman,' Lottie interrupts.

I try to control my smirk. 'Just me to contend with today. My *boss*, Deborah, is still involved, of course.' I jiggle my eyebrows. 'So, let's talk practicalities. The theme is the Twelve Days of Christmas.'

Malika gives a contemplative bob of her head. 'There are twelve students so it works well, one for each day.'

'Perfect. And what sort of size paintings should I expect so I can organise some space to put them?'

'Size? Painting? I can't stymie their creative flow through such rigid framework. No, no, no.' Malika wags a finger at me.

'Sorry?'

'I will give them a lyric and they will produce a work of art. Who knows what they will be inspired to design. Maybe papier-mâché turtle doves, five actual rings rendered in metal or a watercolour of ten lords leaping.' Her hands gesture with passion. 'You cannot bridle their creativity with size constraints.' She picks up a small roller and runs it through the paint.

Flummoxed, I glance from my notes to Malika and back again, while she attacks the canvas with red swipes.

'Please can I have Seven Swans, oh pleeease,' Lottie begs in the background.

Don't be phased, Holly. I plough on with the planning. 'The Christmas gala is in about three weeks, on the second Thursday in December. We'll need the art work at least two days before so we can get it set up in time for the event.'

Malika steps back from the canvas. 'That should be manageable. Will you come here to collect it?'

'Grandpops will get all that organised, I'm sure of it,' announces Lottie. 'Now, about my swan piece....' She diverts Malika's attention and starts talking about chicken wire.

I look back to my notebook and then across to the art teacher. Malika and Lottie are now trying to calculate how many bags of feathers may need to be ordered.

With a little cough, I try to catch their attention. 'I think that's everything.'

'Hmmm?' Malika briefly raises her head. 'Yes, I think so.'

'Okay. I'll call to confirm collection arrangements.'

'Thank you. Oh, and when should we send you the bill?' Malika gives a bright toothed smile.

'Bill?' My forehead scrunches.

'Yes, the invoice for the art supplies and things.'

'I hadn't rea-'

Lottie interrupts again, 'Grandpops is so generous, isn't he? Will you need the cash in advance, Miss Jones?'

'Oh no, I can send an itemised invoice afterwards.'

Setting my shoulders straight, I try to act business-like. 'Of course. Excellent.'

Malika and Lottie's attention has drifted again.

'I'll see myself out. Pleasure doing...' My voice peters out, I say a quiet 'bye' and back out of the class room.

The wall outside the classroom door is cool against my back. That didn't go exactly as expected. Had Montague genuinely promised his granddaughter all those things? What about the budget? Does Deborah know? She's going to freak out if not. Oh God, and I've yet to tell her about inviting Barbara from STARS. Now I know how that woman in blue feels.

CHAPTER 10

'Out of the question,' replies Deborah when she hears my report of the meeting. 'Invoicing us? There's no budget for that. Especially not if you're inviting all and sundry like that Barbara and her grubby *projects* all of a sudden.' Deborah almost spits the words with distaste.

'But Malika said Montague said…'

'Really, Holly. I'd hoped you'd handle this better.' Deborah moves in uncomfortably close. With her eyes narrowed she whispers, 'Montague is merely a figurehead, he has no idea about running the company.'

'We can't expect the college to pay for the privilege of providing us with the artwork for our gala, can we?'

Her laugh is more like a bark, Deborah's eyes spark. 'You're so keen to take this gala on, aren't you?'

'Yes, I want to show you-'

With a dangerously quiet voice, Deborah interrupts me. 'You find the money in the budget.'

A buzzing sound breaks the tense discussion. Nicola, crackles out over the intercom. 'Mr Young for you.'

'Put him through,' calls out Deborah while flapping her hand to dismiss me.

'Everything okay?' asks Amber as I sit down at my desk and let out a heavy sigh.

I give a resolute nod. 'I said I was capable of taking on responsibility for this event, now I've got to live up to it… I almost forgot. Here, I got us a treat.' I pass Amber a paper bag.

'What is it?'

'Terribly important bit of equipment for the gala dinner. Crucial, in fact.'

Amber pulls a black sequinned notebook out and strokes the cover. 'Soooo pretty! I love the glitz! Thank you.'

'The first rule of event planning, other than ensuring you book things for the correct date, is having on-point stationery. It's black because we need to take this event very seriously. But it's sequinned because, well-'

'*Christmas!*' Amber joins in at the same time, and we giggle.

The phone buzzes, surprising me. 'Everything okay, Nicola?'

'I've got a message for you from your musicians.'

'You can put them through if you want.'

'No, they've already gone. They said to tell you they're cancelling December twelfth.'

'What?'

'Sorry, Holly. Just passing the message on.'

Nicola hangs up. Reality has stabbed a hole in my tiny air-balloon of fun, I'm plummeting back down to earth. I fill my lungs, trying to centre my thoughts.

'I'm sure it's not too late to organise some more,' I say to no one in particular. 'Everything is under control.'

Searching for a replacement quartet is a nightmare, all of Deborah's pre-approved choices are booked. The only options available at late notice are eye-wateringly extortionate so definitely not in the budget. Tapping on my computer, a new email icon pulls my attention. Clicking on it, I see it's from Montague, and open it up immediately.

Deborah, I love the idea of having STARS representatives at the gala. If Mark's happy to do a speech then I'd be very grateful. Well done, this is right on the company line for nurturing talent from a grass roots level. I'm cc-ing Holly in- can you make this happen? All the best, MY

I move in closer to the screen. What am I reading? It feels like I've been punched in the stomach. Did Deborah steal my idea about Mark doing a speech and dress it up as her own? I can just picture Deborah sat smugly in her office, belittling my endeavours but shamelessly filching my ideas. I shouldn't have shared Mark's details so naively, I may as well have handed him to Deborah on a Christmas themed platter.

My sigh is weighty.

'What's happened?' Asks Amber, from behind a pile of post.

'Poor judgment on my behalf, apparently.'

'Huh?'

Blinking away rapidly rising tears, all of Deborah's condescending and inane decrees pass through my head. Indignation starts to rise, blossoming into a fiery passion. I've been micro-managed, patronised and stabbed in the back for the last time. 'I've had enough of this.'

'What? You're not leaving, are you?'

'Not after everything I've gone through to get this far!' Sitting up straighter, I steel myself. I swipe a finger across each cheek and lock eyes with Amber. 'I need to show Deborah - show Montague in fact - what I'm made of.'

'Yeah!' Amber, catches on to the tone of my rousing address.

'This is going to be the best bloody gala MY-Technology has ever seen.'

'Yeah!'

'And then finally Deborah can do one!'

'Yeah! Wait. Do you think Deborah will ever back off?'

'Yes. I've just got to prove myself. And solving her latest poisoned task is the first step.'

With a few clicks on my computer, I pull up the expenses spreadsheet. 'Jeez.'

'Anything I can help you with? Devilish Debs has got me twiddling my thumbs again.'

I roll my eyes at Amber's nickname for our boss. 'She's probably got the office bugged!' I warn. 'Short of helping conjure some money from the budget, I don't think you can help me.'

Amber cocks her head to the side. 'What do you mean?'

'Unless there's some sort of manna from heaven, I think I'm going to have to disappoint a whole class of students.'

'Miss Jones up to her usual tricks?'

'How do you know the art teacher?'

'That's what I keep trying to tell you! I used to go to that college.'

'Why didn't you say so?' My voice raises a couple of octaves.

'No one would let me!' Amber mimics in the same pitch and laughs. 'The art teacher is so ballsy. Did she ask you for money then? To be fair the college is kind of poor.'

'Yes, she did, and then Montague's grand-daughter was there and they sort of ganged up on me.'

'I can't believe Lottie's still there.'

'You know Lottie too?'

'I did try and say in the meeting. And again yesterday. Lottie was in my year but kept changing her course so she's still not graduated.'

'So, do you know lots of people in the college?'

With a confident air, Amber nods. 'It's not

huge, you get to know most teachers.'

'Pull up a chair. Let's go through this together. The aim is to spend as little as possible but to pull off an incredible event nevertheless. We're raising money for STARS.'

'Stars?'

'It stands for Students' Training, Advice, Relief and Support. They work to help keep teens and young adults in education.'

'Is that the group Mark was talking about the other day?'

'Yes. We want to raise as much money as possible for them. And, of course, that then makes us look good.' Amber comes to sit by my desk, an excited glow on her face. 'Let's see if we can trim some fat...' I say, scrolling through the file.

We study the numbers in detail until Amber squeaks, 'How much for a string quartet?'

'We need music for the ambiance.'

'I bet the orchestra would do it for a free meal. They're pretty good too. Won an award last year.'

I make a note and feel the inklings of an idea begin to kindle.

We spend the rest of the day making notes and then some tentative enquiries at the college until finally my plan is completely set ablaze in my head.

'How much does that save?' Amber asks as I finish running the numbers.

'Nearly ten grand.'

'Whoa!'

'It's amazing. We can outsource so many of our requirements to the college.' I go through the list. 'They've agreed we can use a couple of the college minibuses to provide our staff transport and also fetch the art installations. If we use some of the college orchestra to provide the music we cut out the cost of replacing the quartet too.'

'I love the idea of enlisting the choir to sing the carol.' Amber's face shines with excitement.

'Do you think we could get the whole drama department involved?'

'We can ask.'

'Right, we need a meeting with Deborah to present the new plan to her. Can you get Nicola to see when she's free, please?'

After a quick call, Amber places the receiver down and shakes her head. 'She's having an urgent meeting with Montague. Nicola says she probably won't be back at her desk today.'

'Even better. You and me get to leave on time and we can present it to her in the morning.'

'An evening off? Now you've no excuse not to get yourself out there and meet people!' Amber playfully spins around in her wheelie chair.

'Very funny but the gala is three weeks today! Now I've *really* got to concentrate on it. It's my number one priority.' While I'm speaking a vision of Rory probes at the edges of my mind, but I brush it aside.

Determined to deliver the event of the century and confident in the new plans, I'm excited when I go into Deborah's office to fill her in on the proposed changes. She seems distracted but I plough on nonetheless.

'We've run the numbers and have worked out how to maintain the same level of quality whilst actually saving money. We thought the saved money could then be donated to the charity and to Lottie's college, who'll be providing so much of the entertainment.'

'Sounds fabulous,' says Deborah, absorbed in staring at her screen.

'Don't you want to see the new spreadsheet?'

'No, I'm sure it'll be splendid.'

'So, shall I just crack on and get it all finalised?'

'Ummmm,' Deborah's manicure taps on the keyboard with impatience. Pausing from her work, she looks up at me with narrowed eyes. 'Actually Holly, I've put you in charge, I think you need to just get on with it. I've been given a very important task by Montague which I need to concentrate on; I shouldn't need to hold your hand through all this.'

Did that just happen? I retreat from the office while Deborah's attention goes back to her computer.

CHAPTER 11

A mber bundles into the office, unwrapping her scarf from around her neck. 'Morning! Only three days to go! I can't believe how quickly time is flying.'

'I know!' I match her enthusiasm. 'It's really not long now. Luckily, it's all starting to come together.'

Without Deborah's manic control tormenting my every move, I've managed to relax and even enjoy finalising the arrangements for the gala. The caterers are confirmed, the entertainment is in place and the running order has been revised. The last few weeks have passed without a hitch and it's all taken shape beautifully.

'Is Demented Debs out of the office again today?'

'Seems like it. She's off doing something for Montague.'

'Oh, to have minions doing all your work for you so you can swan off.'

'You did want more responsibility. Now she's given it to you.' I indicate to a pile of post waiting on Amber's desk.

'That will help distract me for about five minutes. I'm so excited about the gala!' She bounces over to her chair.

'Is Mark all set for his speech?'

'I think so. I'm so pleased he's going too, then he can see what we've been working so hard on.'

'So, it's going well, you and Mark?'

A delicate blush creeps to Amber's cheeks. 'We've been on quite a few dates over the last few weeks. I think I really like him.'

We're interrupted by Nicola on the intercom. 'Malika Jones on the line for you.'

'I'd better take this.' I sweep my hair from my shoulder and pick up the phone to talk to the art teacher.

She updates me with the progress so far and I reply, 'Fantastic, so are all the pieces ready to collect?'

'We're still waiting on the First Day of Christmas to be completed but I'm sure it won't be long. All artists have their own process. Greatness can't be rushed.'

'So, we're just waiting on one? We can work with that.'

'I can bring the final piece on the day.' Malika offers. 'It'll fit in with the choir and musicians.'

'Great, I'll collect the other eleven today and pick up a minibus too.'

As I replace the handset I smile at Amber. 'Fancy a trip down memory lane? I'm heading to your old college.'

'Yes please!' Amber starts to wind her scarf on again.

'Fab, let's grab a cab over and I can drive us back.'

While our taxi is making its way to the college, I locate Cherrywell Manor's phone number and press dial.

'Hello, Mr Barnes. It's Holly from MYTechnology. Could I speak with Mr Perdreau please? He's busy?' *He's always busy.* 'Is there any chance we can drop off some items in advance of the event on the twelfth?'

I waggle my eyebrows up and down to Amber while waiting on hold. 'You can? Wonderful. Is about midday okay? See you then.'

With a satisfied tap, I end the call. 'All sorted.'

Indicating out of the window, Amber says, 'Look, we're nearly there.'

The college comes into view ahead of us and soon we pull up outside the flagstone steps. Paying the driver, I exit the cab with excitement. 'I can't wait to see the art work!'

'It feels funny being back here as an adult,' comments Amber. 'Are we picking up a minibus first?'

'Yes, from reception,'

'That's this way,' she calls as she strides off into her old stomping ground.

We take our time loading up the precious cargo under Malika's watchful eye. Most submissions seem to be straightforward canvases wrapped in protective brown paper, but there are some sculptures and seven large square boxes which I'm pretty confident contain Lottie's swans. I can't wait to unveil these masterpieces. After securing everything in the back, we climb into the front.

'See you on Thursday at Cherrywell Manor,' Malika calls out, giving the minibus a couple of friendly bangs on the side.

'You sure you can drive this thing?' Amber doesn't sound convinced.

I adjust the rear-view mirror. 'Of course.'

Bunny hopping the vehicle forwards, I grit my teeth and then remember to ease the clutch.

'Are you even insured?'

'Yes, it's all covered through work's policy. Are you okay? It's not like you to fuss.'

Amber's wrapping her scarf around her neck and face like some sort of security barrier. I should be outraged she has no confidence in me, but then I grind the gears.

'I'm good, thanks.' She sinks into her seat with a wince.

CHAPTER 12

A tingle shivers across my skin as the manor comes in to view. An unbidden warmth is spreading to my stomach.

'Wow,' gasps Amber.

'Yep.' I slow right down, conscious of the uneven driveway lurching the minibus, and savour our approach. 'Can you imagine what it'd be like to live here, or work here, even?'

'It's a far cry from the city.'

'I love this place. I can't wait to show you.' *And I can't wait to see if Rory is here again.*

After parking up as best I can, I lead Amber to the front door, giving it a firm rap.

A minute passes, Amber whispers, 'Should we knock more loudly?' She rubs her hands together in the cold.

'Mr Barnes needs a bit of time to answer. Maybe we should have gone around to the back or something?'

'Like a servant? It feels like we are in a film set in the nineteen twenties,' says Amber.

'It does a bit.' I squint over my shoulder expecting a vintage Bentley to draw up.

The familiar sound of feet crunching the gravel approaches. Turning to look, a spectre like cloud erupts as I let out a pleased breath seeing Rory emerge. Regulation cap and wellies once again in situ.

'I thought I heard visitors,' he says, a smile playing on his lips. 'Can I help?'

My pulse starts to rush. 'Hi, we're just dropping off some art work. Mr Barnes is expecting us. I called ahead.' I'm gabbling.

Rory's gaze hasn't moved from my face. 'Best to load straight into the side entrance. Do you need a hand carrying things?'

'We don't want to be any trouble,' I say, as Amber starts to say, 'yes'.

Rory glances between us both with a wry grin. 'It's not a problem.'

'This is Amber.' I suddenly remember to introduce them.

The three of us carry one of the seven boxes each to the side entrance and start piling the load just inside the door. After four more trips the rest of the art work had joined it. Utilising his gardener's strength, Rory silently carries all of the heaviest packages while Amber and I manage the rest. Amber keeps up a constant stream of chuntering while I try to chivvy her along. She's dedicated, but she's not used to hard graft.

'I'll get back to work now, unless there's anything else I can do for you?' Rory's gaze is piercing as he looks at me intensely.

'You've done more than enough, thanks.'

He spins and lopes away, his wellies giving a small squeak with every other step.

'That was handy,' I say to Amber.

She grins. 'Yes. And he was rather attractive.'

'You're terrible, what about Mark?' I roll my eyes.

'I wasn't looking for me!'

'You mean me?' I feign shock. The thought absolutely hasn't entered my head. Much.

'He seemed pleased to see you. Do you two know each other?'

'He gave me a… tour when I was last here.' I don't feel like sharing his gift with Amber; she'd probably blow it all out of proportion.

'You must have left a good impression. I think he was interested.'

'Hardly.'

'For sure.'

'Amber, I can't get distracted now, there's lots to do. Shall we start with a look around?'

It's Amber's turn to roll her eyes but she nods anyway.

'This is the main room we'll be in.' I sweep around with my arm. 'The Ballroom. We use this room and the one next to it on the night, so the staff have chance to set up for the dinner and then clear the tables away before the dance.'

Amber's eyes sweep around the huge space. 'Sounds like a wedding.'

'It is a bit. So, I think we should put the art

work in the ante-room next door. That way, the guests have a chance to peruse it with their welcome drinks when they arrive and then again after dinner.'

The doorway is disguised in the same duck egg blue to give a seamless effect. With a push on the handle, I throw open the door and lead Amber into the next room.

'This is the *ante*-room?'

I bob my head. 'The Oak Room.' I can't explain it but I've a certain pride showing off the venue to Amber. It's stunning and seems to lean itself to being the home to wonderful parties.

'My whole flat could fit in this.'

Although large, the room is darker than the ballroom and with a simpler decor. Wooden panelling adorns the walls and a deep burgundy swirled carpet cushions under foot, rather than the polished parquet floor next door.

'We've got about two hundred and fifty guests coming, we definitely need all this space.'

Amber settles her gaze back on me. With a jerk of her head to the empty room she says, 'What are you thinking?'

I can't wait to get stuck into setting everything up. I point a finger to the side wall. 'The bar is going along there, leading to the art display following on in number order around the edge. People will naturally mill around so hopefully it will encourage them to move away from the bar so it doesn't bottle neck.' During my meeting with Mr Barnes, two weeks before, the layout had occurred to me instantly, like it was meant to be.

'Sounds good.'

'First, let's put the trestle tables out for the bar and then we can unpack the art.'

There's a pile of tables folded against the wall and I partially lift one up, offering the other half to my colleague.

Amber huffs. 'Where's that Rory when you need him?'

'This is all part of our job, you know. Sometimes you've got to get your hands dirty and muck in.'

Amber lifts the rest of the table into the air and snorts through her nose.

We heave the tables around and set them up securely. They're ugly but practical. Like a blanket of snow, we cover them up with a few simple white sheets transforming them into something much more elegant.

Propping herself on the edge of the makeshift bar, Amber pants to catch her breath. 'So, that Rory guy...'

'The gardener?'

'Will he be coming to the gala?'

'I doubt it. I've allocated space for Mr Perdreau plus one but I'm not sure if he's even coming.'

'I didn't think Dull Debs approved of plus ones.'

'Not for the likes of us. There's different rules for the other half though.'

'Who would you invite if you were allowed to?'

Who would *I invite?* My social life's taken a back seat to my career ambitions, so much so it's in the boot. 'There's not really a special someone.'

'It's because you work so hard. Work-life balance is extremely important, you know. You don't want to burn out.'

She's relentless! 'All right, you're right! I should put myself back out there.' I gesture to the ether.

Amber gives a little clap of excitement.

'Once this is all over I can concentrate on sorting a love life. But right now, I'm too busy.' A vision of Rory flashes across my conscience but I bat it away.

'Keep your eyes peeled and your mind open, you never know,' says Amber, sagely.

'Right, back to work. Perhaps when we know what's what, we can use those tables to display the sculptures.' I indicate over to some dainty occasion tables dotting the perimeter of the room.

'Are we allowed to?'

'Yes. Mr Barnes said I can make use of anything in these two rooms. He has also said we can borrow their stage.'

'*Stage?*'

'Well, more like *slightly raised platform*. That

must be it in the corner. I remember it from last year, it's fairly straightforward to put up. Albeit heavy.'

With a resurgence of energy, we set to work erecting a small stage at the far end of the ballroom.

I dab at my brow with a sleeve. 'I think I need a drink after all that. That's my exercise for the rest of the year.'

Amber peers into the hallway. 'I wonder where the rest of the staff are? I thought there'd be more help.'

'I did ask Deborah for more hands but she's only signed off for you and me from MYTechnology and, as far as I can remember, there aren't many people who work here. We get in external caterers and waiting staff. We just use Cherrywell Manor as the venue but it's an empty shell really. I think the owner lives in a few rooms upstairs.'

Amber studies the vast room. 'Seems like a waste to me. How are we going to get that drink then? I'm gasping for a coffee.'

'Let's see if there's something in the kitchen.'

Heading out of the room brings us into the grand entrance hall, complete with open staircase sweeping up to a gallery level and then further up to the rest of the house. The space is inspiring and, like a shooting star, a vision of the foyer filled with a huge shining tree suddenly streaks through my mind. Sparks of possibility seem to glimmer from the very fabric of this building.

'If I remember rightly it's through there and down the stairs.' I point to a small recess off to the side. The door opens into a well of darkness. 'I'm sure there's a light switch somewhere.'

Amber drops behind. 'Looks a bit gloomy.'

'I'll use the torch on my phone.' I pull it from my pocket and swipe the screen until a piercing white light erupts. The green baize lining on the door glows emerald and dust motes float in the narrow beam as I shine it down the stairs into a grey pit.

'Why don't I hang back and start unpacking the art?'

'Are you a chicken?'

'No-no, just want to make best use of our time here. Still seems like there's a lot to do.' Amber disappears with haste. Typical.

Nothing to be worried about. Deep breath. I plunge into the darkness. Shining the light along the wall, I find a switch sticking out and flick it up and down but nothing happens. Straightening my shoulders with determination I continue on, phone gripped in hand, illuminating the way. At the bottom of the staircase is another door which opens into the dull afternoon light filtering through the narrow basement windows.

As you'd expect in an old manor house, the kitchen is set below stairs. The traditional features are clad with an armour of modern stainless-steel ovens, surfaces and industrial style cupboards. A portmanteau of old and new. I start rummaging, on the quest for some coffee, mugs or even a kettle. The doors and drawers open and shut with unruly clangs. *Bingo!* Triumphant, I pull two mugs from a high ledge but dislodge a third which falls to the floor with a shrill shatter.

Crouching down, I start to clear up the mess. 'Rats.'

'I hope not,' says a voice.

'Waaaa!' I can't stop the squeal of terror. Reeling backwards, I land on my bottom with a thump. 'You frightened the life out of me.'

CHAPTER 13

Rory grins from below his cap. 'Sorry. I heard you thumping around in here and came to see if I could help.'

'I didn't realise I was being that noisy.'

'You weren't, I was just outside in the kitchen garden trying to salvage some herbs.' Rory removes the headwear, revealing a shock of chestnut hair which flops over his eyes.

'I was hunting for coffee.' I hold up the intact mugs with a guilty grin. 'I'm sorry about the breakage.'

'Not to worry.'

'It wasn't some sort of ancient heirloom was it? Should I tell the owner?' Scooping some shards in my hand with care, I show them to Rory.

Rory examines the debris. 'No, it's the kind of mug you get free with an Easter egg. I'm sure he won't mind.'

'I've not even met Lawrence yet.'

'I genuinely wouldn't worry.'

Really? 'Is he very laid back?'

'I'd say so. Let me sort out the coffee. And

what about lunch for later?' Rory moves confidently around the kitchen, bringing out the kettle, a pan and some tins of soup.

'Yes please.'

'I'll do you a flask to take up with you. Where's your friend from the minibus?'

'She didn't fancy the dark so she's up unveiling the art work.'

Rory set about knocking up our fare. 'Dark? Has the light gone again? I'll have to sort that out before the caterers come.'

His dirty jeans cling to his backside, probably pert and strong from all the digging. 'I thought you were the gardener?'

'I try and turn my hand at any job that needs doing round here.'

'Sounds like you're a good man to know.'

He passes me a steaming mug of drink and twitches his eyebrows mischievously.

We chat over our coffees while Rory warms the soup and I fill him in on some plans for the event.

'It's going to be the most festive and fun gala ever; full of merriment and twinkling lights. I can just smell the scent of real Christmas trees and mulled wine now! Can you imagine a giant tree in the entrance hall? Sorry, am I boring you?'

'Not at all. Your plans sound fantastic and a lot more fun than the stuffy formal dos they've had in the past.'

'Montague brought in the idea of the Twelve

Days of Christmas and it's taken on a life of its own since then. I've just gone with it.'

Rory looks impressed. 'I can't wait to see how it turns out. If you need a hand with anything, then let me know.'

'Thanks for your help. I know you're very busy.'

Rory unearths a thermos flask and decants the soup into it.

'That should keep you going. I should get back to work now.' With a flick he smooths his hair back, briefly revealing some startlingly intense brown eyes before pulling his cap down.

'Of course.' I can't help but seek out his gaze from under the peak. Were there really flecks of gold in with all that chocolate? With an impish grin, Rory moves backwards and goes through the rear door.

Clutching the thermos and a mug for Amber, I retrace my steps, emerging back into the opulence of upstairs. Excitement is coursing through me after my encounter with Rory, but it's just because he was so enthusiastic about my ideas. It has nothing to do with the lingering warmth his smile provoked.

Amber's in the Oak Room, her back facing me as I approach.

Holding up the supplies I call out, 'Look what I found!'

Amber twists around, eyes as wide as Christmas baubles, a frown rumples her forehead.

'You're not going to believe this.'

CHAPTER 14

After a few months of working with Amber, I feel adept at being able to read her. She's usually enthusiastic and carefree, sometimes playful and distractible, and always humbly abashed if she makes a rare mistake, but never have I encountered her looking so uneasy.

'What?'

Amber gapes, mute.

Stepping forwards, I frown. 'Tell me.' I place our soup on a nearby table.

With hesitation, Amber steps to the side of a large canvas propped against the wall. It's almost as tall as her hip; brown paper wrap curls on the floor around it. In the style of a Pop Art print, what look like two large brightly coloured ducks seemed to be fornicating rather roughly.

'I don't get it?'

Amber steps aside and pulls out two more of the same print, in different shades.

'Six geese a-laying. It's a triptych.'

All the air vacates my lungs. My eyes roam the pictures frantically, trying to make sense of it.

'But they're not laying eggs.'

'It must be *artistic interpretation*. They're getting laid!'

'What. The. Fu-la-la-la-laaaa-la-la-la-laaa?' I tip my head to the side, I cannot process this. 'This is NOT what a true love would send at Christmas. This is... awful.' A manic laugh burbles out and I shoot a hand to my mouth to stop it.

Eyes magnetised, Amber can't stop herself from staring at the life size graphics. 'What's Daunting Debs going to say? And Montague?'

A cold sweat is creeping across my shoulders and down my spine. Suddenly, my genius money saving plans feel amateur and cheap. More akin to a school jumble sale than glamorous charity evening. Visions of unruly school kids running amok at the gala flash through my head. 'What have I done?' I breathe, finally.

'It's not your fault. The art was Montague's idea.'

'But I've taken the concept to a whole new tacky level. What was I thinking?'

'Deborah okayed the plans. It's not all on you.'

'She's distracted with that new venture.' Casting a glance around, it dawns on me how much remains to be done. Okay, my imagination may be in overdrive right now; the event won't actually be overrun by infants, the college students are young adults after all. But there is still a terrifying amount of work left. 'Oh my goodness-this was my one chance to prove myself and I'm blowing it.' Because I'm too bloody busy thinking about Rory.

'Don't panic. Couldn't we just paint some eggs on or something, make it look like they're laying rather than shagging?'

I shake my head. 'It's not just that... thing. Look at this place. The gala's the day after tomorrow.' Grabbing hold of the running order, I scan what's left on the schedule. 'We have so much work to do if we're going to pull this event off.'

'This place just needs a few strings of fairy lights and it'll be fine.'

'We need to get back to the office.' I pace. 'We've got to pick up the decorations and maybe we should try and book those expensive musicians after all. If we can make this do look as classy as possible, then no one will notice the art. What's the rest like?'

'It's actually good. Just a partridge in a pear tree missing, but we knew about that. Have faith in all your planning so far. Let's try not to panic.'

'I'm not panicking. I'm just trying not to ruin Christmas.' Breathe! I give a single, definitive, nod. 'Okay. There's a lot riding on this event but we can do it.'

'I'll do whatever I can to help.'

Inhaling deeply, I force my shoulders down, trying to relax. 'So, new plan: Head back, make some phone calls and get as many decorations as we can to disguise *that*.'

And stop getting distracted by enigmatic gardener.

Perhaps sensing the gravity of the matter, Amber doesn't quibble but gathers up our things in a flash. We hurry outside. I've got barely three days left to prove to Deborah I've got what it takes; my professional reputation's at stake!

I load my bag on the minibus and turn to Amber. 'Can you help make some calls on the journey please?'

'Of course.'

Gravel spins out from under the wheels as I drive off.

'First of all, please can you go online and order twenty more strings of fairy lights and at least sixty batteries from my work account. Get them delivered direct to Cherrywell Manor for tomorrow.'

'On it,' says Amber. A couple of minutes later she announces, 'Done!' with triumph.

'Fab, thanks. Next, can you dial that exorbitant string quartet for me and put them on speaker phone? They might not have booked yet.'

Soon the airwaves are filled with a ringing tone and a clipped voice answered. 'Yes?'

'Hello, I just wondered if you have any availability for this Thursday.'

There's a harsh laugh. 'We are fully booked until well into the New Year.'

'Okay, thanks,' I reply but the voice merely continues to cackle until Amber puts us out of our misery and hangs up.

'I'll phone around some others,' she offers.

When nothing comes to fruition, I concede that we should trust in the youth orchestra who are already arranged; they've won some regional awards after all. We travel the next mile in thoughtful silence until I have another brainwave.

'We should call Malika, she might be able to get the person to change the painting.'

Amber locates the number and then hits speaker phone as the line starts ringing.

'Hi Malika, it's Holly.'

'Hi, how's the art looking? Such wonderful and varied pieces, aren't they?'

'Well about that... it's mostly fantastic. I just have my reservations about the sixth day of Christmas.' I fiddle with the steering wheel, picking my words.

'That's Bethany's, such an interesting interpretation, isn't it?'

'Interesting, yes. But it's not overly Christmassy.'

'She's not feeling *Christmassy*, she's just discovered her boyfriend cheating on her. It's brought amazing texture to her work at the moment.'

'Is there any chance she could tweak it?' Silence. 'Just a bit?'

Malika inhales loudly. 'Censoring art is the first step towards losing freedom of speech! I abhor any sort of iconoclastic nonsense. It's anti-democratic. What would be next? Controlling what people wear? What they eat?'

'Okay, no problem. It was just a query,' I manage to interject. 'I didn't mean any malice by it. The art stays.' Forcing enthusiasm, I add, 'And what a talking piece it will be too.'

After a few more placations, I end the call. 'I hope I haven't upset Malika, that's the last thing I wanted to do,'

'Miss Jones loves playing the injured and misunderstood card. Just ignore her,' says Amber with a shrug. 'She's an artist; she loves drama.'

'Business relationships are delicate. She's Montague's granddaughter's teacher, I can't just offend her. Even if she is massively overreacting.'

We both sit, biting our tongues.

My phone starts ringing, breaking the impasse. Amber checks the screen. 'It's Demonic Debs.'

'Can you see what she wants, please?'

After several yeses and other sounds of agreement, Amber hangs up. 'She wants help finding an outfit for the gala and also with planning a complete makeover.'

'What?'

'That's what she said. She said she knows everything is ready to go for the gala so there should be no problem.'

'But we can't do that, we've still got it all to sort out. There's all the decorating to do.' The fear starts clawing its way back up my spine.

'Shall I call her back and say no?'

I struggle to keep the minibus driving straight as I exclaim, 'No!'

Amber flinches.

Chill, Holly. Breathe, remember.

I find a calmer voice. 'You'll have to help her. I've got to be the one on the ground at Cherrywell.'

'What?' Amber's incredulous.

'You wanted her to delegate more things to you. Besides, her asking something like this is because she's starting to trust us, if we let her down now, who knows when she'd let us back in. You help her with her new look.'

'Are you sure? Who's going to help you with all the set up?'

'I can manage. I just need to trust my instincts, have faith in what we planned... and hope that a little bit of Christmas magic helps me along the way.'

CHAPTER 15

After a late night and fitful sleep, I wake early and unrefreshed. Adrenaline pulses through me. With only two days to go I'm desperate to get everything back on track. Salvaging the gala will mean the salvation of my career. I won't entertain the notion of what failure would mean.

A combination of Deborah's last-minute rearrangements and *that* painting has laid waste to my meticulous planning. There's still a whole art display to curate! As she has stolen my sidekick, I try and call in some favours from my colleagues, but no one's free to help with the set up, so it's up to me to sort the crisis on my own.

'This is *my* gala, so I'm going to fix it,' I say to my reflection.

Having spent yesterday evening loading the decorations at the office into the minibus, all that's needed now is to get back to Cherrywell Manor and finish the job. While the kettle is boiling, I work on some deep breathing exercises, trying to top up on some relaxation. Then I fill a travel mug with gingerbread flavoured coffee and stash some stollen into my bag as a snack. Today will be fuelled by caffeine and sugar and hopefully enough sparkle and festive themed props to bring that much-needed Christmas magic too.

I tune the minibus's radio to a station solely playing seasonal songs; now I can spend the journey belting out crooners and cheesy pop classics. Windshields are an invisibility filter, aren't they? No one can see me dancing in my seat. The warming feeling you get when you drive home for Christmas stirs inside me.

Arriving at Cherrywell Manor, I'm psyched for action and, if my reflection in the rear-view mirror is anything to go by, rosy cheeked. Getting as close to the side entrance as possible, I park. Eager to begin, I leap out and rap on the door. Once again there's no answer. I strain my ears and am disappointed, there's no appearance of Rory on this occasion. Still, that's for the best. I didn't really believe I'd be lucky enough to see him again anyway. *Must focus on task at hand.* Trying the door handle, I find it open, so go in calling out a, 'Hello?'

Creeping towards the door is Mr Barnes. He smiles when he sees me but his jaw is set, determined. 'Miss Holly, I am sorry to keep you waiting.'

'It's no problem. Are you okay?'

He gives a strained nod. 'Don't you worry about me. Do you need any help or shall I leave you to your own devices?'

Even taking another step might finish him off, so I decline. 'I'll be fine. Can I carry on setting up?'

'Please do. I'm sure your endeavours will be quite marvellous.' Mr Barnes's deep tones are comforting.

'I appreciate you saying that, thank you.'

Mr Barnes gives a slow dip of his head 'A delivery has arrived for you. I took the liberty of putting it in the corner, ready for you.'

'Thank you.' He staggers off, leaving me alone in the huge, nearly empty room.

Casting my eyes around the space the scale of the task fully dawns on me and my merry glow begins to fade. But hang on a minute, Mr Barnes keeps ploughing on, resilient. I'm not going to let a little last-minute snafu deter me. I've got the lights, the props, the art and some sheer determination. I steel myself for the task ahead and without a second's more hesitation throw myself in to creating a Twelve Days of Christmas Wonderland (in just two days).

The twinkling wintery trees radiate a soft warm glow and now they're set up satisfactorily, I start sprinkling the other garlands and ornaments around the room. Pulling a chair over to a large ornate mirror I string the last set of fairy lights around the baroque frame. The reflection shows the grand room behind me, festooned with a delicate smattering of festive cheer, but, surveying it critically, there just isn't enough.

Carefully I climb down, then double check my supplies. To my horror I realise I've already used everything. All the decorations I'd brought and the extras I'd ordered. The prestige of the company is riding on this event, all the teenagers and support workers at the charity are relying on me, not to mention my future career prospects. I'm not giving up. I just need to hunt out some more adornments, perhaps the nearest town will have something I can buy? Surely the house manager can recommend something. But where to find him? This place is huge and most of it is unknown territory.

'Mr Barnes?' I call out as I step into the hallway.

An icy chill greets me. The front door is open, welcoming the frosty weather inside. From around the frame peeks the white hair and kind face of the elderly man.

'Can I help you, Miss Holly?' His voice quivers.

I rush to him. 'Mr Barnes, are you okay?'

'I'm just putting up the wreath, it's one of my favourite jobs of the season.'

The huge leafy garland is lying on the front step. The dark fir fronds bejewelled with real ruby holly berries, silvery eucalyptus leaves and amber hued orange and cinnamon clusters.

'That's stunning.'

Mr Barnes puffs his chest proudly. 'All foraged

for in the garden. Rory put it together. It's my job to put it up.'

'Do you want me to help?'

'I do not want to put you out, Miss Holly.'

'I'd be happy to.'

The butler reaches towards the wreath but with a gasp, he falters.

I try to support him, my hand on his arm. 'Please, I'll lift it.'

Mr Barnes dips his head and straightens his posture. I'll take that as a yes. Careful to avoid any prickles, I grasp it and heave upwards.

'Gosh, this is heavier than expected.' I stagger for a step before righting myself.

'The ring is soaked in water over night to keep it fresh for as long as possible, and it is brimming with rather a lot of greenery. Perhaps Rory got carried away. There is so much going to waste in the grounds.' Mr Barnes gives a soft chuckle.

With minimal direction, I secure the wreath on the door, and check to see if Mr Barnes approves.

'Miss Holly, I could not have placed it better myself.'

'It's the least I could do, especially as you've given me a wonderful idea.'

'Have I really?' Mr Barnes rubs his hands to bring some warmth back into them.

'Is it okay if I use a bit of the greenery from the grounds to decorate inside, for the gala?'

'Absolutely, would you like me to show you

where to go?'

'No, thank you. Just point me in the right direction and then get inside and warm up.'

'Certainly.'

Excitement blooms in my chest as I stride off, following Mr Barnes's directions into the frosty surroundings.

CHAPTER 16

Gathering a wheelbarrow and some seca-
teurs from where Mr Barnes advised, I
march past the French formal garden
and off into some woodland. The manor house
is soon obscured behind the thickening trees.
The squeak of the barrow is interrupted by a
dull, grating noise. Emerging through some firs,
I come across the welcome sight of a rather pert
bottom, clad in corduroys. Lying sideways on
the ground, the owner is working hard at sawing
the base of a stunning spruce. *There he is!*

Okay, I know I'm here to work but I was starting to worry that I genuinely wouldn't see him
again. I park the wheelbarrow and watch with
wonder. The conversation with Amber loops
through my mind. Find someone after the gala
not during.

The conifer is felled in a flash and quickly up
jumps the pert bottom, along with the rest of
the man, complete with faded baseball cap and
squeaky wellies.

'Hi, Rory.'

Rory startles and turns. 'Your turn to frighten

me this time!'

'Yes, sorry about that. I should have given you some warning I was here, what with the saw and all.' He's holding an impressive piece of kit which looks deadly.

'No harm done. What are you doing all the way out here?' Rory's eyes find the wheelbarrow at my feet.

'Mr Barnes said I could get some foliage to decorate inside.'

Rory raises an eyebrow. Perhaps this is a bad idea.

'For the charity gala...' I explain, feeling guilty. Am I overstepping the mark?

'If Barnes is happy for you to help yourself, then who am I to stop you?'

'Are you sure? I mean, you are the gardener. Sorry, I should have asked you...' Stop rabbiting, Holly.

He holds his hands up as if in surrender. 'It's fine.'

'Do you think Mr Perdreau will mind?'

'Honestly, if you've got Barnes' approval then you won't have a problem. He's a hard cookie to crumble.'

'Really? He seems lovely.'

'He's obviously taken a shine to you. He's the stubbornest man I've ever met.'

'Is that so?' I smile at the thought of him letting me help him; that must be a compliment. I point to the ground. 'Is that what I think it is?'

'If you think it's a fifteen-year-old Norwegian Spruce that's been pruned to symmetrical perfection then, yes, it is!'

I approach the tree. 'Is it a Christmas tree for the house?'

'Kind of. It's for you.'

'What?' I bend down to look closer. Gently rubbing the thick needles between my fingers causes a rich scent of pine to waft into my nose.

'You painted such a beautiful image of your vision for the gala yesterday, I thought it'd help if you had the giant tree you described.'

My attention goes back to Rory. 'This is amazing. Thank you.'

He shrugs. 'There's hardly any household in for Christmas this year so no one had bothered with a tree. But I thought...' He shrugs again, stuffing his hands into his pockets.

Suddenly I'm on my feet, my arms flung around Rory and we're falling. The springy evergreen branches cushion our landing. I don't know what came over me. 'Sorry!' I stand and hastily brush loose needles from my knees. 'Are you okay?'

He's lying sprawled out, hands trapped in his pockets, laughter shaking his broad chest. My hair swings forwards as I reach to help him. The blazing look he gives me as he catches my hand is knee-weakening. He barely puts any weight through me as he hauls himself up, but his grip remains strong. Suddenly he is standing very tall, very close.

'Yes, thanks,' his voice is gruff, strained.

He reaches up to my hair and I'm rooted to the spot. He plucks out a leaf which flutters to the ground. The moment seems to stretch and then, in an instant, it's over as a squawk reverberates through the trees. An amorous squirrel perches on a nearby branch, squealing to attract a mate.

Focusing back on Rory, I say, 'Is the tree okay?'

I bite my lip and his gaze is drawn to my mouth. He swallows, blinks and looks to the tree. 'It'll be fine.' He straightens his cap. The intensity has left his face, now a cheeky glint catches his features. 'We can just put that bit at the back if not, no one will know.'

'We?'

Rory pretends to be outraged. 'You're not making me do it all on my own, are you? Not after I've chopped it down and carried it all the way back to the house.'

I nearly crushed him to death and he's flirting with me! 'You've not strictly carried it back yet. How about, you help prune the greenery for some festive foliage and I'll let you borrow my wheelbarrow to cart it back? Then, if you're lucky, I'll let you help me decorate it.' My coquettish skills are a bit rusty but I'm loving dusting them off.

'*Your* wheelbarrow?'

'Mr Barnes did say I could use it.'

'And he is in charge. In that case, let's get trimming.'

We laugh and chat as while we hack down bunches of holly, spools of ivy and sprigs of other pretty greenery. I keep stealing secret glimpses of Rory at work. A warm glow creeps through me, from my toes all the way to my chest. These feelings aren't exactly new to me, it's just that I haven't had them for quite a while.

But wait.

Lusting after handsome gardener should really not be distracting me right now. *Concentrate, Holly. You've got a gala to run!*

Rory's a very able assistant and after climbing up many a tree to reach the exact sprigs and fronds I desire, he then helps lug it all back to the house.

Things are starting to be on the up; I've solved the problem of the decorations and had the pleasure of Rory's company to boot. Perhaps I *can* harmlessly flirt with Rory and still pull a fabulous event together.

On our final run, Rory is pushing the huge tree through the forest and towards Cherrywell Manor. The trusty wheelbarrow is hidden under the precariously balanced, bouncing spruce, with only the handles on show.

'I'll get the tree stand and put it up, while you sort out the greenery in the other room,' suggests Rory, planning our next move.

'Sounds good. I'm starving, do you want some stollen?' I reach into my bag and break some off to snack on.

'Yes please.'

I hold out a piece towards Rory but he's occupied supporting our cumbersome load. Without thinking, I find myself reaching up and popping it into his mouth. As my fingers brush his lips, the warm glow in my chest explodes into a sudden, melting hot yearning. I'm so close I can see how his pupils dilate. The cheeky flirtation between us has intensified into something entirely different.

'Fanks,' he replies through a marzipan-bound mouth, his eyes blazing at me.

Have I gone too far? I smile and turn away, taking a bite of the stollen to give my heart a chance to quell its tattoo against my ribs. I was so wrong. Harmless flirting is not in my repertoire.

CHAPTER 17

The garish tableau of the Sixth Day of Christmas is waiting for me when I walk into the bar area. The gander has a crazed dissolute gleam in its eye which manages to watch me as I move around the room. Regarding it with contempt, I back out into the hall to find Rory wrestling with the tree. He's thrown his faded cap over the finial on the bannister and his crop of dark hair sticks up roughly with a couple of pine needles jutting out. Although I love the manly look, being able to see his gorgeous face more clearly is definitely an improvement to the ensemble.

Some chuntering escapes from under his breath.

'Can I give you a hand?'

'Please. If you can steady the top part, I can tighten the base up so it's symmetrical.'

Spreading a couple of the boughs to move in closer to the trunk, I grip amongst the spikey needles and hold it steady. From here I have an excellent view of Rory, lying on his side a glimpse of toned torso peeping out where his shirt has ridden up while he labours to secure the tree.

'Uch-hum.' Mr Barnes announces his arrival.

Eyes forward! I can feel my cheeks colouring like the berries with which I share my name. Totally busted.

Before I dig myself into a hole trying to explain, Rory arches out from his sprawl. 'I thought you were going to rest, Barnes?' He stands, brushing off some errant needles.

'The caterers are here-'

'I'll see to them,' Rory interrupts, waving his arms in front of him. They exchange a look which I can't quite place. 'You go and rest that back, or I'll have no excuse but to call out the doctor.'

Mr Barnes gives a slow bow-like bob, winces and moves away.

'Sorry, I'd better go and sort that out. They need to prepare.'

'It's no problem, I feel I'm keeping you from your work.'

'Not at all.' Rory's face is sincere. 'I've been really enjoying getting all this set up with you.'

'Me too.'

'You need anything before I go?'

'Do you have a ladder I could use please? I need to get the foliage up high but there's no rush.'

'Sure. I'll get it for you when I'm back.' His eyes twinkle as he smiles. *God, those eyes.*

'Thanks, I'll make a start on the low bits.'

Back to the task at hand. First, I use a red ribbon to secure some mistletoe into pretty bunches. Then, being careful not to get pricked, I swathe the mantlepiece in a garland of holly. I'm separating the ivy and other greenery into thirty piles, enough to give a festive flourish to each of the art installations and have some spare for the ballroom too, when Rory appears, clanking a paint-speckled ladder.

'It's looking fantastic,' he exclaims, casting his eyes around the room.

'Almost there, I've just got to arrange the art work with some of the greenery.'

Shit, he's going to see those bloody geese. I step backwards in an attempt to obscure his view as he places the ladder down.

With curiosity scrunching his brow, Rory peers around me to see what I'm hiding. There's a split-second freeze before he erupts into hysterics.

'Pa-ha-ha! What's that!'

'Oh don't! It's awful, isn't it?'

'It's certainly something.' He moves closer and pulls out the stack of three canvases to get the full effect of the triptych.

'I'm twisting myself into knots over this, I don't know what to do. Do you think if I disguise it with some of this foliage then no one will notice?'

'No, don't hide it.' Rory's gaze roams across the trio of pictures. 'It's a statement about the lost meaning of Christmas to the corporate, commercial world. A salute to the nineties controversial Britartists combined into a kitschy parody of the pop art movement. It's quite genius.'

'Genius?' I rake some wayward strands of hair from my face. 'It's a disaster.'

'I beg to differ, it's probably the most honest art work that Cherrywell Manor has ever hosted.'

I can feel that vein pulse in my temple, as my blood pressure mounts. 'This is supposed to be a Christmas gala to raise money to support students to continue into further education.'

'And what a fantastic talking point, much better than the usual banalities.'

Are you an art critic now?

'It's three geese getting assaulted. And anyway, how would you know?'

Rory opens his mouth and then shuts it again. 'Anything else I can do for you?' He asks with a sudden change of tone.

'Sorry.' I gnaw my lip with my teeth. 'That was rude of me. I'm so stressed about this... situation. I know it's just a gala but it's so important... I feel like I've ruined Christmas.'

Rory's laugh is kind this time. 'I've seen a couple of galas held here in my time, already I can tell this one's far superior.'

'It's just not classy enough and I'm worried those bloody geese are the final straw.'

'It's beautiful, but in a homely way. It's re-claiming Christmas from all the corporate non-sense. And having students' art and their families here to be able to appreciate it, that's a really special gift. It's a truly wonderful idea.'

'I can't take credit for it, that's Montague's concept.'

'Which you ran with and transformed it into something entirely magical.'

Taking one of those deep breaths, the ones that are supposed to calm me, I look up into Rory's kind eyes. 'Thank you. I've been getting in a tizz about this and hearing that has really helped.'

'My pleasure. Now, how else can I help you?'

'If you have time, I'd love to get this lot up.' I gesture at the stacks of art piled against the wall. 'But I don't want to stop you from your work.'

'Not a problem, let's get this vision of yours *and Montague's* realised.' Rory flicks open the ladder and gets to work hanging the canvases and frames from the picture rail under my careful direction.

CHAPTER 18

The sun is setting, the rose-tinted landscape is lit up with the final flare of afternoon light. The silhouette of bare trees in the distance stand out like a legion of burnt matches. There seems to be a cruel frost in the air, trapping everything under a frozen mantle. Buzz! My phone vibrates, breaking my reverie.

It feels close to midnight but a quick glance at the time shows it's only mid-afternoon. There's a message from Deborah demanding my presence back in the office, so I'd better call it a day. A heavy sadness settles inside as I realise I have to return to the real world. In my head I've spent a fairytale-like day primping a palatial manor, getting it ready for a magical party. When, in fact, I'm more like Cinderella before the ball; slogging away to make things perfect for other people to enjoy. Does that make Rory my fairy godfather? Or my prince?

I find Rory tinkering with the switch for the light on the kitchen stairs. 'I really appreciate your help today.'

'I enjoyed it. Are you off then?'

'Yes, I've got to get back to the office. I'll be back tomorrow to finish the tree and do any last-minute bits. There's still the 'First Day of Christmas' exhibit to set up and I'm sure Deborah will think of things to keep me busy.'

Rory parts his lips as if to say something but a blast of wind interrupts, swinging the servants' door shut.

'Rory, are you there?' A rasping voice calls.

Startled, Rory almost falls down the stairs. He lunges out with his hand, knocking the switch off, plunging us into darkness. I grab for him and he clings to me. As I pull him in close I drink in the pine and musk fragrance from his neck before we manage to regain our balance. His hands feel scorching against my body. I don't want to let go.

'Thanks,' he gasps. I feel his arms tighten around me.

The voice calls out once more.

With a fumble, we find the door handle and stagger into the hallway.

'Barnes!' Rory calls out, sounding huskier than usual. 'Are you okay?'

The butler has braced himself against the wall, his knuckles whitened by his grip. Rory untangles himself and rushes to him.

'Terribly sorry, I appear to have disturbed you.'

'Don't be silly. Is it your back? We need to get you a doctor I think.'

I follow, straightening my clothes. 'Anything I can do?'

Mr Barnes lets out a small groan. 'I don't wish to be a nuisance.'

The last thing Mr Barnes wants is an audience. 'I've got some painkillers in my bag. I'll go and get them.'

Moving towards the Oak Room, I hear Rory say, 'Let's just try and get you upright and somewhere you can rest. You can't do the stairs, I'll set you up along here…'

It takes a minute to locate the packet of pills at the very bottom of my bag. Heart pounding in my throat, I race back out to find the entrance hall deserted. I can't leave them like this, what else can I do? I slip down to the kitchen to see if I can find some inspiration. After rummaging around I locate a wheat bag and an ice pack. Not sure what Mr Barnes would prefer I prepare both, carefully wrapping the ice pack in a tea towel to protect his skin. While microwaving the wheat bag I notice the flask from yesterday, washed up and drying on the side. I make a flask of tea, sure Rory could do with it even if Mr Barnes doesn't fancy any.

Rory's pacing the entrance hall when I return, his phone pressed to his ear. Mr Barnes is nowhere to be seen.

I hold up the blister pack of pills and Rory takes it, mouthing a grateful, "thank you" before talking into the phone and explaining what's happened. I place the rest of the supplies on the bottom step of the staircase. Should I stay and help? I don't want to get in the way.

I indicate to Rory that I'm leaving. He covers the receiver and mouths, "sorry" then drags his fingers through his dishevelled hair, attention tuned back to the call. The memory of his body crushed against me in the stairwell crosses my mind. Reluctantly, I wave and leave.

A heaviness settles over me as I depart Cherry-well Manor; I feel sorry to see Mr Barnes in so much pain and guilty for leaving Rory on his own to deal with it. I can't explain it but I'm drawn to the place and the people. Driving away feels like I'm heading in the wrong direction.

Arriving at the office, Amber greets me. 'It's nice to have you back. Deborah will be pleased too.'

'She will?'

'Everything's been "Holly usually does it this way" and "Holly usually does that" and "Holly usually kisses my arse".'

I grimace. 'Sorry.'

'It's not your fault. I got my own back anyway.'

'You did? How?'

'Gave her full fat milk in her coffee.' Amber flicks her hair with sass. 'It all adds up.'

'You're incorrigible! Did she say what this latest venture is that's got her so stressed out?'

'No but I'm keeping my ears open, don't worry. Did you sort out the goose-aster?'

'Kind of. In the end I thought if I do something weird to it, it'll draw more attention so I've just left it as it is. But I've filled the room with so much Christmas cheer that even that questionable piece of art can't detract from it.'

'Sounds sensible. What's left to do tomorrow?'

'Just the last exhibit to display and a Christmas tree to decorate.'

'Awesome, it's all in hand then. Nothing more can go wrong!'

Well, now she's cursed it!

Deborah wafts into the office, fingering her new, savagely cut bob with one hand. The strip lights glint off her manicure, now a more festive berry colour than the usual blood red.

'You look nice. Did you fancy a change?'

Deborah's eyes narrow as if trying to detect whether I'm serious or not. Ignoring the question, she asks, 'Is everything ready for tomorrow?'

'Yes, would you like a lift to Cherrywell? I've got to take a few last-minute bits but there'll be room in the minibus.'

Deborah gives a curt nod and sweeps off saying, 'Pick me up at nine.'

Once the clack of Deborah's heels has receded, Amber whispers, 'Do you truthfully think she looked nice?'

'Yeah, it's quite a severe change but actually, I liked it. Did you help her chose it?'

Amber nods.

'Did she say what it's all in aid of?'

'Not in so many words.'

'I get the feeling she's trying to reinvent herself a bit.'

'Get down with the kids,' Amber jokes, swaggering about. 'Perhaps she could give her policy on office relationships an overhaul.'

'Hmmm.' In this stark fluorescent lighting, my reality is brought into sharp focus. I've been getting carried away. Deborah will never allow a relationship with someone from the venue, it would be *unprofessional.* Who am I kidding? Rory and Cherrywell are a silly pipe dream, which, by this weekend, will be distant memory. Right now, the only thing I need to focus on is the gala.

It'd be frowned upon if I leave the building before Deborah, so I'm tinkering with some last-minute things at my desk. But my mind keeps wandering back to Rory. He'd said he'd enjoyed setting things up with me and, God, I really had too. He's funny, kind and frightfully easy on the eye. The mouth-watering glimpses of what lies beneath his shirt flicker across my memory. Trying to dislodge the thoughts I shake my head. I categorically cannot let myself get distracted now, not with him, and not with the gala so close I can almost touch it.

CHAPTER 19

The dress's luxurious black velvet feels entirely incongruous compared to the scruffy jeans and woolly sweater combo I'm currently wearing. Pausing for just a moment to ensure I've packed everything, I then zip away my gala outfit in a protective bag and hang it by the door, ready to go. Shovelling a few mouthfuls of porridge in my mouth and scorching my tongue on a cup of coffee, I rush, daring not to spare another minute getting ready for the big day. Within minutes I'm trundling through the darkened streets in the minibus, squinting into the headlights of the other early birds already on the road.

As I pull up outside Amber's flat, a face disappears from a window. Soon she bounds on board with a flurry of bags, her scarf and a large thermos.

'Thanks for collecting me. I like your hairband. I brought us some coffee. It's cold isn't it? I hate these winter mornings.' Her babble streams all the way to the office.

I'm feeling quietly proud. The last few days

of practice must have paid off because, after a smooth journey, I park in a visitor's space outside the building without a single jolt or bunny hop. 'We just need to do a last-minute sweep here, grab the last boxes and anything we may have forgotten-'

'And Dirty Deb's outfit,' interjects Amber.

I nod. 'And *Deborah's* outfit. And then hightail it to the venue, picking up Deborah on the way, to make sure everything is ship-shape.'

'Aye aye, captain.'

While I collect the last couple of boxes from under my desk, Amber storms through the office like a black Friday shopper with a preview to the sales, stuffing anything that might come in handy into a sturdy jute shopping bag. Sticky tape, batteries, the fairy lights from around our computer screens, marker pens, scissors, envelopes and a stapler all go in, forming a messy soup of stationery.

Noticing the bemused expression on my face as I watch her, Amber says, 'Be prepared, that's what the Scouts say,' with an authoritative tone.

'I think the Scouts would have carefully planned their survival kit rather than ransacking the office, sweeping everything bar the coffee machine off the surfaces and into the nearest receptacle.'

'True, but then again, I'm not a Scout.'

'Me neither, we're more like elves anyway.' I gesture to Amber's Christmas sweater emblazoned with the inarguable elf uniform of green tunic and golden buttons, and then up to my elfish Alice band, complete with pointy elf ears and a conical hat. 'What would an elf slogan be?'

'Pack everything you can find because you never know when you might need a bulldog clip?' Amber shrugs.

'We need to work on that.' I laugh.

Feeling like I need all the lucky charms, voodoo and superstition that I can get, I pick up my rosemary cutting with care, give it a little sniff and then tuck it into my handbag. 'That should help ensure we remember everything today. Are we ready?'

'Just "The Outfit" and we're done. I didn't spend five hours outside various changing rooms yesterday only to forget the blasted thing today.'

'You said you wanted more responsibility.'

Amber rolls her eyes. 'I don't know about that, but at least it was better than just being the coffee bearer.'

The sun has come up by the time we leave the office. My phone vibrates as I slam the side-door of the minibus closed.

'It's a message from Malika. We need to collect the First Day of Christmas piece now as she won't have enough room to fit it in.'

Amber studies her watch. 'Have we got time?'

'Yes, but only if we leave right now or we'll be late for Deborah.'

Malika is standing on the steps at the front of the college when we pull up. A rough wooden crate is next to her, as high as her waist and wide and deep enough to fit a person in.

'What is it?' Amber asks as she exits the mini bus and bounds up to the box.

'The First Day of Christmas,' replies Malika with an eyebrow raised.

'Can I see?'

'No!' Malika's reply is stern.

'Is it heavy?' I ask as I arrive.

'Not particularly, just make sure you keep it this way up.'

Amber helps me to hoist it up into the rear of the minibus and secure it to some grab handles with bungee cords and ropes to help tether it.

Consulting my notebook, I see the names that Malika has given me to add to the guest list. There's a fair few. 'Can you manage everyone else that's coming?'

'Yes, some of the parents are car-pooling and the students and props are sorted. We'll be fine.'

'See you at Cherrywell Manor tonight then.' I wave cheerfully and drive off in the direction of Deborah's townhouse.

'Was she a bit "off" then?' Amber chews her lip, hesitant.

'I usually find her quite terrifying so no more than normal.' I shrug.

'I thought she seemed funny. Right, time to get

Dame Debs.'

We draw up outside Deborah's *pied-a-terre* as she likes to refer to it, and I twist to Amber, setting my face in as serious an expression as I can muster.

'This is a really important event.' I keep my voice low and controlled, trying to convey the gravity of our task ahead.

'Yes.'

'Nothing will go wrong; it's going to be the best gala dinner ever.'

'Yes.' Amber's eyes are wide as she listens with reverence.

'We are going to make sure of it. We are event ninjas. No one knows we are there. We're just quietly getting the job done.'

'Yes.'

'And we are doing it well.'

'Yes.'

'Anything that doesn't go to plan we just... Sort. It. Out. Deborah doesn't need to know, she just needs to be happy.'

'Yes.'

'And for the love of everything that is Christmas, we do not call her Debs.'

'Really?'

Raising an eyebrow, I tilt my head.

'Got it.' We hold eye contact until the side door suddenly rumbles open.

'Well, this is jolly, isn't it?' Remarks Deborah as she pokes her head into the back of the minibus.

Amber's trying to catch my eye again but I'm determined not to meet it. I know she'll roll her eyes and I'll snigger like the teenager I really am. 'Morning!'

Deborah's attempt to remain dignified as she hauls herself into the minibus is akin to a pole-vaulter's warm up but she manages to launch herself into a seat and then primps her hair and faux fur coat to ensure all is in order.

'Would you like to sit in the front?' Amber asks.

'No thanks, I can enjoy the journey, and my coffee back here.' She shakes her travel cup with a jewel encrusted hand. 'Gosh, are you wearing that ridiculous hairband for a bet, Holly?'

My hand moves up to my Christmassy elf headwear. 'Pardon?'

'I presume it's just for the journey? You're in charge today remember. You want to be taken seriously.'

Way to snow on my parade, Deborah. I quite liked my festive themed accessory. I try to cover up my humiliation. 'Of course. Next stop, Cherrywell Manor,' I announce as I press the accelerator.

'Ohhh,' proclaims a surprised Deborah.

As I steer to a junction there's a gulping sound behind me.

'All okay, back there?'

'Yes,' comes a small reply. Peering in the rear-view mirror I can see Deborah clawing at the roof.

As I continue to drive, another gasp comes from the back. Amber nudges my knee but, I refuse engage. I'm concentrating on driving. Knocking the indicator, I approach a round-about. 'Hold on to your hats.'

'Blaaaaa-' wails Deborah as the minibus banks around to the right.

With a clunk, the travel cup is propelled to the rear of the minibus and the scent of spilled coffee permeates the air. I glance briefly behind me. A twang reverberates as Deborah manically grabs out for anything to steady her and dis-lodges the cable tie which I'd hooked above her seat. Concentration back on the road, I open my mouth to ask if everything is alright but my words fade on my lips as a series of bumps and crunches clang out, only just audible above Deb-orah's screams.

'Eeeeeek!' Amber cries out, covering her head with her scarf.

I take the exit and then pull off the road as soon as it is safe to. 'What's happened?' Looking back, all I can see are Deborah's five-inch heeled ankle boots kicking in the air.

'Oh my goodness, are you alright?' Amber leaps from the vehicle and wrenches at the rear side door while I put on the hazard lights on and clamber out and round to the back.

A shaken Deborah extricates herself from

amongst the boxes. Amber helps her to get out and brushes some splinters off her as she sits on the high step.

Deborah gives a strained cackle as she composes herself. 'Your driving, Holly! Goodness, that was unexpected.'

I raise my eyes from appraising the wreckage that's covering the inside of the minibus. 'My driving?'

'I got thrown around back there like a loose sail luffing on a yacht.'

'Were you wearing your seatbelt?'

'And ruin this gorgeous coat? I don't think so.'

Eyeballing the carnage again, I try to survey the damage Deborah's caused. My ears start to burn but I'm determined to keep my cool. 'We'd better check this box, it's taken a real battering.'

With a flourish of her arm, Deborah checks her gold watch. 'There's no time. I'm sure it's fine. We must get to the venue.'

'Do you want to sit in the front?' offers Amber again.

'Yes, I don't think my poor constitution could take any more of me travelling in the back.'

'Nor mine,' I mutter under my breath.

'Sorry?' asks Deborah.

She heard. 'On time,' I say in a trice, trying to cover up my chuntering. 'I'm an eager beaver to get there on time. Let's go.'

Amber catches my attention and does her signature eye roll. 'I'll just re-secure these ropes.'

'Good idea,' says Deborah as she launches herself into the front seat. 'They can't have been tied particularly well. It's terribly dangerous of you, Holly.'

With gritted teeth I get back into the driving seat and carry on the remainder of the journey. *Deep breaths*.

CHAPTER 20

'I'll leave you girls to sort the unloading while I go in and see what you've done so far. I expect to be wowed, Holly. This is your big chance.' Deborah snaps the sun-visor up, having reapplied her lipstick in the mirror.

Once she's out of ear shot, I sag from the tension and let out a sigh. 'Just got to hold this together for a few hours and then I'll be free of her.'

'Free?' Amber unclips her belt and sits forwards.

'Well, I'll never be free of her, but once I've proven I can do this job she'll breathe down my neck slightly less.' She must. Levering myself up with the head rest, I peer into the back of the minibus. 'I daren't know what kind of damage she's done back there.'

'It'll be okay,' says Amber, unconvincingly. Then fear crumples her face. 'The new dress!' She scrambles out and rushes around to the back.

With sadness I remove my elf-themed hair band. My hair hangs loose to my shoulders. Curses to Deborah; I haven't brought anything else to tie it up with. Still, that's the least of my worries.

'It's okay!' Amber calls, 'The garment bag protected it.'

'That was a lucky escape.' I get out, cold air and wood-smoke stings my nose. I rub my arms to warm up. 'Brrr. Let's get everything inside where it's warm and see what's what.'

'Now we know that bloody outfit's okay, we can cope with anything else.'

I force my posture taller, more resolute. 'Let's do this.'

We lug our load into the Oak Room. It's aglow with the lights and decorations already in place.

'How are we supposed to open it?' asks Amber as we set the wooden crate down.

Fishing out some sturdy scissors from the bag of random office supplies, I use them like a crowbar to prize off the lid.

A leafy tangle fills the inside.

'It seems alright so far.' Reaching in with care, I grasp a spindly trunk. Lifting the fake plant upwards and out of the box there's a clatter as unseen parts fall off, back into the box and scattering over the floor.

'Oh.' Amber watches a plastic pear roll over to the fire place.

'Indeed.' I hold up a battered and bare plant. 'This must have been the *pear tree.* It's ruined.'

'Where's the partridge?'

'Something fell back into the box.' I set the plant and its pot down into a space on the floor.

Amber reaches into the box. 'There's a couple more pears and this.'

She pulls out a model bird. The rich orange plumage shines in the fairy lights and its emerald green head glistens with velvety feathers. Fingering the long stripy tail feathers, Amber's frowns. 'I didn't think I'd seen a partridge before, but I'm sure I've seen these running around countryside roads.'

I cover my eyes with despair. 'That's not a partridge.'

'What?'

'That's a pheasant.'

'But isn't the song *A Partridge in a Pear Tree*?'

'Yes. But that is unequivocally a pheasant.' Crouching down, I bury my head in my knees with a groan.

'I don't get it.'

'I'm not sure what's worse; Deborah destroying the exhibit or the actual exhibit.'

'Can we fix it?' asks Amber.

'I don't where to begin.'

'Listen, you're the best event planner in the business. I know you'll come up with something good. And I'll do whatever I can to help.'

'Thank you.' I give Amber a quick squeeze. 'Okay, deep breaths. We've got this.'

'That's the spirit.'

'First, I need to confess.' Just as I'm reaching in to my pocket to make the awkward phone call, my mobile starts to vibrate. Malika's name flashes up on the screen.

'Hi, there must be something in the airwaves. I was about to call you.'

'I won't keep you long. I'm calling to finalise our numbers.'

'Okay, what's it going to be so I can update the caterers.'

There's a small cough. 'Three less than anticipated.'

'Oh?'

'One of my students has found the path to being an artiste too difficult a journey to navigate.'

'I'm sorry to hear that.'

'They realised that to be a true creator you need to examine your soul and tell the truth of what you find there.'

Amber's trying to listen in. I give her a befuddled look. 'Right…'

'In truth, I suspect they found an echo-y empty cavern. They've quit the course. They aren't coming and neither are their guests.'

'Okay…'

'It's a relief, their submission to your display was abysmal at best. You'll need to withdraw it.'

Not another disaster! Scanning all the exhibits, I try to work out which one it could be. They're quirky, yes, but they all seem to have had a lot of thought and effort invested. 'Which day were they?'

'The First Day of course. I spent longer packing it into the box than they did producing it. Have you opened it yet?'

Santa is real! Holding my phone in one hand, I hug my free arm to my chest. 'I wanted to talk to you about that piece actually.'

'I was so embarrassed to hand it over to you. I strongly suggest you pull it from the display, it detracts from the other students work. Feel free to use it as you wish.' In a lower voice she mumbles, 'Kindling would probably be best.'

Phew! But wait, should I confess the accident anyway or just be grateful I've got away scot-free and never speak of it again?

Malika fills the silence. 'I look forward to seeing what you replace it with.'

'What *I* replace it with?' Disbelief quickly replaces my jubilation.

'Yes. You've only got eleven of the days now, haven't you?'

'Would one of your students be happy to-'

'Oh no, no, no, no.' I can picture her wagging a finger. 'They have coursework due. Plus, it's a late night for them mid-week. I can't expect to put any more work on to them. I won't keep you any longer I know you must be busy-busy. See you later.'

Staring at my phone screen long after I hang up, my gaze is unfocused while my brain scrambles.

'Everything okay? Was that Malika?'

'Yep.' I've forgotten how to blink.

'She does terrify you, doesn't she? What did she say? Did she go all political on you again? Is she mad about the artwork?'

'No.' I snap out of my daze and give Amber a tight smile. 'We need to pull it from the exhibition. And it's up to me to replace it!'

Just as Amber gives me a commiserating look, Deborah stalks into the room.

'There you are. I've done a quick inspection but I want you to walk me through the event as if I'm a guest arriving. So I know you've thought of everything.'

I scramble on my feet and try to obscure the travesty of the pear tree with my body. 'Okay, let's go now.'

Deborah regards me with curiosity and then tries to glance over my shoulder. 'Okay,' she says with uncertainty, giving a faint scowl.

'Let's start at the front door.' I march off in that direction, holding out my arms dramatically. 'Big beautiful festive wreath, ding-dong, the guests get shown into the great hall.' I sweep through the door for effect.

The huge tree that Rory and I had wrestled with yesterday towers majestically from its position by the stairs. It's still naked but is now surrounded by some large cardboard boxes brimming with decorations; some unexpected gifts under the tree. Rory must have put them there.

'This will never do,' tuts Deborah. 'I thought

you were on top of everything.'

'I am- I was about to-'

'Really, Holly. This isn't good enough.' With an extravagant sigh, Deborah announces, 'I'll sort this out with Amber. You go and sort whatever that was that you didn't want me to see in the other room.'

As heat floods my cheeks, some footsteps start pounding down the stairs. From above descends Rory. I admonish my ridiculous heart, all aflutter like a schoolgirl. *Behave!*

'I thought I heard voices.' Rory rounds the last flight.

Did he hear that remonstration from Deborah? I daren't catch his eye. I stare at his lovely chest instead.

'Oh, hello. We were just about to decorate the tree, care to join us?' Deborah's voice is unusually friendly.

'That sounds fun,' replies Rory. 'But I'd hate to tread on anyone's toes or ruin the vision by misplacing a bauble.'

'I'm sure you have some important things to be doing.' Deborah gives him a white toothed grin, then turning to Amber, announces, 'We shall do the tree. Holly, you run along.'

Amber appears decidedly unimpressed at being lumbered with Deborah, again.

Despite feeling belittled, I take the opportunity to flee so I can panic about the pear tree in private. And lessen the chance of Deborah mocking me in front of Rory- *cringe.* But why was Deborah so friendly to Rory? Normally a gardener wouldn't register on her radar.

CHAPTER 21

In the Oak Room, I drop to my knees and collect the loose pears into a pile with the pheasant and spindly tree next to them, in a dishevelled kind of line up.

'Not another one,' comes a voice from behind me.

I whip around. Rory is standing by the door. His eyes are dancing despite desperately trying to keep his face straight.

'If you mean another disastrous piece of artwork, then yes.'

'What happened this time? Is it one of those flat-pack artworks that you need to assemble yourself?' Rory's features light up as he chuckles, letting me know he's only teasing. 'No? You hated it so much you decided to destroy it?'

'It arrived like this.' I assume a falsely perky tone as I say, 'It's okay though, I don't need to fix it, I need to replace it with something entirely new... and different... and better.'

Squinting at the objects in question, Rory says, 'Is that a pheasant?' His shoulders shake, unable to hold his laughter back any more.

'Don't ask!' Grabbing the stuffed bird, I swat him on the leg with the long tail feathers.

Laughing even more, Rory swipes at the bird, taking it from me and cuddling it under his arm. 'I quite like it.'

The pears make great ammunition as I fire them at him. They bounce off his chest and arms, one after the other. 'It's not funny!'

Rory fumbles to catch the pears and sings, '*And a pheas-ant in a pear treeee.*'

Running out of fruit, I huff, 'Unless you've got a bright idea of how to solve this catastrophe, you can keep your carolling to yourself.'

'Does that mean if I have a bright idea then I can keep singing?'

'Only if the idea works.'

Rory waggles his eyebrows and gives a very knowing look. 'Well, in that case... *On the first day of Christmas my true love sent to meeee-*' He swivels on the ball of his foot and starts striding off.

'Huh?' I jump up. 'Wait. Have you got an idea? What is it?' He's going outside so I grab my coat, and scamper to catch him up as his long legs take him out of the side doors and across the gravel drive.

'Where are we going?'

Rory keeps up the song for the whole way, even singing both tempos for the five gold rings stanza. I trot along next to him having given up asking questions by the sixth verse.

With a hand on the doorknob of a gleaming glassy outhouse, Rory finishes the song and then flings the door open with a flourish. He stands back and bows dramatically to let me in.

'Where are we?'

'The orangery. Quick, before we let all the cold air in.'

An earthy scent hits my nose, while my cheeks warm in the comparative heat. Several large terracotta pots containing fruit trees line one side of the large green house, while across the side wall is a potting table. A yellow hose, lying dormant, snakes across the floor.

'Are we going to change the song to 'a pheasant in an orange tree' and hope no one notices?'

'That would be a bold move, but, no. I don't just grow oranges in here.' Rory retrieves a trolley from one corner and pulls it over to one of the pots.

'Is that a *real* pear tree?' There are some yellow-green fruits nestled amongst the leaves.

'Oh to be a pear tree - any tree in bloom! With kissing bees singing of the beginning of the world-' quotes Rory. Who is this gardener guy who can quote Zora Neale Hurston? He goes on to say, 'I have pomegranates too but thought this would be more appropriate.'

'But it's December. It's still bearing fruit.'

'One of the reasons I love my greenhouse. Off season harvests. So, will this help solve your problem?'

'Yes! Thank you.'

'You hold the trolley steady and I'll lift it on.'

'The plant's not going to go into shock if we take it outside, is it?'

'It'll be okay, but we can wrap it in some fleece if it will make you feel better?'

Bracing my arms on the handlebar to keep the trolley steady, I reply, 'Yes please, I'd hate to be responsible for losing one of your trees.'

Rory manoeuvres the tree onto the flat bed and secures the container with some rope. As he retrieves some horticultural fleece from a high shelf, I'm given another tantalising glimpse of his torso as he reaches up. The muscular V line tempts my gaze down past his waistband. Completely mesmerised, I can't help nibble my bottom lip.

He shoots me a grin as he dismounts the ladder. He totally knew I was ogling him. I can feel my face flame up. It's just because it's warm in here.

Wordlessly we swaddle the tree in the material.

'That ought to do it.' Rory appraises our work.

'Have you got any bright ideas for the partridge aspect of my dilemma?' I hold the door of the greenhouse open.

'I do, as a matter of fact.' Rory gives a cheeky eyebrow quirk and then reprises his vocals. *'On the first day of Christmas...'*

I shut the door behind him and have to scurry

to keep up, once again I'm unable to get any proper answers from Rory, just his very alluring smile.

The sounds of bickering drifts through from the entrance hall, where Amber and Deborah are decorating the tree.

Rory unloads the pear tree with ease and stands it between the bar and a painting of two turtle doves.

'That's exactly where I was imaging it, thank you. And now for the partridge?' The rather battered pheasant is in the middle of the floor.

'Come with me.' Rory takes my hand. His fingers sear a trail like the melting wax of a candle. I barely notice where he's taking me - we're outside again and then we go in another door at the back. I should be making mental notes but my brain is busy repeating a useless mantra of 'don't get distracted now' while every other fibre of my being is consumed with the feeling of his hand in mine.

We go up several flights of narrow stairs, I'm not counting, through another baize lined door, and we emerge on an upper level. The noises from the entrance hall are now filtering up from far below.

'Should we be-' I start to ask if we'll get in trouble but Rory presses a finger to his lips.

He looks over his shoulders and then takes a small peek around a corner. Rory jerks his head indicating along a lengthy corridor. His hand, still engulfing mine, pulls me with him as he runs. I try to keep light on my feet. I daren't breathe. Reaching the end, he turns a brassy knob and ushers me into a room, closing the door behind us.

As the door clicks shut, we are plunged into darkness. I grab out for Rory. We hunch forward, into each other, giggling. His forehead rests against mine; I can feel his breath on my face. Panting from our covert exploits, Rory's huddled so close I'm sure he can feel my chest heaving up and down. Mental note, must do more cardio.

Warm lips brush against mine, setting my heart racing for a whole other reason. As I respond, he pulls me in even closer, his mouth greedy. *Finally!* My skin feels electrified where he's touching my back, my waist, moving into my hair. I've been imagining the feel of his hands on me for weeks. I shut my eyes, letting myself be swept away by his kiss.

'Master Perdreau?' The voice is a long way away but it snaps me out of my trance. Suddenly, I'm upright, pulling away from Rory. 'Whoa-'

Rory gives a quiet shushing sound; a gentle finger soothes my lips. I squint through my eyelashes, I haven't adjusted to the gloom but I can sense he's also frozen to the spot.

After a minute, Rory lets out a low whistle and moves away. A giggle escapes from my mouth, my hand flies up to try and stop it. 'Why do I feel like I'm about to get a detention or something?'

A dim light is flicked on. Rory turns and gives me a smouldering look which sobers me up instantly. 'Were you naughty at school?' His voice is suddenly deeper, loaded.

My stomach dips. My reply of, 'Straight A's,' comes out as a gasp.

'I'm not surprised. If you were in my class, I'd have tried to lead you astray.'

'Well, you're managing it now.' I cast my eyes around the gloomy room, feeling awkward and nervous. 'I'd hate for us to get in trouble for being up here.'

'It's fine.' Rory marches over to the other side of the room and pulls open some heavy lined curtains. The winter sun filters in, revealing a cluttered space, full of unused furniture, piles of boxes and stacks of frames.

'Where are we?'

'It's kind of a storage room. We keep the curtains shut to stop the light fading things.'

Rory pauses and scans the room. He walks over to a wall crowded with artwork and lifts off a small painting. A dark square of navy paint is left behind, the exposed paint around it having faded over time. With a quick short blow on the picture to dust it, Rory then holds it out to me.

'What are you doing?' All my feelings of lust doused by alarm.

'Solving your problem.'

'I don't understand.' I look to the door, hoping we're not busted.

'This can be your partridge.' Rory offers the portrait.

I move over to Rory, thoroughly confused. 'What?' Unconsciously, I reach for the frame to examine it more closely. A noble looking man wearing a burgundy jacket stares back.

'That is Lawrence Perdreau, the first.'

'I'm really not following.'

'Perdreau is French for partridge. You can put that in the tree. Problem solved.'

'But wouldn't it be *stealing*?' The last word comes out as an anxious hiss. 'And wouldn't the actual, current, Lawrence notice?'

'It's fine. Really.' Rory's features crease into a laugh.

Unable to keep from scowling, I implore, 'But how do you know? Aren't you worried we'll get in trouble?'

'If I say it's okay, then trust me, it's okay.'

I'm entirely sceptical. 'Really?'

'There's something I should probably explain. I'm not who you think I am.'

CHAPTER 22

A disorderly lock of hair tickles my face, frustrated, I tuck it behind my ear. 'You're not Rory the gardener?'

Rory's eyes are dancing, amused. 'I'm Rory alright and I do prefer to be in the garden, but I'm not the gardener.'

Indignant, I brace a hand on my hip. 'But you told me that-'

'Not exactly. You presumed that and I didn't correct you.'

'Handyman then! You said you do any job around here that needs doing.'

Rory jiggles his head.

'So, who are you?'

'Lawrence Perdreau, the fourth.' Rory points to the portrait. 'He's my great-grandfather. Rory is what my friends call me. People I don't know, or like, call me Lawrence.'

What?!

Pacing the room, a myriad of thoughts run through my head.

How dare he lie!

What a jerk!

Deborah's going to kill me!

She'd always said not to mix business with pleasure and kissing the son of the owner of the venue does more than just blur those lines a smidgeon.

'You're Lawrence.' I don't expect an answer, I'm just trying to get my head straight. 'I did wonder why I hadn't met him yet.' And it explains how Deborah knew him.

I flump down on the nearest chair, a rather opulent, upholstered affair that's not especially comfortable. I press at my forehead.

'I wouldn't sit on that.' Rory says with a wrinkled nose.

'What?'

Rory shakes his head. 'Prized family antique. That's an original Queen Anne chair. A gift from George the third.'

I leap up. 'Oh gosh, I'm so sorry.'

'Joking! It's a replica. Just trying to lighten the mood.'

Not for the first time, I want to throw something at him, but I'm still clutching the portrait, and there's nothing else to hand. Better not.

I study his face. I can tell his clowning around is masking something. His eyes have that same solemn look I saw on the terrace weeks ago. I should be raging at him but instead I'm worried about him.

My curiosity wins out over my outrage. 'Are you some sort of lord or something?'

'No, my dad's the one chasing a peerage. I'm just a normal guy, wanting a normal life.'

'Why did you lie?'

'It was never meant as a lie as such.' Rory inhales deeply, as if to fortify himself. 'It was a relief when you didn't know who I actually was. You didn't treat me differently and I liked that. Then I was too scared to tell you, I was enjoying the anonymity. I... I liked you and if you knew who I was then...'

'I wouldn't have treated you differently.'

Would I?

'Yes, you would.'

Yeah, he's probably right.

'People always do. Deborah's one of the worst! Look, I'm just a simple guy. I didn't ask for all this.'

'The grand house and the name you mean?'

Rubbing his forehead, he sighs. 'The pressure.' He swallows and continues, 'Dad's completely left me in the lurch to organise this place, to *save* Cherrywell. But I'm not the noble, sophisticated type he wants me to be.' He tugs at his chequered shirt as if to explain. 'I'm just a normal person who likes gardening and fixing things.' He looks at me, all vulnerable and pleading. Those puppy eyes are going to be the death of me.

Reluctantly, I have to admit I understand why he fibbed. I soften my voice to let him know I'm not mad. 'So, why are you doing all this?'

'Hosting this gala is a big deal to Dad. He and

Montague go way back. School buddies. Montague is a bit like an uncle to me. Plus, Dad has ideas of converting the house into a venue, to help generate some money to keep it going. He wants me to *take the helm*.' He assumes a posh accent. 'But I can't do it, not on my own. This place is massive and takes a lot of work.' He examines his shoes. 'Sorry, I shouldn't be burdening you with all this.'

'It's okay, I'm happy to listen. I remember you said the other day there was a lot of work to do. I hadn't realised quite how much.' I squeeze his arm, wishing I could do more to console him. 'It strikes me as though you're doing a great job so far.'

A shy smile peeks out. 'It's all you, to be honest. You've got some amazing ideas for the place. The last few weeks have felt like a weight's been lifted.' There go my cheeks, burning again. 'I was panicking about letting him down and messing things up. I'm no good with all the formal stuff and I hate all the networking and falseness. I've hidden upstairs when there's been many a gala held here.' He shudders to emphasise the point.

'That explains why I haven't seen you before.'

'Or I, you. And then you blazed in like some sort of revelation.'

'Well, I've had a lot of help,' I bumble, overcome. 'Plus, my future career is riding on this so I've really tried to go the extra mile. Do you know what you're going to do after the gala?

With the house and other events and things?'

'I feel trapped. If I don't help out I'll be letting Dad down. But it's too much for me on my own and you've seen Barnes, I can't burden him.' Rory runs a hand through his hair.

'What happens if you say 'no' to it all?'

'This place is a money pit. The house would fall into disrepair. Good people would lose their jobs. Not doing something is not an option.'

Poor Mr Barnes! 'What are you going to do?'

'I don't know.' He fills his chest and exhales slowly. 'If I can't think of something then Dad's just going to have to come back from the Caribbean and do it himself. It's his vision after all.'

'How's that going to go down?'

Rory grimaces. 'Horrifically. I'm going to have to let him down gently, pick my time with care or risk certain... alienation.'

There's clearly more to this than I could begin to imagine. What a nightmare for him. 'Wouldn't it be better to tell him sooner rather than later?'

'You're right. I've been putting it off for too long. I'll phone him.' He rubs at his forehead. 'Once the gala's gone off with a bang and he's in a good mood. Then hopefully he'll take it better.'

'No pressure then,' I quip. 'I'm going to need your help to ensure this event is outstanding, otherwise we'll both be in trouble.'

Rory fixes me with a reassuring look. 'I know it will be. I've seen you working. You're exceptionally dedicated to your job. This truly will be the best gala ever.'

'Speaking of which…'

'We should get back, I need to see what Barnes wanted.'

'And I need to keep Deborah happy.'

We leave the room. He's not holding my hand as we retrace our steps. Perhaps now I know the truth he's not interested? Maybe I was just a fantasy for him and now his secret's discovered, I'm not desirable? My heart feels heavy. I grasp the portrait to my chest, wishing it was Rory pressed there instead.

CHAPTER 23

'Tell me about this exhibit.' Deborah gestures to the newly installed First Day of Christmas. 'It's not particularly in keeping with the other pieces from the college.'

Fighting the urge to retort that it was Deborah who gave the kiss of death to the already abysmal submission, I grit my teeth. 'Due to unforeseen circumstances, that particular composition has been withdrawn, so I liaised with a contact here at Cherrywell and we produced this. It's literally a family tree of the Perdreaus. I thought it tied in well with Montague's theme and his specification to bring back family in to the meaning of Christmas.' Maintaining a cool, professional poise my brain whirrs frantically, like one of those seven swans swimming on a lake, she's not able to see the chaos below the surface.

'And you have all the relevant approval to use their painting?'

'Yes.'

'Well, I have to say, other than the lack of organisation with the Christmas tree, all appears to be in order. The gala should be satisfactory.'

And there it is. My glowing accolade. I check the clock. 'We have an hour before the first guests arrive. Let's get ready.'

'Mr Perdreau usually makes a room available for me upstairs, but we don't want to assume this kindness for everyone, so you and Amber should use the basement.' Deborah pivots and strides from the room.

Eyeballing Amber, I silently implore her not to quibble as we follow Deborah, leaving the Oak Room and enter the main hallway. Deborah heads upwards, she knows her way around pretty well, while we continue down to where us minions belong, the basement. Only once we've gone downstairs, do we and turn to each other and groan about Deborah. We duck through the frantic activity of the caterers in the kitchen to a small room further at the back.

'You get yourself ready. I need to get my dress from the minibus. See you soon.' I nip away.

There's a churning in my insides; excitement, apprehension and a tinge of sorrow. The thought of the gala finally happening is wonderful although I'm anxious for it to be a success. And if it is a success then that means it's finished, it'll all be over. I'm going to miss Cherrywell Manor... and Rory.

The last few days I've spent with him have been dreamlike, despite a couple of nightmare situations. But I guess that's just what they were, a dream, a castle in the sky. In a bid to shake the thoughts free, I twitch my head. Right now, I need to stay focused and he's far too distracting and completely out of reach.

Cherrywell Manor is so big, I'm sure I've never walked the same route twice. Taking a circuitous journey to get one last fill of the great house, I go out of the small room, through another parlour up some narrow stairs and then outside, finding myself in the kitchen garden. The sun descended long ago, it's pitch-black save only for the illumination of a security light. Rory's silhouette is digging underneath it.

A smile creeps across my face at the welcome surprise. 'Hi, Rory.' God, I'm pathetic.

'Hey! Everything okay? Another art work emergency?' Rory works over the muddy ground with vigour.

'Not this time, I'm just going to get my dress.'

Rory's eyes shine brightly as he looks up. He buries the prongs of the fork into the mud with a thunk. 'I'm sad I'll be missing out on seeing that!'

'What? Are you not going to be there tonight?'

He shakes his head. 'I thought I should keep Barnes company. And socialising at galas- like I said earlier, it's really not my scene.'

Disappointed, I fiddle with my keys. 'Okay, well, thanks for all your help and everything.' I hate the way my voice tapers off.

Rory pauses, holding my gaze. After a moment, he says, 'I know you need to get ready, but will you meet me under the Christmas tree before it all kicks off. So I can wish you luck, or break a leg, or whatever event organisers get wished.'

Yes. Absolutely, yes.

But play it cool, Holly. 'Okay.' *Good job.* I check the time. 'See you there in half an hour?'

'Great.' Rory dusts his hands off. 'I'll just go and get cleaned up myself then.'

After watching him disappear through the back door, I continue in the direction of the minibus, trying not to leap into the air clicking my heels. The chilly air doesn't even register. My heart's pounding, adrenaline's coursing. It's not because of the night ahead. It's entirely because of Rory.

CHAPTER 24

With Amber distracted by sticking on some false eyelashes, I move quickly through the basement and up the narrow stairs to our rendezvous point, worried that Rory has given up waiting for me. Pinning my curls up into an ornate clip had taken longer than I'd anticipated.

Lit by the glow of a thousand fairy lights swathed up the tall tree, the hall looks truly magical. The space is deserted. I check around the tree, the boughs are laden with decorations, but Rory's nowhere to be seen. I've missed my chance.

'Pssst.' A noise comes from above, I snap my head around to locate it.

Up in the gallery stands a tall figure. Clad in an excellently cut black tuxedo and with his hair slicked back, Rory beckons to me. *Oh, give me some of that figgy pudding!* He looks steaming hot.

I mount the stairs as gracefully as I can muster. The thick carpet muffles the sound of my shoes and my velvet dress swings silently around my legs.

'You look beautiful,' says Rory with a wide smile. His eyes roam up and down from my swept back hair to my golden heels and all the slinky black dress in between.

'This old thing?' I mutter. Never have I been gladder I get to dress up for swanky events. 'You've not scrubbed up too badly yourself.' He's freshly shaven and resembles a model from a designer watch advert. 'I didn't think you were coming?'

'Changed my mind. I want to help if I can.'

I cock my head. 'I'll need all the help I can get.'

'Don't worry. Believe in yourself.' Moving in close, Rory runs his fingers through a loose tendril of hair, gently grazing my cheek before looping it behind my ear. My breath catches in my chest. 'I believe in you,' he whispers before brushing his lips against the side of my face.

My heart hammers in my rib cage like it's pounding to get out. As he lingers in close, the smell of his aftershave fills my nose. I can feel his smooth skin against mine. My brain is screaming that now is really not the time and I try and stop from turning towards him. He pauses, sensing my movement. Instinctively my hand goes to the lapel of his tuxedo.

Rory gently cups my face, his thumb tilts my chin upwards and our eyes lock. Slowly his lips find mine. I slide my hands up and into the curl of hair at the nape of his neck.

With a whispered growl, Rory pulls away ever

so slightly. 'I wasn't sure if... after my confession... if you'd let me kiss you again.'

'You make a very compelling argument for it.'

His breath is ragged as he chuckles, 'Well, that's promising.'

'Promising?' I move back a little and raise an eyebrow.

'I'm hoping... After tonight... Can I take you out to dinner?'

Cartwheels would be in order if I wasn't in such ridiculous clothes. I answer by tightening my fingers through his hair, and drawing his face back to mine again. I melt into his kiss as he tightens his grip. I press in closer as an icy draft swirls around my bare shoulders. Suddenly, the loud creak of a shutting door interrupts and I jump backwards in shock.

As Rory asks if I'm okay, a voice calls out, 'Hello?'

I peek over the gallery rail; Mark is standing in the entrance way.

'Mark?' Patting at my hair clip, I move to the top of the stairs.

'Hi, Holly.' He peers past me up to where Rory is. 'Is Amber around?'

'Yes, she's here somewhere.' I glance around surreptitiously and start moving towards him. 'You're here early.'

'I was hoping to see her before everything kicked off.'

Reaching the bottom of the stairs, I say, 'I'll

just see if I can find her. Wait here.' Turning to face the gallery, I give Rory an apologetic look. His eyes are ablaze with frustration but a resigned grin steals across his jaw.

Down in the basement, I search for Amber but she's nowhere to be found. Her bag with her working clothes is packed neatly in the room we got changed in, but otherwise there's no sign of her. Asking a couple of the catering staff if they've seen her results in some confused shrugs, so I grab my trusty notebook and make my way back up the stairs once more. She's somewhere in this maze of a house, I just need to find her.

As I approach the baize door, I hear jovial chatting in the entrance hall. No, no, no! It's too early for the guests to be arriving.

I open the door a crack and see Mark shaking hands with Rory and an older man who bears a striking resemblance to the portrait hanging on the pear tree, but with a better tan. The similarity only hits me now I'm seeing him in person.

'Well, it's jolly good to meet you. I'm sorry, you've caught me unprepared. I'm not quite dressed for the gala yet. My son here, Lawrence, has been organising it all. I've just flown in this afternoon.'

Clenching his teeth into a forced smile, Rory says, 'We'd have come to get you from the airport if you'd have told us you were coming.'

'I must let you prepare for your speech, it's an honour to meet someone who knows the charity so well. You'll be an inspiration, I'm sure.' Lawrence Perdreau the third turns to Rory and irritation flashes across his face before he regains his polished façade. We've never formally been introduced, Deborah usually schmoozes him, but I've always thought there was something disconcerting about him. Beneath his polite exterior there's a serpent ready to strike. 'Show him the way and I'll go and get ready. And where's that Barnes?'

Poor Rory, his dad materialising out of the blue is not what he needs. I have to help. I approach the men. 'I'll show Mark where to go. I'm sure you must be busy.' Meaningfully I meet Rory's eye and see a flash of anguish and appreciation. I lead Mark away, into the Oak Room.

Rory's hushed mutters are drowned out as I close the door. 'Dad, you could have warned me!'

'This is impressive,' says Mark, surveying the grandeur of the Oak Room.

'Thanks, we try.'

'It's a big event. Now I know why those reprints were so important.'

'Yep, they set the tone for the whole affair.' I smile as I follow his gaze, taking in the grand room through fresh eyes.

With his hands plunged into his chino pockets, Mark winces. 'I'm starting to feel a little under-dressed.' A bead of perspiration appears on his temple.

Patting Mark on the arm, I reassure him. 'Really don't worry. Grab a drink from the bar, relax, and I'll see if I can round up Amber.'

'Whiskey, please,' says Mark to the barman as I head into the ballroom.

CHAPTER 25

A buzzing hive of activity meets me as the caterers set about their last-minute preparations. Taking a careful lap through the room, I hunt for Amber in all the chaos. She's got to be here somewhere but finding myself back where I started, I'm at a loss for where she can be.

Moving back into the Oak Room, I locate Mark propped against the bar. He's chatting with both Amber and Deborah. My sparkling feet freeze to the parquet. There are already two empty whiskey glasses on the bar, and another filled one in Mark's hand. And neither Amber or Deborah drink whiskey as far as I know.

A cold dread starts to creep across my skin as I scuttle towards them. I can't explain the sudden ominous feeling but I know I must get there as soon as possible.

Amber's doing her awkward 'I'm sure everything will be fine' smile, Deborah's wearing her scathing 'I'm not impressed' expression, while Mark's animatedly retelling a story. '… I look up and see Holly snogging this bloke, who only

157

turns out to be Lawrence, the son of the owner of this place.'

Shock crosses Amber's features while Deborah merely narrows her eyes.

Shiiiit.

As I move even closer, desperate to do some damage control, Deborah's fingers whiten around her clutch.

Oblivious to the situation, Mark carries on, 'Nice guys though. Anyway, is it hot in here?' He fiddles with his tie. 'I think I need another drink.'

Catching sight of me, Deborah strides over to intercept. In a barely audible whisper, she leans in and utters, 'This is entirely inappropriate.' Her fingers pinch in tightly to my elbow. 'Fraternising with Mr Perdreau's son, indeed. What sort of impression do you think you're giving?'

'But-' I try to interrupt.

'This reflects badly on not only you, but on me, on MY Technology, on Montague, even.'

'But-'

'No buts. Consider yourself on a warning. This event has been plagued by your mistakes; the Christmas tree, the *pear* tree, the budget. Anymore antics like this, if there's even a bauble out of place, then you're fired.'

Another 'but' dies on my lips.

'Now, get back to work. And have a little... decorum.' Deborah swivels on a stiletto heel and marches off in the direction of the hall.

Shocked, I'm frozen to the floor, unable to get

my thoughts in order.

Amber crosses over to me. 'What the hell? You snogged the owner's son? Why didn't you tell me?!' she hisses.

'It's all a massive mess,' I whisper.

'But what was Mark saying?' Two brackets dimple between her eyebrows.

'He saw me kiss *Rory*, he's the son of the owner. I had no idea. I thought he was a gardener.'

'Way to go Hols! And I thought you were too busy to sort out a love life.'

'It's hardly that. It's... I don't even know what it is.'

'Tell me everything.'

'He's been helping me a lot with the event and well we kind of... we were chatting and then we were flirting and then that led to kissing...'

'Kissing plural?'

I pull a gawky face. 'Plural.'

'Wait. You like this guy, don't you?'

I nod, my eyes opening wide and imploring. *Oh God, I do.* 'I really do. I know we've not known each other for long, but I feel a connection.' I rub at my forehead. 'Urgh, that sounds cheesy.'

Amber shrugs. 'When you know, you know. So why has Dramatic Debs got her knickers in a twist? This can hardly count as fraternizing with a co-worker.'

'I think she's extending that rule to business associates. She said I'm giving Montague, the whole company in fact, a bad name and that I've been making too many mistakes with the gala.'

'What? You're single-handedly reviving it.'

'And if there're any more then I'm fired.' I press my fingertips to the corner of my eyes, trying to block the threatening tears without smudging my make-up.

'Okay, damage control. You get some coffee into Mark. I think he's drinking too much and babbling from nerves. I'll go and see if I can sort out the misunderstanding with Deborah.'

'Okay.' I sniff.

'It'll be alright.' Amber gives me a quick squeeze.

'How are you so sure?'

'Solving crises? I learnt from the best!' With a wink Amber is gone.

In my head I cycle through every expletive under the sun, while forcing myself to appear cool and composed.

I am completely in control.

Everything will be fine.

A drunk Mark slurring through a speech is the last thing I need. It would surely the be the coup de grâce to my career, especially as I pushed for his attendance. It would be a disaster for MY-Technology not to mention STARS. Eyeballing my watch, I note there's still a chance I can sober him up, if I intervene immediately.

I take a deep, calming breath. In through the nose. Out through the mouth. And then focus on the task at hand.

'Hey, Mark.' I approach him cautiously. 'Might want to go steady on the whiskey. Can I get you a coffee?'

'Holly!' Mark engulfs me in a hug. 'Coffee would be good. And biscuits. I love biscuits. I'm really hungry. I haven't eaten all day.'

'You don't say.' I prise the glass out of his grasp and replace it with my hand. 'Let's go and find you something to eat.'

Leading him away from the bar, I turn back to catch the barman's eye. I give a crooked smile and mime a slice at my neck, indicating he needs to cut off Mark's supply. I hope he doesn't serve him any more booze. Although I could sure do with some.

CHAPTER 26

Pausing in the entrance hall, I appraise the door down to the kitchen. The madness down there is not the best place to leave Mark, he needs calm so he can sober up and rehearse his speech.

Shit!

What to do?

Where to go?

My feet start to lead us to the previously unexplored east wing of the house, hoping to find him asylum. The darkened hallway indicates that there might be somewhere quiet for him to recover. With a gentle shhhing, I guide him along, his chatter echoes down the hall.

'Is that you, Miss Holly?' Mr Barnes's calls through a closed doorway.

'Hello?' I reply, moving towards the sound.

'Come on in, dear.'

Grappling Mark's elbow to stop him wandering off, I steer him through the door.

'Sorry Mr Barnes, I'm afraid I've brought some trouble,' I say with a worried smile as I enter a cosy parlour.

Mr Barnes is stood, his hand clenching on to a walking stick. His jaw is set with determination, but the pain that had creased his face has eased.

'It looks like I'm missing out on all the fun. Who do we have here?'

'This is Mark, he's a friend - a work contact - and happens to be delivering a speech during the dinner. But he may have over indulged on the Dutch courage. I'm just searching for somewhere he can recover.'

'I see. Now, Miss Holly, I wonder if I could prevail upon you for a favour?' Mr Barnes's eyes twinkle with guile. 'Perhaps you could be so kind as to find someone to keep me company, I am getting frightfully bored in here, confined to the makeshift quarters Rory has set up. This is usually the morning room.'

What a lifesaver! 'Mark, do you think you'd be able to hang out with Mr Barnes until your speech? You'd be doing me a big favour.'

Oblivious to our unspoken plan, Mark agrees with a nod, gawping around distracted.

With a knowing look Mr Barnes says, 'I am a bit peckish. Do you fancy some toast?'

'Toast?' asks Mark, lighting up. 'I'm great at toast. I'll make some toast.'

A cupboard, doubling as a make-shift kitchen-ette, with a kettle and toaster perched on top, stands in one corner. As Mark bundles over to it, I murmur to Mr Barnes, 'I can't thank you enough.'

'It is you doing me the favour,' replies Mr

Barnes. 'Are you sure you can spare him? I know you must be very busy.'

Busy saving my job, saving the reputation of the company, saving Rory... I set my jaw, determined. *I can do this.* 'Really, you have no idea how much this is helping. How are you feeling now?'

'The doctor prescribed some most excellent pain killers and I am gently trying to get moving again. I hate this blasted thing though.' Mr Barnes knocks the foot of the stick down on the floor.

'Why don't you wander down to see the entertainment later?'

'I would love to see how it has all come together, but I feel I should keep out of the way.'

'You really don't need to hide away. I've planned it so that everyone's welcome. That's what Montague wanted. And you're the house manager. If you need an excuse you could say you need to oversee things?'

Mr Barnes glances at his stick, hesitant. He's not confident to be out and about yet, I decide, but I can't have him hidden away in here, missing out.

'Perhaps, after your snack, you could help Mark find his way back?'

Mr Barnes gives a comforted smile. 'Marvellous, Miss Holly. Thank you.'

The sound of a toaster pops in the background and I waggle my eyebrows. 'I'll see you in a little while.'

Relief washes over me as I shut the door to Mr Barnes's quarters behind me. But it doesn't last long. On returning to the main entrance, I find Malika and all the students have arrived. They throng in the entrance hall with an excited buzz.

Amber approaches with her strained grin. 'Miss Jones is just asking where they can all go to get ready, you know, before the performance and things.'

I give my automatic everything-is-fine look while I check my notebook. On the page dedicated to co-ordinating the students, I had scribbled the words:

Use the morning room as a suitable changing room.

I'd jotted them down when I'd attended my first site visit.

But that's where Mr Barnes and Mark are recuperating!

My brain starts to reel. Before the clutches of anxiety fully dig its nails in, Rory swoops by, looking all suave and sophisticated. The 007 of Cherrywell.

'You must be from the college. Welcome, we're delighted to have you here at Cherrywell Manor. There's been a slight change of accommodation, I've got a couple of lovely rooms through here for you if you need to get changed and leave your things.'

Malika seems smitten and rather thrilled

with the turn of events. 'Thank you, she purrs.

'Follow me.' Rory twitches me a wink as he leads them away.

I exhale in gratitude and move over to the edge of the foyer to confer with Amber.

'What was it we said earlier about nothing going wrong?' she grumbles.

'We're event ninjas not event whingers. Crisis averted and Deborah doesn't need to know. Now, let's get back to it. We need this event to go without a hitch, my reputation and any future job prospects are counting on it.' Not to mention what's at stake for Rory.

CHAPTER 27

The guests are an eclectic mix of the company's most lucrative accountholders, shareholders, clients and anyone that Montague might know who would support a good cause. I barely have a moment to stop and think now everyone's started arriving.

'Barbara, so pleased you could make it,' I call out to the director of STARS, who has pottered into the entrance foyer looking slightly overwhelmed.

Barbara pats at her bushy curls and pushes her glasses up her nose, magnifying her eyes. 'Thank you for having me. My assistant wasn't able to come, it's just me. Is that okay, dear?'

'Of course. I hope you enjoy tonight.'

Clutching my arm, she stage-whispers, 'I can't wait to see how the other half live.'

I chuckle. 'I hope we do STARS proud tonight.'

'Sure you will. Now, you must be very busy.' Barbara smooths her hands over the polka-dot pattern of her red satin dress. 'Which way should I go?'

'Head to the bar and get a complimentary

drink before you browse through the art display. I'll try and catch up with you later.' I usher her in the right direction.

The Oak Room is a vibrant hive of activity with glitzy dresses and smart suits parading around, tall glasses of champagne in hand. The art work is a fabulous ice breaker, drawing people together to chat and discuss as they wander along.

In a rare moment of calm, I survey the site and find Rory's eyes across the room. He gives me a smouldering glare, causing my cheeks to flare from ten metres away. Flustered, I look down to my black sequined notebook and write out *CONCENTRATE* in capitals across the top of a blank page.

Peeking up, I find Rory closing in. I flip the page over to hide it and then flash him a smile.

'Hi.' His voice is deep. Loaded.

'Thanks for sorting out the college party's changing area.'

'I'm sorry! I'd forgotten that room was for the students when I put Barnes in there, it was all a bit of a muddle last night.'

'Don't worry, you've had a lot on your plate. I think they've enjoyed the rooms you found them so it was all fine in the end.'

He heaves a relieved sigh.

'So, your dad's back. That's-'

'Unexpected. Obtrusive. A complete bloody nightmare.'

'We found space for him on Montague's table. No biggie.'

'Thanks for that.'

'How are you finding it all? It's a bit much isn't it.'

Rory surveys the room and swallows. Then he leans in and whispers, 'It's okay. Not such a heavy cross to bear; I've got an ulterior motive. This act of chivalry is entirely selfish.' He is so close, his breath tickles my cheek. I have to resist the urge to kiss him right here and now. Job be-damned.

'Are you trying to drive me crazy?' I bite my lip and his eyebrows twitch with mischief.

Casting my eye around for Deborah, I fiddle with my notebook and try to look professional. His presence is deliciously distracting.

'I was going to ask you the same. It was bad enough when you were wiggling around the place in your sensible work attire.'

Amber approaches, striding with purpose. Rory straightens up, saying a degree too loudly, 'If it's okay with you, I'm going to stick to the background but let me know if you need any-thing.'

'I really appreciate that.'

He gives me another of his blazing looks and backs away.

Amber jiggles her watch. 'Almost ready?'

I glance at the attendee list, everyone is pre-sent and accounted for. 'Show time!'

Now all the guests have arrived, they're called through to the ballroom to find their places. An aisle has been left down the middle, the tables set out equally on either side. Each is laid beautifully with sprigs of greenery from the garden tied around the napkins to give a warm, festive feel to the grandeur. As soon as the guests have settled down, there's the tinkling of a bell to call silence and then one solitary voice rings out, singing an elegant soprano. With a gasp, the guests all twist in their seats to find the sound.

Through the door walks the choir, a quartet, now all of them joining in with the soloist, who leads them to stand on the stage.

'Wow, I've got goose bumps,' whispers Amber.

As the song reaches the fifth verse, suddenly through the door erupts a couple of gymnasts twirling and juggling five gold painted hula hoops. With a flourish they spin the glittering rings as they join the group at the front. Steadily, in march more and more students with a different prop or skill for each verse. A couple of oboes quack as the geese, seven dancers in tutus glide in as the swans and ten 'lords' leap and tumble down the aisle, top hats and all.

'This is incredible!' I squeak.

'It seems like they brought the entire drama, dance, music *and* PE department.' Amber starts counting the students under her breath. 'Thank God they've allowed for artistic licence and haven't tried to have someone actually represent each different part.' She tries to add it up on her fingers and gives up. 'However many that would be, we wouldn't fit them all in.'

Various members of the choir suddenly pull out some long pipes and pretend to be the pipers piping. For the last verse, twelve of the ensemble bend forwards, offering their bottoms to the sky and twelve more pretend to tap on them like bongo drums. The audience roars with laughter.

One by one, they give their final flourishes as the song winds down until there's suddenly silence and then the soloist belts out, *'and a partridge in a pear treeeeee.'*

From our position at the side, Amber and I jump up and down clapping, while the diners push their chairs back and stand to applaud. With modest bows the students grin and as the uproar settles down they file down the aisle and back out of the door.

'I got the caterers to put them on a bit of a buffet in there.' I jerk my head towards the Oak Room. 'I can't seat everyone in here and I think they'll need something after that!'

'Do you mind if I go and say hello? I think I recognise some of the faces.'

'Of course, Malika and the art students will be in there too. Can you let them know they can dig into the buffet and that they're welcome to stay around to enjoy the evening? The orchestra has put together a band so there'll be music and dancing later.'

As Amber leaves, I survey my domain. The serving staff have already brought out the starters and our guests are noisily tucking in to their winter soups. A student violinist plays some delicate background music from one corner. I check my schedule and tick off a couple of tasks. All seems in order and Deborah and Montague seem happy so far.

Loitering over at the back is Mr Barnes and a much soberer Mark. I beam as I approach, my notebook clasped to my chest. 'Did you manage to see any of that?'

'We caught the last few. Incredible!' Mark's eyes are bright and alert.

Mr Barnes gives a knowing smile. 'I knew we could expect great things from you, Miss Holly.'

'That was all them, not me. How's everyone feeling?' I look between the two men.

'This young man made some excellent toast and after a bit of a chat gave me the confidence to walk down. I feel much better being up and about again, reclaiming my position as house manager. I can oversee things from the back here.'

'And Mr Barnes has helped me calm down about the whole speech thing. We ran through it a couple of times so I'm feeling better about it.'

'That's wonderful. I'm pleased you two could help each other out.'

'I'm on after the first course, I think.' Mark regards the rapidly emptying bowls.

I check the schedule. 'Yep, you're on in ten minutes.'

'Jeez,' Mark replies.

'You'll be fab. I'll be up there near the front with you. Montague is going to introduce you and you just need to talk about yourself- you can't get it wrong. And no one will know if you do.'

Mark rolls his lips in together and takes a deep breath. 'I can do this.'

'Yep, and whatever you do, don't distract yourself by picturing the whole audience naked.'

'Absolutely not!' says Amber as she joins us. 'Just focus on me and Mr Barnes here at the back. We'll be rooting you on.'

'And fully clothed!' Adds Mr Barnes with a raised eyebrow.

CHAPTER 28

'**T**hank you all for joining us this evening for this very special cause.' Montague, usually an unassuming man, has swapped his regular cardigan for a well-tailored tuxedo, making his geeky grandpa vibe switch up to timeless silver fox. Ordinarily hunched behind a computer screen, he commands the audience like a pro.

'You're gonna be great,' I whisper to Mark at the edge of the stage.

With the audience enraptured, Montague continues, 'When I started MYTechnology my aim was to provide software that was accessible to all and so STARS is a charity very close to my heart and I'm delighted we are able to support it for another year. It provides emotional, financial and practical support to keep young people in further education. Here is Mark Gutenberg to give you a more personal perspective so you can see how important the cause is...'

On hearing his name repeated, Mark steps forward to take Montague's place. His eyes settle on Amber and he gives a tight smile. 'Thank you for having me here tonight. I have to admit, I'm a bit nervous-'

A chuckle goes around. Mark swallows then continues, 'Quite simply, I wouldn't be here today without STARS. Growing up, I was in no position to access college or university and my career prospects were bleak. Luckily, I had a very good teacher at school who recognised my situation and put me in contact with STARS. They arranged an apprenticeship, a mentor, supported me through a business qualification and now the rest, as they say, is history. I am very proud to run my own ethical printing business.'

I feel so proud listening to Mark go on to explain how his business is carbon positive and environmentally friendly. I had no idea when I discovered him how far he'd come.

'...we maintain a personal relationship with our clients, while providing a commercial standard service.' Mark's nervous smile broadens into a grin as he keeps eye contact with Amber.

'A most excellent product I think you'll agree,' calls out Montague, holding one of the invitations aloft. 'Thank you, Mark...'

The audience give a rapturous applause. By the side exit, a shadow catches my eye. Rory does a small wave, trying to be inconspicuous. He jerks his head to indicate I follow him through the drapes to the doors outside. He disappears in a blur of fabric.

As the audience quietens, the caterers bring out the main course. Deborah, pan-faced and difficult to read, sits by Montague's side, silently judging everything. Once I'm convinced everything is going smoothly I set my eyes on the side door and stealthily make my way towards it.

The cold air takes my breath away as I slip behind the heavy curtain and out into the night. An icy light from the moon tinges everything bluish, and frost sparkles in the glow.

'Rory?' I whisper.

Suddenly warmth enrobes me as Rory, approaching from behind, encircles me with his arms.

'Hey.' His voice is husky in my ear.

I turn to face him. 'Hey yourself.'

'So... On the stairs... We were interrupted.'

I shiver. 'Mmm.' The memory of his most excellent lip work flashes across my mind.

'Where exactly were we?' Rory finds a sweet spot on my neck and kisses me, grazing his teeth lightly up to my jaw.

This feels divine. A white fog erupts and then vanishes as I sigh.

Something inside pulls me to towards him. I press against him, wishing for more. I find his lips and devour them, entirely forgetting my need to be on my best behaviour.

Rory's mouth tickles my earlobe and he whispers, 'I've been dying to get you to myself again.

Watching you work the floor, all commanding and in charge while slinking around in this.' He tugs gently on my dress, swirling his fingers in the velvet and tracing the curves of my body downwards.

My chattering teeth mask my giggle, he's hit a particularly sensitive spot.

'Sorry, you're freezing.' Rory's voice is suddenly full of concern. He swings his jacket over my shoulders and then pulls me in close to his chest. 'I couldn't resist pulling you out here,' he confesses. 'I keep catching glimpses of you floating around, working your magic and it's been driving me nuts.'

'You've been rather distracting, yourself.'

I smooth my hands over his shirt. Rory lowers his head and captures my lips again, murmuring into my mouth, 'Terribly sorry. I should have stayed hidden upstairs.'

I know he's joking but I pull back a little, just so he can see my no-nonsense face. 'Absolutely not! I'm glad you changed your mind about helping out.'

'Me too. It was hardly a tough decision. Spending time with those sycophants is totally tolerable with you here.'

'And here I was just thinking you were just being a good Samaritan.'

'Good? Nope. Ever since I saw you with all that crazy, sexy hair billowing around I've been having *very* naughty thoughts.'

'You'll have to tell me sometime.'

'Tell you?' He pretends to be appalled. 'I can't repeat something like that to a lady...'

I give him a curious look, twitching up an eyebrow.

'I'll have to show you instead.' Suddenly Rory takes a hold of my arms, a serious expression on his face. 'I've been thinking. What about when this is all over?' His eyes are soulful, studying me. 'I don't want it to be over for us. It feels like we're only just getting started.'

A battle mounts inside. My somersaulting heart is paying no heed to the voice of reason in my head, reminding me of Deborah's warning. Every muscle fibre of my being seems to be urging me towards him. I'm so torn. I'm such a wimp. I move my lips to his to try and buy more time to work out what I need to do, what I want to do. It doesn't work though, I get lost in him again.

My hands find their way across his back and start exploring south. I hook a finger into his belt, grazing the top of his backside. His whole body seems to respond and he stifles a breathy moan, making the tiny hairs on the back of my neck tingle.

Clattering and laughter from inside the manor drifts through the sash windows, drawing me back to the present. Somehow, I manage to say, 'I shouldn't be here.'

'It's too cold, I know.'

'It's not that. I can't get caught kissing *the owner's son.*'

'You're right. Very unprofessional.' He punctuates each sentence with another kiss. 'Really don't want to get you in the doghouse.'

I kiss him back but then force a hand on to his chest, stopping him. 'Other than the risk of hypothermia and losing my job, believe me, I'd love to stay. But we should get back inside or I'll be missed...and in trouble.' I hand him his jacket.

Rory gives me another knee quivering kiss and then leads me to the door. 'This is still unfinished business by the way.' He looks meaningfully at me. 'I'll slip back inside in a minute.' He plants one final kiss on my forehead before melting into the darkness.

With a flick of my hand over my hair to check it's in place, I round the curtain and blend in with the crowd.

Back to work now. Best behaviour. Nothing to see here.

CHAPTER 29

I throw myself back into the gala, distancing myself from my distractor. I just hope I've done enough to make this gala a success. Not even for lovely Montague, but for Barbara, and her students.

Glancing around, I seek out Mark to congratulate him on his speech. Malika is talking with him as I approach.

'Miss Jones was a student teacher at my school,' Mark tells me as I arrive.

'Small world!'

'I'm impressed with the art exhibition, Holly.' Malika shifts towards me with a beam. 'It's better than I could have hoped for.'

'Thank you. But it's all down to the fabulous submissions.' I nod appreciatively to the students mingling nearby.

'You know, the new *First Day* made me chuckle - how did you come up with that?'

'I can't take credit for that either, that was Ro-Lawrence Perdreau's idea.' Raising on to my tiptoes to peer around the room, I'm unable to see if he's come back in. *Where did he go?*

'It's wonderful to see the students' hard work being enjoyed. We've had some lovely feedback about their pieces. Talking with the guests has been an incredible experience for the class too. I always say that art, once it has been created doesn't belong to the artist anymore. To live it needs to be free, like a bird leaving the nest.' Malika's voice is soulful, ethereal.

'I'm so pleased it's been a beneficial experience for everyone.' My mind starts reeling. I start talking before my idea has fully cemented. 'I have a proposal.'

'Yes?'

'If it suits you and your students, you could donate the art for a silent auction.'

Malika grasps my elbow and rounds me to the side. 'That's a-'

Oh God, I've offended her again. 'If you and the class are happy of course,' I garble, worried I've overstepped a line. 'The proceeds would go to STARS-'

Malika interrupts, 'and it would be a great accolade for their portfolios.'

She likes the idea!

The nearby students have noticed our exchange and are listening with interest, nodding along.

Lottie calls out, 'Yes! Let's do it!' There's a consensus of approval.

'That's so generous, thank you.' I have no idea how to do this, but I'll make it work. Ideas whizz

181

through my mind and I start thinking aloud. 'We need some way of recording the bids...'

Having listened to the discussion, Mark speaks up. 'I've got some excellent sample card in the boot of my car, you could use that.'

'Yes please, and I've definitely got some pens somewhere.' Amber's emergency kit is about to prove its worth.

Collaring Amber, I leave her in charge to troubleshoot any issues that arise during the rest of the dinner, and set up a work station on the bar next door. Lottie offers her handwriting skills and soon the forms are drawn up for the guests to write their names and bids down. I can't believe Deborah's never done this before. *Surely it's fundraising 101?*

As the dessert course draws to a close, I spy Deborah whispering in Montague's ear. From their table at the rear, I can see her eyes flick around the room and Montague's brow furrow. A prickle on my skin tells me that I'm was the object of their disagreement. Deborah's probably trash-talking me. Lottie's seven swans catch my eye; if I had feathers like them (four bags worth if I recall) they'd most certainly be ruffled.

I'm not about to roll over and give up my job without a fight. Surely my qualifications carry more clout than a kiss? And who knows if it was *just* a kiss or two, a fling, or, in fact, the start of something meaningful and wonderful and totally divine.... That will become clear over time but in the meanwhile I can't lose everything I've worked so hard for. Not because of Deborah's outdated attitude. I need to prove to Montague what an asset I am, he'll see for himself that I've done a bloody good job and then Deborah can't fire me. Before I can over think it, my feet take me up towards the stage.

The mic squeaks a little as I approach it, causing all eyes to shoot towards me. The audience looks quite daunting from on the small stage. If only I'd had some of Mark's Dutch courage before climbing up here without a plan. The sea of up-turned faces undulates like a kaleidoscope until I find Mr Barnes's kind features. I latch on to him like a life ring and deliver my announcement.

'Ladies and Gentleman, in addition to our schedule of events this evening, I'm thrilled to announce our first ever silent auction.'

A twitter of excitement ripples around the room as I go on to explain that the Christmas artworks will be up for auction.

'You have until eleven o'clock, then we will announce the results - the highest bid wins! All proceeds will go towards STARS.'

Barbara's eyes are damp as she watches on. She clutches her heart and beams at me.

As I descend from the stage my kitten heels feel as wobbly as stilts, and my heart thunders in my chest. It was a foolish play, if this unexpected change of plan pisses Deborah off then that's it, I'll be out of a job for certain. But, catching snippets of chatter such as, "great for the work bulletin", "a talking point for that magazine interview" and "tax deductible", I realise the suggestion may be rather profitable, for STARS at least, if not myself.

Feeling both Deborah's and Montague's eyes boring into me, I paste on a smile and glide to the back of the ballroom to meet them. The meal has ended and the guests are making their way back to the Oak Room for some postprandial drinks and hopefully to make some bids. I can hear the distant sound of a booming laugh over all the chatter. Through the melange of people, Amber converges to their table at the same time as I do, a fierce expression of solidarity on her face.

'What an interesting addition to the event, Holly,' says Montague when I arrive. 'A fantastic idea. A fantastic night!'

'I can't take the credit. Amber's been instrumental. The students have all been fantastic-'

Amber elbows me in the ribs. 'Holly's worked so hard on tonight, hasn't she? And it's really paying off.'

It's Deborah's turn to interrupt. 'We should leave these girls to their work, Monty. Shall we head back out and chat with our guests.'

'Oh,' Montague sighs. 'You're probably right, okay.' He gives me a sad look and shuffles off after Deborah. I get the feeling he puts on a wonderful yet exhausting act of being the big cheese. He'd much rather be at home in his slippers. He reminds me a bit of Rory in that respect.

'Thanks for trying to big me up,' I mumble in Amber's ear.

'Is she trying to make it seem like it's all her doing?' Amber's incredulous.

'I do wonder what she's thinking sometimes.'

'She's probably worried you'll outshine her.'

'Maybe that's why she's gunning to get rid of me.'

'I think you should try and get Montague on his own. Fight for your job!'

With a set jaw, I whole heartedly agree and march in to the Oak Room, raring to set the record straight. Now the gala's well underway, I decide it's high time I stand up for myself.

As ever, Deborah's glued to Montague's side, muttering something in his ear.

My resolve falters as I approach. Deborah's glowering at me, her piercing eyes could cut through ice. 'Perhaps Holly can explain now, Monty. Here she is.'

Montague spins and as he moves he reveals Lawrence, Mr Perdreau Senior, standing tall in a black dinner jacket, looking perplexed. 'Holly, it appears-'

'Are you auctioning off a family heirloom?' Mr Perdreau interrupts, his voice curt.

'Sorry?' I utter.

'A rather hefty sum of money has been placed on my grandfather's head. I had no idea he'd be up for sale. Or that he'd garner so much.'

'What?' All my arguments die on my lips. Panic floods to my pores. Family heirloom?

Shit.

The painting.

The First bloody Day of Christmas.

I trip over my heels, as I skitter to the bar where the bidding sheets have been set up. He's right. I'd forgotten to omit that particular piece from the bidding. Under the title "A Partridge in a Pear Tree" are the initials FB and a pledge for five hundred pounds.

A strand of hair falls loose as I whip back around to face the group. 'I'll sort this out. I promise.'

'I'm incredibly disappointed, Holly.' Deborah's eyes glint while Lawrence raises an unimpressed eyebrow. A crowd of milling guests engulf them and I'm left clutching the bid.

I beckon the barman over and ask if he'd seen who'd made the pledge. He shrugs a no.

Poised over the sheet like a bird of prey, I quickly scribble *'bidding closed'* under the initials. I can't risk a higher stake being placed and I can't just withdraw the bid, that would be like stealing from STARS, from Barbara and all those students. No, if I can find out who made the pledge, I can apologise and buy it off them, keeping the painting here and ensuring STARS still gets their precious funding. It's going to sting, especially with no job, and it being just before

Christmas. But anything more would certainly ruin me.

More guests approach the bar, topping up their glasses whilst filling in the ledgers so I move out of their way. Flicking through my sequined notebook I consult the guest list. After a quick skim, I can't find any guests with the initials F B or B F.

A movement through the doorway catches my attention as Rory enters the room. He scans about and his face lights up when he finds me. Unable to force a smile, I give a bug-eyed grimace in his direction. He looks searchingly at me as he comes over.

'I've been hunting for you. I want to ask you something. Everything okay?'

'No.' I cast a glance around. Not wanting to make a scene, I whisper, 'I've royally buggered up.'

'What? Impossible. The gala's a huge success. That's what I've been wanting to talk to you about.'

'Seriously. You know the family heirloom you leant me to solve my last crisis? I've accidentally auctioned it. And I don't know who to.'

Rory's nostrils flare as he tries to contain a snort of laughter. 'I hope you're not always this careless. Otherwise I'll have to rethink the offer I'm about to make.'

CHAPTER 30

T he urge to batter him with a pheasant re-
surfaces. 'I can't think about dinner plans
now.'

'I'm well past talking about dinner plans,'
Rory intonates. 'All this time spent lurking in
the background this evening, it's given me a
chance to think. I can't stand the thought of not
having you around all the time. Come and work
with me.'

'Be serious, I've got a major problem I need to
solve. I can do without you messing around.'

'I am being serious. And I'm sure we can solve
this together, like all the other hurdles. It's been
fun setting this up with you.' He runs a finger
down my arm. 'And fun sneaking around too.'

'It's all fun and games until your job's on the
line.'

'We'll work it out. Don't worry.'

'My whole reputation is resting on this event.
I can't not worry. There's Malika-' I lurch away
from Rory. 'Malika, have any of the parents or
students made a bid, do you know?'

'I think a couple have, on their kids work.

Why?'

'Anyone on the pear tree one?'

'I don't know. I-'

'Does anyone have the initials F and B?'

'No, Holly, what's all this a-'

'Never mind. Sorry, gotta dash.'

I run back over to the bidding sheets. They're thick with black inky scrawls. Panic sets in once more as I try to locate the one I want, I should have held on to it. Riffling through I eventually find it and scrutinise the entry again. It's definitely an F and a B, penned in an elegant cursive script. I look around the room trying to detect the perpetrator. I can't very well go around asking each guest individually. Can I?

Rory's at my side. 'So, what do you think? About the job?'

'Rory, I can't think straight. I've got to find out who made this bid so I can explain it's not for sale and hopefully pay them off or something.' I indicate to the bidder's details.

'I never knew Barnes had that kind of cash.'

'Pardon?'

'Barnes. Five hundred quid on great-grandpa. I'd have given it to him if I'd known he'd liked it so much.'

'This is Mr Barnes's handwriting?'

'Yes.'

'Oh, thank goodness for that.' My whirling suddenly comes to an end and I sag against the bar. 'Hopefully he'll understand.'

'Another crisis averted.' Rory chuckles.

'Any idea where he is?'

With a shake of his head, Rory peers through the crowd.

'I don't normally drink when I'm working but I need one after that. What do you fancy?'

'Whatever you're having, thanks.'

'Two proseccos, please.' I place our order and then turn to Rory. 'It's been quite a night.'

'It's been a laugh though.'

'I thought you hated events.'

'I do. But it's not the organising per se, it's the hosting, the schmoozing, the standing around with everyone gawking at me that I detest. It's just so fake. I wasn't lying before; setting it all up with you has been so much fun. You had everything taken care of.' He shrugs. 'You've made it seem so easy.'

'Until that.' I thumb towards the painting.

'No harm done. Ugly picture anyway, I wouldn't have minded if it had been sold. Nothing else has gone wrong has it?'

The barman delivers our drinks and waves away my attempts to pay him. I take a well-earned swig. *God, that hits the spot.*

'Well, the night is still young and there's the small matter of me being fired.'

'Fired? Are you crazy?'

'No. Deborah heard from Mark about our *kiss*.' Suddenly I can't make eye contact with him.

Rory leans right in to my ear and whispers,

'Which one?' before giving my lobe a nip.

I squirm away from him as he chuckles. 'And she said I'd caused too many problems and that if anything else went wrong, she'd fire me.'

'That's ridiculous, she doesn't have any grounds to fire you. You're the reason the gala's the success it is.'

'Until I started auctioning off your dad's worldly goods. Now Deborah has the excuse she's been looking for. She's always given me a hard time, maybe she's been waiting for a reason to get rid of me.'

'Still, it's worked out perfectly though.'

I nearly spit a sip of fizz back out. 'Perfect? I kind of liked being employed and having a roof over my head.'

'But now you can work with me.'

'Are you seriously serious?'

'Deadly.'

Having fought so hard to keep my job it feels odd to suddenly consider giving it up. But maybe that's what I need to do to get the autonomy and satisfaction that I crave. I've been so bogged down with striving to be successful at MYTechnology that I'd failed to consider I could be successful somewhere else.

I cast my eyes around the Oak Room. It's the perfect space for events like this. My gaze tracks to the sparkling ballroom being revealed through an opening door, while the band strikes up, ready for the dancing to commence. Absolutely perfect.

Then I study Rory. There's kindness in the creases of his face. He has every reason to be an arrogant prick like his dad, but he's endearingly earnest and entirely unassuming.

He's waiting for me to answer. His eyes are wide with anticipation while my brain starts to process the full extent of his offer.

It's been more than fun working with him. I've loved every second. So why aren't I leaping at this chance? Why is there a sinking feeling in my stomach?

Somehow, my mouth forms the words that my mind is struggling to identify. Words it doesn't want to accept. 'Wouldn't it be weird to work together?'

'I think we've done pretty well so far.'

'Your dad isn't impressed with me. He thinks I'm trying to steal prized family heirlooms.'

'He doesn't know you. Besides, Barnes likes you. And honestly, that's the most important thing.'

Something's jarring. I can't place my finger on it. I glance around again, seeing the potential brimming. 'I've got so many ideas for the place. Working here would be like a dream come true.'

'So, is that a yes?' Excitement tweaks at his lips, his unspeakably attractive features all pulled together, beseeching me to say yes.

I take a deep breath.

'No.'

The light sparkling in Rory's eyes dims as he withdraws. 'Oh.'

'It's not you it's-'

'Me?' Rory finishes the lame sentence for me. 'I understand. Sorry. Must have my wires crossed. I thought I felt something. I thought you did too. I'm sorry.'

No-no-no-no-no, you're misunderstanding. 'I did. I do.'

Abruptly, Amber interrupts, 'Rory, you're needed in the ballroom. Your father wants you.'

Rory holds my gaze as he moves away.

'Please let me explain,' I call out.

'I'd better...' he looks to the door and then back again with a sad smile. 'I should go.'

I watch as he retreats into the melee.

'Sorry,' Amber says, 'did I interrupt?'

'You weren't to know. In fact, a few seconds earlier and you may have stopped me making a huge mistake.'

Amber looks curious so I explain Rory's offer.

'And why aren't you biting his perfectly muscular arm off? Are you mad?'

'That's the trouble. I reeeaally like him. And my God, I'd love to work here.' I fiddle with a fold of cloth covering the bar. 'It would certainly help him out of a bind. But I don't want our poor fledgling relationship ruined by stresses of work. Work that I think he'll end up hating.'

'I get it but-'

'I know what you're thinking. I've probably

ruined everything already by rejecting him.' Tears sting and threaten but I don't let them fall. 'There won't even be a relationship.'

We move into the ballroom and stand on the edge, observing the party.

'I didn't say that.'

'You thought it, and I'm thinking it too.' I massage my forehead and then scour the room looking for Rory.

From across the floor, doing an impression of a ladybird perched on a wall flower, Barbara is sitting on a chair, watching the dancers peel past. She catches my eye and I give a little wave. A curl of excitement starts to travel up from my stomach.

'But I've just thought of a possible solution, for Rory at least.'

I pick my way over to her through the revelling crowd.

CHAPTER 31

After a lucrative chat, I leave Barbara at the bar with a bottle of prosecco and three glasses, heading off to find Rory. I'm going to sort this mess out if it's the last thing I do. Although, in fact, I hope it will be just the start of something.

Rory is standing with his father and Mr Barnes; they are leaning close together whispering heatedly. I catch a snippet of a conversation as I move closer.

Mr Perdreau is frowning. 'Lawrence, after the debacle with your sister I'd have expected better from you and what exactly have *you* been doing, Barnes?' He sees me approach and, after casting a derisory sneer, he stalks off.

'Miss Holly,' says Mr Barnes when he sees me move in, before excusing himself with a dip of his head. I'll have to explain the mishap with the painting to him later, right now I have something much more urgent to solve.

Rory looks up. He doesn't say anything, but he doesn't move away either.

'I'm sorry about earlier. I got my words wrong

and I messed up.'

'So, is it a yes then?' He's trying to sound non-chalant but he's chewing his bottom lip.

'No, but let me explain.' My words come out in a rush. 'Perhaps Deborah has a point, about mixing business with pleasure.'

Rory's shoulders sag slightly.

'I mean, a little is fine, but this much busi-ness... with this much pleasure...' I grab out for his hand and pull him closer. 'I'm worried about working so closely together suddenly, when we're only just getting to know each other. You being my boss and my- I don't know what this is yet.'

'I guess you have a point. I was just enjoying doing this with you so much, I thought maybe I could make a go of this place as a venue, if I had you working alongside me.'

'It was a really sweet thought. It's an amazing offer for me... and it would solve things with your dad too. But you told me you absolutely hate doing events! When the fun wears off, I'd hate it to ruin things with us.'

Rory sighs. 'Sorry. You're right. I got carried away. I do hate all the hob-nobbing.' He gives a small smile. 'Time to think of a plan B.'

I lean up on my tip toes and peck him on the lips, without a care for who sees.

'I've already got the perfect solution.'

Rory shoots me a sideways glance. 'Go on.'

'I'd like you to meet someone.' Linking my

arm through his, I pick our way over to the bar area. 'There's someone who I think would genuinely be able to help you out and, at the same time, I think you'd be doing her a massive favour.'

Locating Barbara, I can't hide my grin as I introduce them. 'Rory, this is Barbara Bridges, managing director of STARS. Barbara, this is Rory, or Lawrence Perdreau, the fourth.'

They shake hands and Rory says, 'Please, Rory is fine.' He looks to me, intrigue etched on his face.

'Barbara, here, is looking to move her premises out of the city to not only house the STARS headquarters, but also store equipment and even host enrichment days, fundraising opportunities, training events and overnight stays.' I turn to Barbara and say, 'Rory has been charged by his father to fill Cherrywell with events, the proceeds of which will ensure the upkeep and future of the manor.' I check with Rory, 'Did I get that right?'

'More or less.' He jiggles his head.

'Perhaps it would be worth exploring if STARS and Cherrywell Manor could have a more long-term relationship?' I suggest.

Barbara shifts to face Rory fully, adjusting her glasses with a pat. 'Rory, it's a wonderful location you have here. Is renting out a small portion of the property something you'd consider?'

'If the terms were right for both of us, then

absolutely.'

'Well.' Barbara winks at me. 'My newly appointed events co-ordinator would need to be involved. As, I expect, would Mr Perdreau Senior?'

A curious furrow flashes across his brow, as his eyes dance between us.

'Holly, could you set up a meeting please?' Barbara asks with a wry grin.

'It would be my pleasure.'

'Hang on. What's happening?' Rory can't quite believe the scene unfolding in front of him.

'When I accosted Barbara to see if she'd be interested in exploring Cherrywell Manor as a solution to the problems she'd told me about, she offered me a job.'

'It's been such a pleasure working with Holly on this gala. I've been very impressed with her work,' Barbara explains. 'I was planning on squaring it all with Montague first. He's been so good to us, I feel a bit naughty poaching one of his employees.'

I survey the room, my gaze settling on Deborah. 'I think it's time for me to move on though.'

'This is fantastic news!' Rory pulls me in for a hug.

'Shall I top us up to toast this venture?' Barbara holds out the bottle.

I can't peel the smile from my face and nod my head vigorously while she pours.

Rory raises his glass. 'To new starts.'

I clink my glass to theirs, my excitement fizzing like the bubbles streaming inside it.

The guests buzz around the ballroom, dancing to some Christmas party anthems. The band had kicked off the party with some live tunes, but now an aspiring DJ from the college has taken over.

Gathering up the completed bidding sheets, I spot Mr Barnes through the melee and hurry over to him before I lose sight of him.

'How's your back doing?' I raise my voice over the music.

'Easing now I have been moving around. I do not want to over-do it so I will go and rest again in a while.' Mr Barnes pauses and then quirks a bushy eyebrow. 'I wanted to hear the result of the silent auction.'

'About that...' *So awkward.* He's going to lose any respect he had for me. How do I even begin?

'Are you trying to tell me there has been a mix up?' His voice rumbles as if in disbelief.

'Yes, I...'

'Miss Holly, it is quite alright. Rory explained everything.' Mr Barnes places his hand on my arm. 'I mean, I admired Mr Perdreau the first immensely. He was still going strong when I started working here as a footman. But I do not need a painting of him.'

'You don't?'

'No, I only bid on the painting to keep it in

Cherrywell Manor.'

'I... How did you... That's such a relief, thank you.'

Mr Barnes tips his head. 'It has been a pleasure having you work here, Miss Holly.' He glances over in the direction of Rory. 'You have brought more than just the house alive. It would have been a shame to have this special night marred with one little slip.'

'Thank you.' I engulf Mr Barnes in a hug.

After initially freezing, he softens into the embrace, giving a gentle squeeze back before moving away. 'It was the least I could do after perpetuating Rory's deceit. I felt terrible about it. In the beginning I only indulged him to try and help him out of this terrible obligation he feels. I was supposed to show you around to take the pressure off, but then, well, it was too late and I did not want to give him away. He needed to tell you himself, it was not my place.' Mr Barnes looks guilty. 'And neither is me telling you this. You seem to have a bewitching effect on the men in this house.'

'Perhaps not *Mr* Perdreau,' I stage-whisper.

Always professional, Mr Barnes merely presses his lips together, but he can't control the twinkle in his eye. 'Now, best to announce the winners so I can go and have a rest. Enjoy the remainder of the night.' With cautious steps, Mr Barnes makes his way to the edge of the ballroom.

I glance down at the sheaves of paper in my hand. It's time to make the announcement. I approach the DJ and, as the song finishes, give a signal and they end their set. Much more confident than earlier, I grab the mic and call everyone's attention.

'Ladies and gentleman, thank you for your generosity tonight. I have the pleasure to announce that the silent auction has raised a further six thousand pounds to add to our total.'

A cheer goes around and I offer a clap to the audience.

'Perhaps the lucky winners could meet the artists by their respective pieces?' I look over to Malika who nods in agreement. Smiling, I continue, 'Without further ado, and in no particular order, the winners are...' The audience gives a polite cheer and clap to each announcement.

'The successful bidder for Six Geese a-Laying is Michael Henson from The Chameleon Group.' I can't help but gawk at the man who had bid on *that* particular monstrosity. He's paid a mighty hefty sum for those poor geese too. It seems to be the highest bid of the lot. He rises up from a table, punching the air like he's won a sailing race. Handsome, yes, but as for the type of person he is, I can only imagine.

I list the winners, ending on Twelve Drummers Drumming and give a final clap to all who've taken part.

With an excited glow, Amber arrives and

passes up a folded piece of paper.

'Woah.' I accidentally exclaim into the microphone as I read the note. The guests titter and look at me expectantly.

'My assistant has just given me the final total of what we've raised tonight and it's a whopping twenty-five thousand pounds.' The audience explode into applause and the thrill of success ripples through me. I can't help notice Deborah standing on the side lines, face unreadable. 'Thank you to everyone who's come tonight. It's been so much fun and you've donated so generously.'

With wide claps and a huge grin, Montague approaches the microphone. 'May I say a few words?'

I pass him the microphone, and step off the stage. Only half listening to Montague thank all the various people involved, my brain is spinning with the amount we've successfully raised. I'm so grateful for everyone's hard work and, dammit, I'm proud of myself for bringing it all together. There's another feeling seeping through, trickling down my neck and across my shoulders. Relief. Yes, I'm relieved it was all so successful but, ultimately, I'm relieved it's all over. Everything. Including working for Deborah.

All eyes and ears are on Montague and there's some intermittent clapping in the background but I'm not paying too much attention. The folded slip of paper is still in my hand, quickly I scribble a few words on the back. A tingling sense that I'm doing the right thing whizzes through me with every pen stroke.

CHAPTER 32

Feeling at least a foot taller I stride towards the back, towards Deborah, towards my past. Deborah steps backwards slightly, confusion rumples her chemically smoothed brow.

'Deborah, it's been a pleasure working for MY-Technology, but I think my time there has come to a natural end. I'm leaving.'

'Don't be foolish. Is this about the kiss? I'm sure something can be worked out.'

'No. I quit.'

'But... but... there's protocol and policy. I need it in writing.'

'I hereby give you my written notice.' I pass Deborah the note I've just scrawled.

The image of a frog pops into my head as Deborah opens and shuts her mouth, eyes bulging. 'But you can't... you need to give notice.'

'I'm owed some annual leave so I won't be in on Monday.'

'You won't get a reference you know,' she hisses. 'And I'll tell Montague what you've done and he-'

'He'll what?' asks Montague, suddenly appearing. Deborah pinches her lips together, her eyes looking like they could ignite ice.

Focusing on me, Montague holds out his hand. 'I hear congratulations are in order? Barbara came over to apologise for her intention of poaching you. I presume you accepted?'

Nodding, I find myself shaking Montague's hand.

'What am I thinking?' Montague suddenly lets go and smothers me in an embrace. 'Really well deserved. It'll be a shame to see you go but I think you've made a smashing decision.'

Bemused, I pat his shoulder until he pulls away. 'I've enjoyed working for you, Montague. I've learned a lot.'

'Well, there's always next Christmas. I trust we can come again next year?'

I nod emphatically, while Deborah taps away on her phone. 'We really must be going Monty.'

'Deborah, I keep telling you, you need to worry less.' He sounds exasperated.

Huh? Surprised, I watch the interchange between Montague and my formidable ex-line manager.

'You pay me to worry.'

'No, I pay you to manage the company. I can't cope if I lose you to a ruptured stomach ulcer or something.'

Deborah's nostrils twitch.

He turns back to me with a shake of his head.

'It's like this latest venture, I just wanted Deborah to organise a fun staff getaway. A sort of bonding and thank you trip for everyone, but it feels so stressed, like I'm about to make a play for a hostile takeover of Microsoft. Which I ruled out long ago...'

Deborah straightens her shoulders with defiance. 'Monty-'

'Bonding trip?' I echo, confused.

'So, you didn't tell Holly about it? Deborah, you need to accept help and delegate. No one can do everything.'

So, this is awkward. 'Sorry, I should-' I try to inch away from Deborah's impromptu appraisal.

'No, I'm sorry. Look, Holly, can I ask you one last favour before you leave?' Montague says frankly.

Wary, I glance towards Deborah. She's standing, gripping her phone with her manicured talons, shoulders set, jaw rigid. But suddenly I see her in a new light. This is a woman who's given her life to the service of the company, the cost of which means she has no life outside the job. A job which she's therefore guarded and protected as if her life depended on it because it really is her whole life. No wonder she wouldn't relinquish her tight grasp.

I feel a bit sad for her.

Being so consumed with work, Deborah's had no way of knowing that times are changing in the real world. Perhaps her struggle to keep a grip on her life's purpose means she's fumbling to hold on all the more.

'I'll help if I can.'

'Can you think of a worthy replacement? As the captain of my ship, I need Deborah to have a trusty first mate. They need to bring ideas that will help keep the company fresh and up to date.' Montague nudges Deborah playfully. 'We are getting on a bit.'

'Speak for yourself.' Deborah's face cracks a rare smile. 'Holly's going to be a real loss, you know Monty. All the flourishes you've loved about tonight, that's all been Holly. I told you it was entirely her idea about getting Mr Gutenberg on board for the speech. And she came in below budget.'

I gape in confusion. Was Deborah actually giving me credit? I'd convinced myself that Deborah stole my suggestions and dressed them up as her own, but maybe I'd just misread the situation. Listening to Deborah counting off a list of my ideas and achievements, it feels strange, as if they're discussing someone else. But Montague's looking at me, smiling, confirming it is, in fact, about me. A thought flutters at the edge of my mind, perhaps I'd misunderstood Deborah all along.

I zone back into the conversation, Montague and Deborah are making a list of my replacement's required attributes. 'And they need to be able to hold their own in discussions,' adds Montague.

Deborah nods. 'I can't abide a wet blanket. Who would you recommend?'

Surprised at Deborah's sudden deference, I do my best not to stutter. 'Do they need much experience?'

'Some. A willingness to learn is more important. And ideas. They need to have a brain in their head.'

'What about the policy on inter-office relationships or fraternising with business associates?'

'What policy?' Montague asks. 'I met Mrs Young at work, she was my secretary.'

'That's why we have *The Policy*, Monty,' tuts Deborah.

Montague shakes his head. 'There's no policy.'

'In that case, I have just the person in mind.'

'You're going to say that temp, aren't you?' Deborah's eyebrows are raised but there's the hint of a smile at her lips.

'She's an intern. And yes, actually. She has some very good ideas.' I address Montague, 'Amber would definitely bring a new perspective and lots of energy. And she meets MYTechnology's target of nurturing talent from a grass roots level.' Amber may be inexperienced but she's got talent by the bucket-load and, knowing Deborah, she'll keep her on a tight leash. Plus, Amber knows exactly what it's like to deal with *Dastardly Debs,* so I'm not worried she'll intimidate her. I think it will be the making of both them.

'Deborah?' Montague turns to his colleague.

'She gave as good as she got when I've worked with her so far. Let's start her on a trial basis.'

'If she says yes to the job,' I say.

'She'll say yes,' replies Deborah. 'I was hard on you, Holly,' she admits. 'But it's because I knew you could handle it. I pushed you to give me your best and you always came through. I have a lot of respect for you and I look forward to working with you in your new role.' She sticks a hand out and I take it. Deborah gives me a firm squeeze, a formal shake and then releases me. 'Wishing you all the best.' She gives a prim dip of her head and then strides off. Classic Deborah.

Montague shrugs and after a kind smile, trots off after her. 'Hey Debs, wait for me.'

Deborah twists and glares at him, while he chuckles like a school boy.

CHAPTER 33

At the end of the gala, everyone gathers outside on the morning terrace, eagerly anticipating some fireworks. A couple of firepits have been ignited giving a dramatic focus to the event's finale. There's a friendly hubbub as the guests huddle close to each other, the crisp winter air making their cheeks red and their breath cloudy.

Standing to one side, ensuring the mob keeps behind the safety barriers and the pyrotechnician executes the fireworks as Montague has requested, I can't help but feel excited; glad this is one job that's not been delegated to students.

'Shooting stars for STARS,' says Rory, melting out of the darkness. Pulling me into his arms from behind. 'Very apt.'

I nuzzle into him, kissing his cheek. 'Have you come to warm me up again?'

'That's an offer I can't refuse.' He gives a low, growl-like chuckle. His hands find their way across the velvet of my dress and down.

'Rory!' I exclaim with a whisper.

'Sorry, I can't help myself. It's been a wonderful night. You're here... Cherrywell looks incredible... there's fireworks... did I mention, you're here?! This is paradise.'

As rockets explode into a shower of stars above our heads, Rory pulls me into a heavenly kiss. My senses are overloaded. Crackles and whizzes, the smell of gun powder, a faint scratch of stubble and Rory's mouth roaming over mine. His hands are everywhere. Sparks streak across my mind, even with my eyes shut.

Sensing the display drawing to an end, Rory pulls away. There's reluctance in his eyes as he says, 'I'd better go in before people notice. This evening should be about the charity, not us.'

'You're probably right,' I sigh. My body already missing his warm imprint. He leaves a tender kiss on my temple before retreating back into the darkness.

My constant mental checklist starts reeling again. There's so much I still need to do. The gala may be over, but my work certainly isn't, not to mention the small matter of paying for that pissing partridge.

Large cars pull on to the gravel driveway, their headlights swinging across the terrace, ready to collect the weary revellers.

Although the number of merrymakers is steadily dwindling, the buzz of the catering staff clearing up gives the ballroom an effervescent feel. It takes a while for me to locate Amber, I should really give her a heads up on my conversation with the boss but I don't want to ruin the surprise. Last time I saw her she was assisting a colleague to load up the seven swans, complete with white feathers and crowns. Montague had successfully bid on Lottie's Christmas creation, insisting they'd make a fun addition to the reception area of MY Technology's offices.

'Amber, I wanted you to hear it from me in person.'

Amber's eyes swell in fear. 'What's gone wrong now?'

'Nothing,' I chuckle. 'Don't worry! I'm leaving MY Technology, I've been offered another job.'

'You've accepted the one with Rory?'

'Not quite. With STARS.'

'Congratulations! They're like buses, aren't they?' Amber flings her arms around my neck. Suddenly, she gasps, 'But what about...'

Pulling away slightly, I grip her shoulders with reassurance. 'Don't worry about your internship. You'll be fine.'

'But if you're not there, who's going to mentor me?'

'I can't say anything but when Deborah comes to speak to you about all this keep an open mind, try not to call her Debs and perhaps push for your idea about going paperless in the office. They are a tech firm after all.'

Amber frowns a little, puzzled, and then returns for another hug. 'I'm so happy for you, but I'll miss you. Stay in touch?'

'Of course I will! Thanks for everything you've done.'

'Thank you, Holly.'

'Can I get in on this hug action?' Mark asks, having wandered over.

I pull him into the embrace too. 'Well done tonight, Mark. You two should go on somewhere to celebrate. I think a minibus is heading back to the city soon.'

'Don't you need a hand clearing up?' Amber bites her lip, looking torn.

'No, I'm happy to do it, it'll help me get my head straight. Go on, don't miss the next ride. Perhaps you can go on somewhere to carry on the party?'

'I've certainly got something in mind.' Amber cheekily waggles her eyebrows and the couple make their way off.

Taking down the fairy lights and spooling them up with care so they don't tangle, I feel peaceful for the first time in weeks. In this moment of tranquillity, I meditate on the rapid change of events. Filling my chest with a slow breath, I look around my new empire. Excitement pulls a faint curl to my lips as visions of banquets and balls dance through my imagination.

'Penny for them,' says Rory, interrupting my musings.

'Only a penny? I'm going to need more than that to settle up for the painting.'

'I've squared all that away, don't worry.'

'You have?' *Oh, thank God!* 'Thank you.' The saying is true, it actually feels like a weight has been lifted from my shoulders.

'It's nothing.' He waves. 'I can write it off. I did ask Barnes if he wanted it up in his quarters but, for some inexplicable reason, he declined.'

'So, have you told your dad about the plan to partner with STARS?'

'Yes... he didn't hate the idea, so that's promising.'

'I'm worried about meeting with him again, I haven't made the best first impression.'

'The success of the gala speaks for itself. I'm sure he'll laugh about that painting one day.'

'He will?'

'Probably not, but I'll disappoint him so much in the future it'll move to the back of his mind. And besides, Barnes was virtually dancing a jig when he found out. We both know it's his opinion that carries all the clout around here.'

'What did he say about us?' I peer up.

Rory takes my hand, threading our fingers together. 'Nothing yet, but I'm incredibly happy there is an *us* so I'm sure he will be too.'

I give him a squeeze. 'Us. It sounds good.' Then taking hold of his collar, I assume a flirty tone. 'What's your company policy on work-place relationships?'

'There isn't one. We should probably start working on that straightaway.' He pulls me in closer and continues, 'Together, of course.'

The fairy lights unravel with a spin as I forget about everything except Rory and his kiss.

The End

TWO TURTLE DOVES

A Christmas Short Story

Angela could hear the approaching tap of a pair of brogues over the rustle of tinsel. She'd recognise the sound that arrogant walk made anywhere. Swallowing back the desire to groan, she lugged the last box out of the store cupboard and turned to greet him, pasting on a smile.

'Good morning, Mr Whittaker. I wasn't expecting to see you.' *This Grinch had better not be here to steal Christmas too.*

His silvery blue eyes looked her up and down, taking in the dust covered Christmas jumper she'd hastily donned. At least she looked festive, unlike his corporate attire.

'Morning, Miss Hart. The Principal called me, he said he wanted volunteers to help set up today.'

'So, you volunteered?' Angela appraised the man in front of her as she lifted her load on to the top of the hand trolley. She'd always seen him like this; hair slicked back, blazer and tie, and why was there a broom handle up his butt?

'Well, it's for the kids isn't it?' He looked towards the entrance foyer. The stark deserted hallway was lined with peeling displays and towering lockers. 'Is it just you and me?'

'Looks like it. I guess Mr Bentley didn't manage to convince anyone else. You needn't stay, I managed just fine by myself last year.'

'You decorated the entire school hall for the Christmas Fair all by yourself?'

'Yep.' Angela gave a small shrug.

He rubbed his closely shaved chin as if tempted to leave but then shook his head. 'No, it's fine. I'm here now. I'm happy to help.' He placed his briefcase neatly by the side of the storeroom.

'Then you might want to ditch your jacket.' Without giving him a chance to respond she tilted back the sack truck and wheeled it off down the corridor, marching towards the dark belly of the school, her ponytail swishing.

She turned back to see him flapping like a demented pigeon trying to half run to keep up with her whilst shimmying out of his jacket. *Urgh, Douglas Whittaker. How was this good-for-nothing thief, Devondale Community School's recently hired Head of Geography? He was so pompous and uptight.*

She considered blowing her whistle to try and speed him up.

'Need a hand?' Angela struggled to keep the contempt out of her voice.

'No, no. I'm fine. Here let me help you.' He tried to squeeze past her to open the door and exhaled heavily.

Is he out of breath? After that tiny jog? Jeez.

'I've got this really, it's no problem.' She stepped forward too and they wrestled over the door handles. They stood pointedly either side of the corridor, each holding a door so the other one could go through. Stalemate.

'After you.'

'No, after you.'

Simultaneously they huffed, moved away from the doors and went to push the trolley. It was only the sudden appearance of a dark shadow dive bombing them from above that stopped the bickering. There was a tremendous whistling and rumble over their heads as a flurry of cool air ruffled their hair and stung their eyes.

'What the-' Douglas jumped back.

'Waaaah!' Angela crouched behind the boxes, covering her head and trying not to hyperventilate.

Steeling herself she turned to see their attacker. A peculiar creature was darting down the hallway. The wintery sun streaming through the doors illuminated its lumpy silhouette; it seemed to have a freaky bulbous head.

'What was THAT?' she asked. Standing up, Angela dusted herself off.

'I think it might have been some sort of bird of prey.'

The creature landed on top of a large hanging bearing the school emblem, a large 'D', which was suspended in the reception area. Angela sensed Douglas look across to her and she tried to appear calm and collected, even though she felt anything but.

'I'll go and check it out.' He took a visibly deep breath, stuck out his chest and walked towards their assailant.

Fierce pride was the only thing that allowed Angela to put one foot in front of the other and follow him. Her heart was still hammering in her chest and the last thing she wanted was to be clawed to death by some sort of man-eating eagle but she wasn't going to let Douglas Whittaker show her up.

Suddenly Douglas started to laugh as the bird gave a gentle trill.

'What is it?' she asked.

She couldn't help but chuckle too when she saw what he was looking at. From underneath what appeared to be a miniature leather flying helmet, peered a beady black and orange eye. It reminded her of a target. She saw the rise and fall of the pinky-grey feathers on its chest. The black and white stripy collar around its neck quivered as it gave another gentle 'turring' quaver.

'No need to worry. It's a turtle dove,' said Douglas confidently. He turned to the bird and said softly, 'What are you doing here, little one?'

'It can't be. Don't they migrate?'

'Well, they should. But seeing as this one's wearing a hat it's probably not wild.'

She admired the rich, gingery, diamond clad plumage on the wings.

'Poor thing must be terrified. What should we do?' he asked. 'Should we call the caretaker?'

'Alf? No, he's away this weekend. I think we should call animal rescue or the vets or something.'

'Wait, what's that on its hat?' Douglas pointed towards the bird.

Angela looked up, but at almost a foot shorter than him she had to admit, 'I can't see.'

Carefully he inched nearer to the dove. 'I think someone's painted something on the top of the helmet.'

He moved closer still and spooked the bird, which squawked and careened off towards the entrance doors.

'Don't let it escape!' hollered Angela, starting after it.

Grabbing hold of her arm, Douglas pulled her towards him. She was surprised by the smell of delicious cinnamon wafting from him, snaking up into her nose.

'Don't you'll scare it,' he whispered. 'It's ok, girl,' he murmured to the bird, 'we won't hurt you.'

It flapped and fluttered against the windows leaving dusty wing prints. Opening out his arms slowly, the bird seemed to sense Douglas's calm presence and settled on the ledge on top of the enclosed notice board. A dollop of white and grey gunk dripped over the poster advertising the school's Christmas Fair.

Angela tried to take control of the situation. 'Right, you shut all the doors off this corridor so it can't go anywhere else and I'll phone… someone to come and get it.'

Douglas methodically worked his way along

the hallway shutting any doors that had been left open, while she made some calls.

'I've phoned around. The vet said we'd need to bring it in to them, there's no answer at the animal rescue centre and the nearest bird charity shelter is over two hours away.'

'I guess we're on our own,' said Douglas. 'I'm worried if we just open the door and let it go it's at risk from attack from bigger birds, and it looks like someone's pet. We need to try and help it.'

'I'll try the animal rescue centre again.'

Angela watched him squint at the bird while she held the line waiting to speak to a ranger. He pulled some horn-rimmed glasses from somewhere and then peered inquisitively towards it. He was studying it closely, but before she could work out why, a voice came on the other end of the line.

'We can get someone out to you in about two to three hours, there are no units available right now.'

'Is there anything we can do while we wait?'

'If you're sure it's a pet, it's best to try to keep it inside and keep it calm. Maybe provide it with some water. If you feel confident about getting it safely into a cage then go ahead, but it may be best to leave it alone.'

After confirming the school address and phone number, she thanked the man and hung up.

'Any joy?' Douglas's piercing eyes were full of concern. His hair was ruffled and his shirt had become untucked, giving him a more relaxed, unkempt vibe. He seemed to have lost the broom stick from what she couldn't help but notice was a rather pert backside.

'It's going to be a few hours. There's nothing much we can do, except maybe give it some water and try not to stress it out.'

'You know, there's definitely something written on its helmet. It looks like an 'I' has been painted on in white.'

'I wonder why? And how did it even get in here? Poor creature. Let's sort out some water for it and then finish what we came here to do while we wait.'

Together they headed back in the direction of the abandoned boxes at the doors to the school hall. Pulling back the handles, Douglas easily manoeuvred the sack truck and she found herself holding a door open for him. Silently Angela berated herself for cooperating so willingly; she didn't want him to march in and take over something else. It must be his kindness towards this bird that had her going soft.

With a series of pings the fluorescent strip lights overhead flicked on, one by one, revealing the stark old gymnasium. It was a multipurpose room meant for assemblies, school performances, indoor PE sessions and, apparently, Christmas fairs, but it wasn't particularly fit for any of them. Ancient climbing apparatus were folded against the back wall, while at the far end there was a mini stage. Uncomfortable plastic chairs were stacked into teetering towers in one corner, some folding tables leaned near them. Court markings on the floor had faded and worn away over time. The scent of sweaty trainers and sandwich crusts lingered in the air from generations of teenagers that had over-run it. It was a dilapidated and run-down hall, but it was *her* dilapidated and run-down hall and she looked around it with a protective feeling.

Douglas swept the loose strands of hair from his forehead back into his messy quiff. 'Getting this place ready for the fair tomorrow is going to be a huge task.'

'You don't have to help.' She felt defensive of her hall and of Christmas for that matter.

'I want to. I'm a sucker for Christmas and the kids deserve some fun.'

She nodded in agreement and reluctantly said, 'Another pair of hands would be appreciated, for sure.' She desperately didn't want to let her students down. The fair was the best fundraiser for the school and they were in dire need of some new sports equipment.

He looked around the blank canvas and she watched him as her trophy cabinet caught his eye. Like a shining lantern on a dark gloomy night, a silvery shimmer was glinting at them. Inside was her crowning glory; above the house points shield, some dulled mini trophies from years past and a couple of framed newspaper cuttings was a huge, ostentatious, gleaming silver cup. It stood towering over the rest of the medals on the display. Etched across the front were the words 'Devondale Doves, Championship Winners'.

Douglas moved towards it, his eyes lighting up. He called out, 'I've found what we can use for the bird's water.'

She felt the creases on her forehead get steadily more furrowed as she saw what he meant.

'You have got to be joking,' she squeaked.

'Why? It's perfect.'

'That's the trophy we won for winning the netball tournament last year. Absolutely no way.'

'It's just an object, like any other. What else are we going to use to try and save this bird's life?'

'Not that! My girls worked so hard to win against the Fotherham Flyers, especially as they tried to sabotage all our matches. Besides, it's the first time the school's won anything for years. You're not desecrating that with bird poop.'

'I can't believe you value some material artefact over something's life. Where's your humanity? Where's your Christmas spirit?'

Angela could feel her heart rate doubling and she struggled to maintain her cool. How dare he suggest using the one thing that represented a year of her hard work as a glorified bird bath. Talk about poop all over her dreams. What more did he want to take from her? And to imply she didn't have Christmas spirit when it was usually only her who worked tirelessly to try and make the school festive for the kids each year. *Outrageous.* Heat soared in her cheeks and she took some deep breaths.

The corners of his eyes creased as he smiled and she realised he was teasing her. *We can both play that game; I'm the master of games after all.* Angela was about to hit him with a witty retort when she heard a plop and his grin faltered. Then something fell through the air and land with a wet thud-thud on his head and shoulder.

'Urggh!' Douglas shuddered and Angela watched as he ducked, throwing his hands up defensively in the air, backing away like a wounded crab. Her eyes tracked up to the ceiling to be greeted by the fluffy backside of a bird as it perched on one of the climbing ropes, which were suspended across the high ceiling. *How on earth did it get back in the gym?* Another splat landed dangerously close to her trainer. She found herself giggling as she sprinted after him, away from target practice.

'It's not funny,' he grumbled.

Angela chuckled again and Douglas caught her eye and started laughing along with her.

'Now we know what the bird thought of your

idea. Come on, you can get cleaned up in here.' She led him over to the girls changing room that was through a door off the side of the hall. Seeing Douglas hesitate before following her inside, Angela smiled. 'It's ok, you're allowed in, it's not like anyone's in there getting changed.'

'I guess it's just instinct to not go in.'

'You're about to discover that the girls' changing room is as boring and gross as the boys' changing room, but with the scent of hair spray and perfume rather than farts and cheap aftershave.'

'So, this is your office?'

Angela tutted. 'I don't get an office. I get a locker and a store cupboard.' She failed to keep the note of irritation and jealousy out of her voice. She indicated to a sink with a mottled, cracked mirror over it and then reached into a large cabinet, pulling out a towel. She threw it at him, expecting him to fumble with it, but he managed to turn and catch it in time.

'Thanks,' he held it gingerly. 'Lost property?'

'Yuck, no. It's mine from home.' He sniffed it cautiously and she rolled her eyes. 'It's clean. Unlike you.'

The mirror reflected the Pollock-like splatters over his hair and shirt and a slight pink tinge to his cheeks.

He caught her eye in the reflection and quipped. 'I'm going to be having nightmares about a 'white' Christmas after this.' He started to unbutton his shirt. He was taking the bird-do-disaster surprisingly well for someone so hung-up about his appearance. Angela was impressed he was maintaining his sense of humour.

'I'll leave you to get cleaned up.' As she turned away, she clocked a surprisingly muscular chest with a small curl of hair escaping from his gaping shirt.

Remembering his question about lost property, Angela had an idea and she ran to the school reception. Sadly, the lost and found box only contained one shoe, some greying socks and two jumpers, both rather small and holey. Nothing remotely big enough for him. A flash of inspiration struck her. She took the bunch of keys from the drawer and made her way to the principal's office. The fifth key she tried let her in. Guiltily, she reached behind the door and grabbed the heavy dry-cleaning bag that hung there, before hastily backing out and locking the door again.

Clutching the cumbersome contraband to her chest, she ran back to the changing room. 'Are you decent?' she called out as she entered.

Woah. Douglas stood in the middle of the room towel drying his hair. Droplets of water gleamed off his toned body. Tight black boxer briefs clung to him, while his lean legs stood braced against the floor. His smart trousers were tossed over one of the benches, seemingly a darker grey from where they must have got soaked in his wash. *Holy-moly where had the geography department been hiding this specimen? Timbuktu?*

He coughed shyly. 'What you got there?'

'Erm, this? I, er, thought I'd find you something else to wear. Here you go.'

Without taking her eyes off him she groped forwards to find a peg and hung the bag from it, then backed out of the room, barely blinking.

Angela leant heavily on the wall outside, feeling breathless. Douglas's sculpted chest was emblazoned on the back of her retinas, she could never un-see it, and she wouldn't want to. She pressed her hand to her forehead to compose herself, but again the image flashed across her mind bringing a smile to her face. She couldn't help but let out a giggle. The sound of gentle 'turring' brought her back to her senses and her attention was drawn to the rafters. Searching the ceiling, she found the bird perched on the top bar of the apparatus. She couldn't fathom how it had got there from the hallway without them noticing. Suddenly a thought crossed her mind; maybe it was *a* bird, not *the* bird. Checking the hallway, Angela's suspicions were confirmed by the sight of a second turtle dove. Her eyes flicked over the cavernous room trying to detect any more.

She spotted a blind moving in the corner. Cautiously, she went to see if another dove was hiding behind it. A window had been propped open;

the breeze outside causing the material to flap. There were no doves here, but at least there was an explanation of how they got in.

The door creaked as Douglas emerged from the changing room. Hearing him come out, she turned slowly and she felt her eyes bulge as she took him in. Although she was a little disappointed to see him wearing clothes again, he looked incredible and she tried not to gape.

'I know what you're thinking,' said Douglas.

'You do?' She hoped he didn't.

'You think I look ridiculous. But I don't care. I feel awesome; I've always wanted to wear one of these bad boys.' He struggled to keep the grin from his face and thumbed the white fur trimming the Santa suit.

'Not at all, I was just thinking...' She scrambled for some words. 'It suits you.' She cut herself off before she started rambling and turned away, pretending to look for the bird again.

It was true though, it wasn't just the cheeky novelty of a sexy Santa that was working for her, but also seeing him relaxed for once; without his shirt buttoned suffocatingly to the top, collar straighteners, tie pin and stuffy attitude to boot.

Moving closer to her, with a loud whisper, Douglas replied, 'I kinda like it.'

'You surprise me, you always seem so... particular in what you wear.'

'It's all about good impressions isn't it? Dress for the job you want and all that.'

She turned back, hand on her hip. 'Are you saying my tracksuits give a bad impression?'

'Not at all.' Douglas raised his hands up in defence. 'You're lucky you get to be so casual at work.'

'You think I don't take my work seriously?'

'No, I'm getting it all wrong. Look, in truth, I still feel like a new guy in the job and a bit of a fraudster. I've been dressing smartly in the hope that no one starts to question why I'm here but I'm not sure it's giving the effect I want. I'm envious of you to be honest. Sorry, I...'

Taken by his candidness, Angela decided to put him out of his misery and interrupted. 'Relax. I'm teasing you.'

He laughed shyly and swept his hair back into position again. 'Are you getting me back for the trophy comments?'

'Yep, we're even now.' She felt like she was a school girl again, being mean to divert him from her rapidly changing feelings. It was all she could do not to push him over and run away.

'Where on earth did you get this?' He indicated to his bright red, festive ensemble.

'Mr Bentley's office. He always insists on dressing up at the school fair.'

'He knows that the kids are teenagers, right?'

'It's just his tradition, I've learnt not to question him too much. It's a good job he had it or we'd be raiding the drama department for costumes.'

'Well, I'm happy. It's a relief to be more comfortable to be honest. Plus, with a waistband like this,' he plucked at the large black belt. 'I could eat my weight in lebkuchen and not worry in the slightest.'

'Lebkuchen?'

'Yeah, it's a German type of gingerbread.'

'I know what it is all right, it's just that most people haven't heard of it.'

'Really? It's one of my favourite things about Christmas.' Douglas's eyes twinkled and the edges creased from his smile.

'Mine too.' Angela's voice caught in her throat and she felt hot. Douglas was stood ever so close to her. What was she thinking, lusting over a guy who only an hour earlier seemed nothing but irritating? She turned away from him and in a bid to change the subject, diverted his attention back to the matter at hand. 'I was just hunting for our feathered friend again and look what I found.'

She showed Douglas the open window and pulled it shut.

'Do you think that's how it got in?'

'How *they* got in. There's two.'

'There's another one?' Douglas scanned the rafters. 'Surely they can't have got in by accident?'

'It's probably just kids playing a joke.'

'A cruel joke. We'd better try and round it up as well.'

She strutted across the room to drag out some of the gym apparatus. Carefully, she climbed up as close to the bird as she dared and they worked as a team to gently encourage the bird into the hallway along with the first one.

'This one has a funny 'E' painted on its helmet,' she called down.

'Does that mean there are more? I wonder what it's going to spell.'

The bird took off from its perch and moved back to the centre of the hall again.

'I've got some sweep nets in my office, we could try and catch it,' Douglas suggested.

'I'll keep an eye on this one while you get them.'

'I've had an idea,' announced Angela as Douglas returned, brandishing a couple of nets. 'It's not an 'I' and an 'E', it's a one and a three on their hats. You know what that means?'

'There's definitely a third one. We need to find number 'two',' said Douglas, catching on quickly. 'Right, we best get started then.'

'These are a great idea,' said Angela, waggling the net as she closed the door on the two birds they'd so far rounded up. 'So, how come you've got nets?'

'It's for my after-school Environment Club.'

'Oh right,' she looked out of the window to the grey landscape. 'What do you do in that then?'

'Various projects, so far we've created a bug

hotel, a bumblebee and butterfly meadow and we're planning a big recycling event next.' His chest swelled proudly.

'Meadow? Is that what you've done with the south end of the field?' The fact that he'd stolen some of her sports land had nettled her for weeks.

'Yep.'

'I thought you'd just let my grass grow.'

'*Your* grass?'

'Yeah, well it was part of the athletics field.' She sighed and sheepishly said, 'I guess it's being repurposed for a noble cause.'

Angela silently cursed the Principal for not explaining why he'd redistributed the land. She'd spent the best part of a term finding Douglas completely irksome because of it and it turns out he was just being a good man. A good, kind, handsome man...

'I hadn't realised that I'd commandeered some of your athletics field.'

'You didn't?'

'I guess you didn't know why it had been commandeered either. I guess...'

'What?'

'It doesn't matter.' Changing the subject, he said, 'Shall we split up and look for number two separately or search together?'

'Let's stick together, we might need each other when we find it.'

'Good plan,' he said and turned away. She just

caught the edge of a grin on his face.

As they left the hall Angela looked forlornly at the abandoned boxes of decorations. She'd get this hall ready for Christmas if it was the last thing she did. Just the easy task of rescuing some birds first. For the first time she was relieved that Douglas was there to help her and she wasn't dealing with this on her own.

In an attempt to shake off her unexpected feelings, she tried to focus on the task at hand. She usually prided herself on her self-discipline, but it was getting hard not to find herself increasingly attracted to the guy in the Santa suit who was pounding the corridors next to her.

As they turned into the food technology lab and Douglas said, 'Nothing in here either.'

Giving the room a cursory glance, Angela spotted an equipment cupboard. 'This might answer one problem though.' She reached into it and pulled out a baking tin. 'Bird bath?'

Douglas nodded, 'Good thinking and that'll save the silverware.' He gave a cheeky waggle of his eyebrows.

They supplied the birds with the water and carried on with the hunt.

Methodically scanning the ceilings and windows, they took it in turns to check each room. With an overzealous flourish, Angela threw open one of the cleaning cupboards and squealed as a collection of mop and brush handles rained down on her from out of the darkness.

'Easy,' Douglas spoke gently as his arm shot out to protect her.

A jolt of something passed right through Angela. His breath felt hot on her face. Paralysed, she stayed where she was, as Douglas pushed the equipment back. She could feel his body move against her, while her stomach did all manner of flips.

'Thanks.'

'No problem. I need you in one piece so we stand a chance of getting the decorations up.'

'I'd never have thought we'd work together so well,' admitted Angela.

She caught his eye as he raised a thoughtful eyebrow. 'Yeah, we make a good team.'

'Mmmm. Whodathunk it?'

'Not me, I got the sense you didn't like me.'

She felt her voice strain into an unnaturally high pitch. 'Me? Not like you?'

'It's ok. You thought I'd stolen your athletics field. I get it.'

'I guess I jumped to conclusions. Sorry I was a little frosty.'

'Sorry I stole your pitch.'

'I wasn't fair on you though. It was Mr Bentley who made the decision, it's not your fault; I should have taken it up with him.'

'Like you said, you've learnt not to question him. I'm glad we've cleared the air though.'

'Do you think he masterminded this whole

thing? To make us work together?'

Rubbing the back of his neck, Douglas smiled. 'Maybe the Christmas fair, but not the doves.'

The principal was getting more than he bargained for Angela thought. Her impression of Douglas as an uptight sycophant was changing as she got to know him. She was beginning to like the real Douglas. The relaxed version.

They carried on their trek around the campus. Angela stopped suddenly and slapped her forehead. 'Stupid!' she exclaimed.

'What?'

'It's the oldest trick in the book.'

'Huh?'

'There isn't a number two! It must be the pranksters trying to make us think there's a number two so we waste time looking for it.'

'Urgh, who would do that?'

'Someone who wants to get at the school. Or more precisely, me; our netball team is called the Devondale Doves after all. This must be meant for us.'

Douglas raised his eyebrows.

'I think I can make a good guess at who's to blame too.'

'Who?'

'The Fotherham Flyers. This is exactly their style.'

'Wow, I had no idea netballers could be so ruthless.'

'You've never watched a match then.'

He shook his head.

'You should come and support us sometime.'

'I think I will. So, we can abandon our search? Shall we decorate what we can while we wait for animal rescue to arrive?'

'Absolutely.'

Douglas gave a mirthful laugh and said, 'Two turtle doves; we should have seen that one coming!'

Angela lead the way back to the hall and went to check on the doves. As they passed the trophy cabinet, she noticed Douglas pause and lean in for a closer look. A thoughtful look crossed his face.

A ngela's stomach rumbled loudly. 'All this hunting has worked up an appetite. Shall we try and raid the kitchen for a snack?'

'I've got something you might appreciate.' Douglas retrieved his briefcase and opened it shyly.

Keen to see what he was hiding, she took a peep inside it. Instead of some dull buff folders and work books, she found it was choc-a-block full of delectable treats. He passed her a bag of lebkuchen and grinned.

'Is that what you carry around in there? I always thought it was to keep your papers in order.'

'Looks can be deceiving,' he replied with a twinkle in his eye.

Sharing Douglas's stash of Christmassy goodies, they got busy sorting out the decorations. The boxes were brimming with the treasures of Christmas' past. There were long shiny foil garlands, reams of sparkling tinsel and voluptuous hanging displays. The ornaments emitted a whiff of dust and plastic and hope as they were lovingly unfurled from their year-long hibernation.

They laughed and joked as they worked and slowly the hall started to take on some Christmas magic. Angela was seeing Douglas in a new light and it wasn't because of all the glitter and shimmer. As he adjusted his glasses, she noticed how they accentuated his chiselled jaw, like a superman transformation in reverse. Oh, Comet and Cupid- she could get completely smitten with this man who wasn't just attractive, but modest, kind and funny too.

The school phone started ringing and Angela excused herself from detangling the strings of twinkling lights. 'That'll be animal rescue. I'll see to them,' she said. Knowing how proud Douglas usually was of his appearance, she didn't want him to be embarrassed by greeting the animal welfare officer in a Santa costume.

'Who'd pull a prank like this?' asked the officer, once both birds were safely stowed in some transport cages.

'My money is on someone at the other local high school, they might still be bitter about our victory last season.'

The officer shook his head in dismay. 'Poor birds. Thank goodness you took such good care of them.'

'And we'll take care of the netball team too,' she said levelly. 'On the court, of course,' she hastily added when she saw the look of concern on his face.

She watched the van drive off and took a deep breath. They still had a lot to do to get the school hall ready for the Christmas Fair. They hadn't even started on the tree yet. Thankfully, she wasn't doing it all on her own this year. But would her and Douglas's efforts be enough?

Douglas's eyes shone with excitement as he approached her in the entrance hall.

'Everything ok?' she asked.

'For sure.' He looped some bushy tinsel around her shoulders. 'Now we can focus on finishing our winter wonderland.'

Angela laughed. 'Just another hundred metres of this stuff and six more hours work and we'll have the place looking spectacular.'

His phone pinged and he glanced at it, a smile crept across his face. 'I've got a surprise for you,' he announced. 'But first of all, you have to put this over your eyes.' He held out a scarf.

She hesitated. 'Really?'

'Trust me, it'll be worth it.'

Their hands brushed as she took it from him and she hoped he didn't notice her involuntary quiver. Tenderly, he led her into the main hall. Her senses were heightened by her sudden blindness and she was aware he was making some sort of silent gesture.

'What's going on?' she asked.

'Ok, you can take it off now... Surprise!'

She removed the blindfold and before her stood a motley young crew including the entire netball team.

'Surprise!' the group of kids called out.

'What? Where have you lot come from?'

'I've managed to purloin some helpers.'

A tall girl came forward. 'Hi, Miss Hart.'

'Hayley, what's going on?'

'We jumped at the chance to help when Mr Whittaker posted that volunteers were needed.'

'Mr Whittaker? Posted?' Angela was clearly lost for words.

'I put a plea out on the school social media page and this lot turned up. My whole environment club has come,' he said proudly. 'I opened up the back when you were out with the doves so they could sneak in.'

Angela shook her head in disbelief again and then turned to Douglas with a huge smile. 'Thank you.'

'My pleasure.' He held her eye for what felt like an endless time and it was all she could do to rip herself away. *Must concentrate.* She scolded herself.

With her usual vigour, Angela started organising everyone and shouting out instructions. One of the teens started playing some Christmas tunes out of their phone and a cheery festive atmosphere immediately engulfed them.

S tanding back, Angela admired the hustle and bustle. The girls from her netball team were helping out the other kids and everyone had a merry look on their face. Particularly Douglas, who was still in the Santa outfit. She really couldn't reconcile the jumped-up, uptight, bore with the fun, relaxed guy who was laughing and joking with the kids. How had she missed how wonderful he was over the last few months?

He caught her eye and started to walk over to her.

'This is amazing,' she called.

The festive songs were belting out and he raised his voice over the music. 'All credit to you and your organising.'

'And the kids,' she said as he joined her.

'And the kids,' he agreed.

'There I was, worried we wouldn't get it sorted for them and they're the ones helping us out.'

He smiled at her before leaning in and whispering, 'It really is beginning to look a lot like

Christmas.' She felt a tingle zip right from her ear to her toes.

'Hey, Sir,' one of the boys from the environment club called out. 'Look up!'

She sensed Douglas brace himself as he looked up, probably expecting to find another feathery derriere in the rafters. But a bunch of greenery greeted them, glistening with pearly white berries.

'Mistletoe,' he said quietly.

Angela peeked up to him, her heart about to explode. He had an intense look in his eyes. As he leaned towards her, she put a firm hand on his chest. 'We shouldn't. Should we? Not in front of the kids.'

'But it *is* Christmas.'

'Just a peck then.'

He pressed his lips to her forehead and she took a deep breath, soaking in the feeling of contentment.

'Aw, Miss!' Interrupted Hayley. 'You two look like a regular couple of love birds,' she cooed as she walked past with a giant candy cane.

Douglas pulled away before scooping up her hands. 'Two turtle doves, that's us.'

The End

THREE FRENCH HENS

A Christmas Short Story

I just couldn't help myself. I flicked through the stiff, creamy pages and inhaled deeply. The scent of decades of knowledge, love and anticipation drifted up my nose as the waft from the fluttering leaves fanned at my fringe. It's like a drug.

Glancing over my shoulder, the shop floor was clear. Just wall to wall forest green shelves stuffed with books. No one had seen me get my high. Tenderly, I closed the book and, running my finger along the shelf, found the right spot and slotted it into place.

'Gabrielle, when you've finished fondling the second-hand stock, we've had a delivery, I think you'll want to see it.'

Busted!

'Okay, Todd. I'll be right there.'

I caught sight of a battered copy of *Matilda* in the children's section. She'd understand. Posting the last few tomes into their correct places, I climbed off the bottom step of the wall ladder and went looking for my boss.

For about three years, I'd been working part-time in Greenway's on a Saturday and picking up extra odd shifts that fell in line with my time-table of lectures. It didn't pay much, but the magic of the books kept luring me back. Todd was the owner and book-buff extraordinaire, sometimes his boyfriend Kyle popped in with coffees and snacks to keep us company. Today it was just me and Todd, and the books.

With eyes twinkling, Todd stood over a huge brown box, unopened on the counter. 'You won't believe this.'

'What is it?'

'Open it up. Go ahead and see.'

I picked up the scissors and carefully ran them along the length of the packing tape, releasing the seal. Lifting out some bubble wrap, only my curiosity helped me resist the urge to pop some. Inside it was chock-a-block packed with books.

I glanced inquisitively at Todd.

'It was a blind auction,' he said by way of explanation. 'No idea what's in there. They're all second hand, but...' He peered inside and read out some of the spines. 'It looks like there's some belters. It only cost me twenty quid plus postage.'

'And you got all of these?'

'Yeah. I thought you'd enjoy helping me sort them out.'

'Perk of the job,' I replied. 'Can I read any I like the look of?'

'You can buy them,' he said with a laugh. 'I'm trying to run a business here!'

I liked bantering with Todd. Usually I was painfully shy and, both being introverts we'd taken at least a year to warm up to each other, but now I considered him one of my very good friends. Plus, he understood how I felt about the books. Books had been a passion my whole life; I loved them. They were always there for you.

They didn't care what you looked like. They wouldn't judge you for what you said or thought. They didn't let you down - and if they did, if the characters broke your heart or made you mad, there was always a myriad of other books to make you feel better. It was because of the books I enjoyed my job in the shop so much, my passion for them overrode any trepidation about interacting with customers.

While I helped sort through the stash, Todd typed them into our inventory.

'It looks like there're some popular classics which should sell well.'

'All be it cheaply,' grumbled Todd.

'And some obscure biographies.' I held up a couple of unheard-of titles.

At the bottom, there was a bundle trussed up like a Christmas turkey. I lifted it out and looked up to Todd. He shrugged and then nodded at me, his curly hair bouncing as he encouraged me to go on. Peeling back the layers, like opening up my own private pass-the-parcel, I finally got down to the last protective sheath. I took a deep breath, preparing myself for whatever masterpiece I was about to unveil.

There was a heavy silence. It felt like the books had eyes, all the characters inside had turned to watch, staring at me, willing me to open up the last layer, just as curious as I was to find out who their new shelf-mate would be.

Todd started up a drumroll on the edge of the

polished wooden counter with a couple of bookmarks, and my laughter broke the tension. As he reached a crescendo, I tore back the last sheet and my gasp caught in my throat.

A rich orange cover was revealed. The gilded pattern of undulating vines glinted in the light being cast from the vintage pendent that was suspended above the till.

The swirls of the art nouveau font spelled out the title. 'Les Trois Poules.' My voice was thick, making the accent I'd assumed husky, 'by Noëlle Fournier.'

'Another obscurity,' Todd sighed.

'Do you have any idea what you have here?'

'You know I'm more into literature than non-fiction.' Todd cast his hand away dismissively. 'Is it any good?'

'Good? This is...'

A flood of memories swamped me. Stood on a chair stirring a bowl, my great-grandma, Mamie, gently guiding me. A long apron string wrapped around and around my waist. Mamie's wispy grey hair bobbing as she pulled a tray from the oven. Her crinkled face beaming at what we had baked. Mamie flicking through a copy of this book, a dusting of flour on her nose.

Mamie had been gone a long time now.

Whatever happened to that book?

Todd sliced through my reverie. 'Limited appeal though. You probably get a kick out of it, what with your French Studies and things.'

'It's a Degree in Translation.' I corrected. 'Fournier is like the grandmother of French cooking; the Mrs Beeton of France.'

Todd shrugged. If I were a cat my hackles would have risen.

'My great-grandma had this book. I remember it from when I was tiny.'

With care I raised the cover. My heart started to pound. 'It's a first edition.'

Todd took it off me and turned it over. 'Bit of damage to the back cover. It might add a bit of interest and international flavour to the second-hand corner.'

'You can't sell it!' My voice squealed.

Todd picked through the pages.

'A few sauce splatters on the Bisque de Langoustines recipe. Might affect the price a bit, but I'll see if I can clean it up.'

'This should be in a museum. It's one of the most famous French recipe books in the world.' I felt drawn to this book, protective of it.

'Now you know I love books. I have printer's ink running in my veins. But I can't keep everything we buy, it's hard enough in this market to keep afloat as it is.' Todd scathingly looked over at the novelty gift books he'd got in for Christmas stocking fillers.

'At least let me read it before you sell it.' A covetous heat rose up within me.

The bell over the door tinkled, drowning out Todd's laugh. 'You could buy it yourself, you know. Staff discount is another perk of working here.'

I glared at him. He had saved me a fortune in textbooks over the years, but I didn't do this job to earn big bucks. My pay just about covered my rent and bills and what with Christmas around the corner I needed every penny to save up for presents.

Catching the eye of the customer, a regular who often dropped in, I smiled. 'I'll be right with you.'

Covering up the book with a protective flourish, I whispered, 'This conversation isn't over. Do NOT sell it. I've got first dibs.' I found my finger poking aggressively at Todd's chest. 'Right?'

'Okay.' Todd laughed again. 'If Tsundoku is where you buy books but don't read them, what's the word for someone who reads books they don't buy?'

'Theft?' Chipped in the customer.

Very cute. I did my best not to scowl at him. Todd gave a flirty laugh and moved the parcel off the counter and headed in the direction of the office.

'Hi, how can I help you today?' I looked at the guy who'd approached the till with scepticism, he often just came in for a browse, rarely buying anything. He was quite tall, his skin a warm, sepia brown. Some headphones perched around his neck.

'Exciting new arrival?'

'I think so. Todd's being a complete philistine about it.'

'What is it?'

Launching into a lengthy explanation, I went into explicit detail of the significance of this particular book. As I spoke, the inklings of an idea seemed to solidify. Not only was the book a portal back to my childhood; a direct line to my long-departed Mamie, but it could form a massive part of my studies this year. Perhaps it could be my source text for my dissertation. I really needed to get that nailed down; I'd been so distracted what with working to raise funds for Christmas.

He started smiling at me, interrupting my monologue. The most exquisite dimple appeared on his left cheek and I faltered. 'Sorry, you probably don't care.'

'I do, actually. It sounds very interesting.'

'It reminds me so much of my great-grand-mother. I guess being a sixteenth French, not to mention a self-confessed bibliophile, I can't help but get carried away. So, anything I can help you with?'

You'd better not buy my book.

That book was going to be mine. I couldn't resist it.

He glanced around, his eyes sweeping the shelves. 'Have you got anything by Patty Aakhus?'

'Let me check for you.' Relieved that my book

was now safely in the back office, I nipped around the corner to retrieve the wall ladder. 'Bear with me, it'll be on the top shelf if we have it.'

'Aanrud and Aaronovitch, but no Aakhus, sorry.' I looked down at him from the top of the ladder noticing his handsome profile from above. No wonder Todd had been flirty. 'Can I order it in for you?'

'That's okay. I'll just carry on having a look around, if that's alright?'

'Of course.'

'Thanks for your help...' His eyes flicked briefly to my chest, seeking out a name badge. 'Gabriella.'

'Gabrielle.' I corrected. He gave a small smile and then sidled off into the back of the shop.

Todd came back out and waggled his eyebrows suggestively.

'You have a boyfriend,' I mouthed.

'No harm in browsing,' he replied loudly. 'Please, take your time,' he said to the customer.

'You don't normally say that,' I said in hushed tones.

Todd looked at me, mischief dancing across his features. 'The browsers aren't normally quite so hot.'

'Have you never seen him before? He's in all the time.' *And how am I only noticing how cute he is now?*

'He's not come in when I've been out front.

Now, speaking about getting people in, have you had any inspiration for tempting shoppers in to spend their Christmas pennies with us?'

'I have actually.' I'd gathered an entire collection of ideas I'd seen around the Internet on my phone. I called it *It's beginning to book a lot like Christmas,* but I wasn't going to confess that much. 'I was thinking in the front window we could create a display of red and green covered books heaped into a kind of pyramid. Wrap some fairy lights around it and, voila, it's like a tree.'

Todd cocked his ear to his shoulder thoughtfully, then gave a nod. 'I like it. Let's set it up tomorrow. Can you start rounding up anything appropriate from the second-hand section.'

'They're not second hand, they're pre-loved!' I replied with passion and then wheeled an empty cart around to the back nook of the shop.

S tanding back, I admired my handiwork. Using festive coloured books that didn't seem to be selling, I piled them up in a tree formation, leaving more room on the shelves for popular stock.

'Looks good from over here,' called out Todd.

'I'm just going to do the lights then it's ready.'

'I'll go and pour out the mulled wine, then we can toast the tree,' Kyle whizzed off to our little kitchenette, brimming with excitement. He'd come in specially to witness The Switch On. I loved his "any excuse to celebrate" attitude.

With a giggle I turned back to the tree. Unspooling the string of fairy lights with care, I wove them around the pyramid, tucking in the wire occasionally to hold it in place. *Jeez, I hope no one wants a book from the bottom of this pile.*

Just as I reached the top I felt some eyes trained on me. Through the window I saw the regular again, the one that never bought anything. *He's pretty fine so I'm going to forgive him for that.* I stretched up to place the last light, the end of the strand, and, as he had caught my eye, gave him a small wave. He gave me a big 'thumbs up' and suddenly the world exploded into colour and dazzling illumination. With a start, I wobbled from my precarious position on the chair and saw the guy's face crease with concern.

Wafting my arm, I regained my balance and shouted over my shoulder, 'Todd, are you trying to kill me?'

'What's wrong?'

'I almost plunged to my death and, what's worse, I could have knocked the tree down.'

'Sorry! I thought it would help if I switched them on, so you could make sure they're even. Are you okay?'

'I'm fine.' *Just my pride that's hurt.*

I looked out the window and couldn't see the guy there, he'd melted away into the gathering crowd. I felt heat rise in my cheeks as I clambered down. How embarrassing, he'd definitely seen me almost topple over. *Way to play it cool, Gabrielle.*

Bridget Jones watched on from her shelf, sending out sympathy. *Thanks, Bridget.*

Our festive display invited in a steady pace of customers all afternoon. I couldn't stop whipping my head up to see who it was with every tinkle, but it was never him. My mind kept replaying my near fall in my head, each time the hottie from the window suddenly appeared, catching me in his strong arms.

Kyle sidled over to me with another serving of mulled wine. 'Loving the display, Gabi. Any more ideas?'

I took a sip. 'Actually, I do. We should do a late-night opening session. Get some more of this on the go for the customers.' I held up my mug, clinking it against Kyle's. 'And maybe some mince pies.'

'Or yule log. No, panettone bites are more elegant. I could be head of catering!'

Absorbed in chatting with Kyle, I didn't notice the window guy come in, or sense his approach but suddenly he was there. All unnecessarily close with his dimple and everything.

'I couldn't help but hear your idea, it sounds great.'

'It does, doesn't it,' replied Kyle. 'She's full of good ideas is Gabrielle.'

Feeling awkward, I shifted my weight and

gave a small smile.

'I'd be happy to spread the word, I have a slot on the student radio station. I could mention it.'

A radio show? Yikes, that's brave! The thought of so many people listening to me, judging me. No thank you!

'Thanks. That'd be fantastic.' Kyle started bouncing up and down.

I grabbed out to calm his clapping hands. 'Let's run it past Todd, first.'

'I'll tell him.' Kyle almost skipped off. 'I love this idea,' he sung over his shoulder as he went. My shoulders slumped, what had I started?

'Sorry, I didn't mean to put you in an awkward spot.' His voice was soft.

'It's really kind of you to offer, I'm not sure how keen my boss, Todd, will be if I let Kyle get too carried away. You should have seen how he got over Hallowe'en.'

'Were all the cobwebs Kyle's work?'

'Yep, no one could find anything on the shelves for a week.'

'I remember.' The guy chuckled.

'Of course, you're in here a lot. Sorry.'

'I'm sure you get a lot of customers. I'm Neo.' He held out his hand.

Without thinking I reached out for it and gave it a shake. 'Gab-'

'Gabrielle,' he said, his eyes twinkling. 'You said the other day.'

I smiled and carried on shaking his hand. It

felt strong, but smooth. Not sweaty. It was a really nice hand. I wondered how it would feel tracing its way under my top... *WHY ARE YOU STILL SHAKING HIS HAND?*

I whipped my hand back and felt my mouth forming my usual sales words on autopilot. 'Anything I can help you with today?'

I didn't hear his response, just the rushing of my heart pounding in my ears, so I murmured, 'I'll go and check our inventory.' *What did he say again? Concentrate. Listen!* I logged on to our computer to check the stock. 'Could you spell it for me?'

A small frown rumpled his brow. 'Errr, S-M-I-T-H,'

I forced a grin. *I am entirely in control of the situation.* 'And first name?'

'M-A-R-K.'

Mark Smith? Typical. Riding out the awkwardness of my now apparent complete ignorance, I made a few unnecessary taps on the keys, just for show, before proclaiming, 'No sorry, was there a particular title I can get in for you?'

He gave a fake tap at his pockets. 'I left my reading list at home, I better double check. Sorry. Bye.'

'See you soon,' I said as he hastily retreated. Poor guy couldn't get away quick enough, which was a shame. There was something about him.

As I watched him go, I caught sight of the huddle outside the window. People pausing to look at my book tree. I moved back to the second-hand nook and stood, hands on my hips, surveying the scene. As I watched, another idea started to take shape in my mind and I began to pile more books onto my trusty trolley.

'What's happening here? There doesn't seem to be any stock at the back of the shop, Gabrielle.' Todd squinted at me from behind his glasses, looking suspicious.

'I thought I'd clear this spot to make room for some more Christmas stock, or give us some space for folk to mingle.'

He started to scowl. 'Folk? Mingling? Is this on the late-night opening that you've started to organise without me?'

'Well...'

'This is a bookshop, not a singles bar.'

'I thought...'

His face broke into a grin. 'I'm messing with you. It's a great idea.'

'Phew! And now you come to mention it, a singles night in a bookshop might be fun as well.'

'Let's just stick to Christmas shopping and see how it goes. What are you going to do with the books?'

'I'm going to do something fun in the other window too.'

'I'll leave you to it. Oh, before I go. Any more thoughts on your French recipe book? I've searched for it online, there's a lot of interest out there.'

I froze. 'What? You can't sell it! I told you. I'm going to buy it.'

'Okay, I can put it on hold for you. But I can't hold it forever. And I've seen offers well above what I was expecting to sell it for.'

'Is in the New Year okay?'

He scrunched his nose. 'Can you do any sooner?'

'Can I have an advance on my wages?' I scrunched my nose right back at him.

Todd pushed his glasses straight. 'I'll hold it until after Christmas.'

I'd fashioned some old sheets into curtains and hung them in the huge arched windows at the front of the shop. No one outside could see the frenzy of activity happening behind them. We were only shutting up the shop for half an hour to get everything thrown together before our evening opening event. Todd, Kyle and I were working like mad to get it all ready.

'All set?' asked Todd with only a minute to go.

'Yes,' I replied. While Kyle called out, 'Roger that,' with a laugh.

'Kyle, you switch off the main lights. Gabrielle, help me pull down the curtains and then when we've moved away from the windows we can turn on the decorations.'

'Good job it gets dark so early at this time of

year,' said Kyle, twitching the sheet. 'It's pitch-black already.'

'No peaking at the audience!' I gently scolded.

'It does feel like the opening night of a play.' Kyle moved over to the main board of light switches.

'Many people out there?' I asked, suddenly feeling nervous.

'You wait and see. Right, I'm in position.'

I could almost feel the books quiver and rustle their pages in excitement.

'Go!' shouted Todd.

Kyle killed the lights, Todd and I swiftly downed our makeshift curtains and scuttled out of the way. Kyle's analogy made me feel like I was part of the crew changing sets on stage.

'Hit it,' Todd gave a loud whisper.

Kyle and I counted down from three and then each flicked the switch so the lights came on at the same time. A warm glow filled the front of the shop and lit up the windows. I could see countless faces outside peering in and heard a collective 'oooohhh' and 'ahhhh' erupt from their lips, like viewers at a fireworks display.

Having repositioned the book tree to the centre of the shop, it had left space for new displays in the two front windows. On one side we had sculpted a cheery scene with Santa reading to some elves in front of a fire; the armchair, table and fire surround were all made out of books. While on the other side, I'd turned the books to spine facing in and created a family of three snowmen out of the white pages. With the lashings of fairy lights, the place couldn't get any cosier.

Kyle stood ready with a tray of mulled wine and Todd flung open the front doors and greeted people as they entered. In poured a fair-sized crowd. Regular customers and new faces, students, pensioners and everyone in between were milling and chatting. It felt very festive, if not a bit overpowering with all the bustle. *I must get better at interacting with real people, not just fictional ones.*

We'd only put up a couple of posters to advertise, so the turnout was surprising. Luckily Kyle always over-catered, ever hopeful to gorge himself on the left-overs.

Kyle seemed to sparkle in the buzz of activity, while Todd, clearly surprised by the crowd, appeared to be having trouble even swallowing. I tried to give him a reassuring look, but I could sense his nerves as he pushed his glasses up his nose and forced a smile.

'Everything okay?' I asked him with a lowered voice.

'Yep.'

Wondering if he was worried about disappointing the hoard of shoppers I had a brainwave. 'We should do a reading. Perhaps in the space at the back of the store.'

'Yeah, good idea, Gabi.' Kyle swept by with a

restocked tray.

Todd visibly bristled. 'I don't think...'

'Something Christmassy.' I persisted. 'To get everyone in the Christmas spirit.'

'Well, I...' Todd started to stutter.

'The Night Before Christmas is nice and short. And your voice will really do it justice.'

Kyle nodded along in agreement.

With a flick of my hand, I removed the poem picture book from the top of a stack and passed it to Todd. His hands fumbled as he took a hold of it.

'No. I appreciate your help with everything but, no.'

Channelling Lizzy Bennet, I decided I could be an obstinate, headstrong girl too. 'But it will make the evening more of an event. Give it some focus.' I was determined to make the night a success.

'No.'

I felt a knot start to tense in my shoulders. Todd wasn't normally so confrontational, but then again, neither was I.

He adjusted his glasses again and it hit me. He's not being stubborn, he's shy. Even shier than me. I should have remembered, us introverts need to stick together.

A few customers had caught wind of our discussion and were watching with a bemused interest.

'How about I do the reading?' *I hate public*

speaking, why am I saying this? If only Neo was here, he'd be able to do a reading no problem.

'I'm happy to do it.' Kyle piped up. 'I played Tony in our school production of West Side Story, you know.'

Relieved, Todd and I exhaled in unison. 'Yes!'

Kyle gave a little shrug. 'Sorted.' Then he wafted off, proffering the welcome drinks to the gathering audience.

There was a wonderful hubbub in the shop, it felt almost magical. I passed around some wicker baskets for the customers to collect their purchases into. There was a steady ding of the till as Christmas presents and literary treats were rung up.

'Gabrielle, it's looking awesome in here.' A familiar voice found my ear.

Spinning round, I found Neo smiling at me and making my insides feel all fuzzy. 'Hi, thanks for coming.'

'No worries. After mentioning it on my radio show today I thought I should really come along so I can report back tomorrow.'

'Wow, that explains the student crowd. Thanks for doing that. Are you looking for anything particular tonight or just here to see what's happening?'

'There is something...' He rubbed his hand across the back of his neck, and gave a nervous smile. He hesitated. *Apparently he's just here to drive me wild.* 'I need some gift ideas for my niece and nephew. My sister has just said "books".'

Of course. He's here for a book, not you. 'You're in the perfect place. No matter how old you are, books are the best. I'm getting everyone books this year.' *Stop babbling, Gabrielle.*

'I'd really appreciate your guidance, I'm a bit clueless about it.'

'No problem, it's why I'm here. How old are they?'

Together we picked out a huge monster encyclopaedia for his seven-year-old nephew and a compendium of stories about inspirational women for his nine-year-old niece.

'Are you sure they'll like them?'

'I'm positive, but it won't hurt to get them some chocolate too.'

'I'm not sure if their mum will be that impressed.'

'But you're their uncle, it's your prerogative to spoil them. And chocolate and books *is* the ultimate combination.' I waggled my eyebrows.

Putting the sale through the till, I passed him his quarry. His eyes held my gaze and there was a stirring in my stomach like a flurry of flipping pages.

'Kyle's going to do a reading in about ten minutes, feel free to mooch about until then.'

'That's brave. I'd rather him than me.'

'I'd have thought with your radio show you'd be super confident at public speaking.'

Neo gave a chuckle. 'It's a bit different sitting

in a sealed booth, speaking into a microphone, with no idea if anyone's really listening. Being able to see the audience? And tell what they're thinking?' He dropped his voice. 'Sounds terrifying.'

'I wouldn't even be able to speak on the radio.' I held up a book. 'I'm much better with words written down.'

Neo looked thoughtful. As if he were about to say something but changed his mind. Eventually, he said, 'I definitely need to work on it though.'

'Maybe you should have it as a New Year's resolution. Confront your fears?'

'Sounds like a good plan. You've given me a good idea for a future show.'

'I have?'

He bobbed his head. 'What would your resolution be?'

'To get my dissertation finished, or at least started.'

'What's it on?'

'I wish I had that fully figured out. I've not even bought the French book I want to try and translate yet. This place is keeping me busy.' With a smile, I looked away, acknowledging an arriving customer.

Neo moved aside, giving me a rueful look. 'Good luck tonight,' he called over his shoulder before he headed off.

Despite not seeing Neo again, the evening was

a real success. Kyle gave an entertaining reading; the kids in the audience were completely enthralled. Books were flying off the shelves and plenty of orders were placed. It was wonderful to see the shop bustling with happy shoppers and, importantly, a happy Todd.

As we tidied the last few bits away and slotted any abandoned books back in their rightful places I felt a satisfied tiredness settle over me, the kind you get after getting a good job done well.

Wiping down his canape tray, Kyle approached me. 'Are you coming out for a drink? Celebrate the reprise of my stage career?'

'Thanks, but not tonight. Straight to bed for me.'

'Curling up with anyone nice?' Kyle's eyes gleamed mischievously.

Neo flashed through my mind. I shook my head. 'Just me and Harry.'

Kyle gave me a funny look, while Todd whipped his head round.

'Harry Potter,' I explained. 'He's my go-to for relaxation.'

'I'm gonna start worrying about you, Gabi.' Kyle placed an arm on my shoulder.

'I'm glad to hear it's not all haute cuisine and complex translation to be honest,' quipped Todd. 'The woman needs some down time.'

'Haute cuisine? Can you cook?'

'Not that well. But there's this amazing book

I'm hoping to translate as part of my thesis.' I dragged Kyle to the back office to show him my stashed copy of *Les Trois Poules*. It was being kept on the top shelf; out of harm's way. I gabbled away with passion until Kyle's eyes started to glaze.

'You really do need to get out more, Gabi. What does it even mean?'

'It's a recipe book from France, from the beginning of last century! *The Three Hens*.'

'The Three French Hens? Ha! Very festive, indeed. It'd make a good Christmas present.'

I elbowed him. 'Well hands off, it's my treat to myself. After Christmas. Todd has promised to hold on to it for me.' I hugged my book to my chest.

'You've not said anything to ease my mind. I'm still worrying about you!' Kyle patted my backside with the tray and walked off chuckling.

C hristmas was only a couple of days away and my lectures had wound up for the holidays. I'd done my shopping, all at work, of course, and picked up as many extra shifts as I could. I needed every penny I could get if I was going to buy the book of my dreams.

The shop's bell tinkled and I straightened up from my position in the front window, tucking the glass cleaning cloth in my apron. I couldn't contain the beam that spread across my face when I saw Neo walk in.

'Hello.' My brain went as blank as a brand-new notebook. Scintillating conversation, I had none.

'Hi,' he replied, returning my grin.

I gazed into his eyes; they sparkled as if they'd been caramelised.

A clock ticked.

Come on Gabrielle, you can do this. Be bold. 'Can I help you with anything?'

'Actually, yes please, do you have anything by Carlos Ruiz Zafón?'

'Let me check. English translations or the original Spanish?'

'Probably best to stick to the English,' replied a dubious Neo.

I knelt down to the bottom shelf of our fiction section and skimmed the spines. 'Here he is.'

Neo crouched next to me. Incredibly close. His knee brushing against mine. 'Anything in particular you'd recommend?'

'I absolutely adore The Shadow of the Wind.' I pulled the book off the shelf with care and passed it to him. His hand engulfed mine as he took it. His dimple creased.

The cursed bell tinkled again and in swept a man, all trench coat and fedora dipped over one eye. He strode over to the counter and looked at me with expectation.

'Thanks,' said Neo, ending our interaction with a sigh.

With a heavy heart I stood and brushed off my knees. As I moved towards the next customer I glanced at the biography section and inwardly rolled my eyes with Humphrey Bogart.

'Hi, can I help?'

'I should hope so.' His voice was clipped and formal. 'I'm looking for some rare books.' He shook a list out of his pocket and placed it on the counter top. A spidery scrawl filled the page and I skimmed through it, not recognising a thing.

'Let me get the manager, Todd. He's a specialist in rare books.'

Talking about books and schmoozing the literati was where Todd really shone. He had the man eating out of his palm, and had me up and down the bookshelf ladder and in and out of the basement. A stack of books, both on and off the impossible list, started to pile up on the counter. Neo continued to browse but I had no time to chat with him.

From the top of the ladder I heard the words I dreaded.

'Just one more thing. I'm trying to find a very old French Recipe book by Noëlle Fournier. Les Trois Poules. I would consider paying *very* good money if I could get my hands on it.'

My feet skidded down the ladder like a toddler on a xylophone, landing with a bang. All gazes turned to me. I eyeballed Todd.

Please don't do it.

Todd gulped. 'Afraid I can't help you there.' He

smiled and pushed his glasses back into place.

As my shoulders unhunched from up around my ears I saw the Bogie wannabe hand over a card. 'If you hear anything then please do let me know.'

Pretentious jackass.

Once he'd taken his bounty, trench coat whipping behind him as he left, I headed over to Todd. 'Thank you.'

'I can't hold onto it indefinitely, Gabrielle.'

I tried to thank him again but he interrupted. 'Plus, although the shop had a good boost in takings the other night, we still need to do better. I can't compete with prices online. If he's offering to pay big for it, I might need to consider it.'

'I know, I know. Just give me until after Christmas. I'm hoping to get some money and-'

'I know. The situation isn't that dire yet. Don't worry. It still has your name on it.'

Neo walked over with his book and our conversation ceased. I could feel his eyes on me, making me feel all warm. My brain flicked into overdrive, thinking about him.

Oblivious, Todd put the sale through the till, chatting happily with Neo. Neo seemed to exude this magnetising power, I couldn't look away. He looked between Todd and I as he chatted, seeming genuinely interested in what was being said.

My mouth went dry which was odd as I was also trying not to salivate over him. Was there something between Neo and I? I couldn't tell with Todd there too. At least there were no awkward pauses in conversation which would have been inevitable if I'd have been left to my own devices.

'Are you in town for Christmas?' Todd asked him.

'Yes, I'm staying at my sister's, she lives pretty close by. Are you?' Neo looked between us both.

'I'm heading back home for a couple of nights with my family.' I looked meaningfully at Todd. 'But I'll be back in work on the twenty-seventh.'

'I'm just having a quiet one with Kyle,' said Todd and then laughed. 'So, he'll cook for about ten people and insist on making me drink my body weight in champagne cocktails and then demand to play board games which he'll sulk over if he loses.'

'Sounds fun,' Neo replied.

'I'd rather be here stock taking and getting the shop in order.'

'You work too hard, Todd,' I said.

Neo tipped his head to one side and held my gaze. 'I'd better get going. Have a merry Christmas, however you spend it.'

I glowed. 'Merry Christmas to you too.'

His eyes continued to linger. I felt as if I could easily fall into them. Just as Neo looked like he was about to say something else, Todd chipped in. 'Yes, Merry Christmas. Have a good one!'

Neo swallowed and dipped his head, moving

away slowly. 'Bye.'

The door tinkled again as he left and I let out a breath.

'Todd!'

'What?'

Eyebrows cocked, I looked at him. *Was it really only me that could sense that?*

'What?' He looked at the door. Cogs whirring. 'That guy?'

My hands found my hips.

'You like that guy? Does he like you?'

'We'll never know now!'

'I didn't realise. Sorry. You need to give me some kind of signal of something.'

'I thought you'd be able to tell!'

'I'm no good at stuff like that. Kyle on the other hand, he'd be able to sense it.'

'Don't say anything to Kyle. He'll make it super awkward if Neo ever comes in again.'

'Awww, but he loves playing cupid. I'm sure he's got a fancy dress bow and arrow some-where.'

'Don't! Besides, you'd just be telling him in order to distract him, so he leaves you alone to work yourself to death.'

'There is that. Speaking of which, I'm heading back to the office to run some more numbers.'

The last hour of the day dragged. A couple of people popped in for some last-minute pur-chases, but there was not much to take my mind off Neo and that dimple.

At closing time, I flipped the open sign to closed and dimmed the shop lights. Grabbing my coat and bag from behind the counter, I hitched them over one arm and then, tapping a few buttons on the till, I opened it up and took out the money tray. It was surprisingly light. With my hands full I gave the office door a couple of kicks as a way of knocking and then stood back.

Todd opened it up, looking sombre. 'Is it that time already?'

'Yep. Here's today's takings.'

'Thanks.' Todd relieved me of the tray and took it over to his desk, looking distracted.

'Shall I see you tomorrow? Same time?'

'Actually, sorry. I don't think I need you tomorrow. It's really not as busy as I hoped it would be for the lead up to Christmas.'

'That's okay. I've got plenty of reading to be doing.'

'Sorry, I know you need the money.'

'It's fine.' I gave as reassuring a look as I could muster. I couldn't complain. I had enough money to survive, just not enough to buy anything.

'I guess it's Merry Christmas, then?' Todd started rummaging in a drawer.

'Merry Christmas. I've got something for you and Kyle.' I reached into my bag.

'We've got a little something for you too.' Todd passed me an envelope with a red ribbon wrapped around it and a cellophane bag of what appeared to be chocolate truffles.

'Kyle's own special recipe,' said Todd, tapping the packet.

'Well, I'm glad you two are up for home-made gifts as I devised this for you.'

I passed him a little rectangular package, wrapped in brown paper and string.

'Thanks,' we said, simultaneously.

Todd had already started ripping in to his gift as I said, 'I think I'll save mine until the big day.'

'Ah, Kyle normally shreds any gifts on sight so I have to get stuck in when I get the chance.' Todd only looked a little bit guilty but paused nonetheless.

'Go ahead.'

He pulled out a stack of cards and started flicking through them with wonder.

'It's literary top trumps.' I explained. 'I made it, so I think you'll find that anything written by Austen and her peers will score quite highly.'

Todd engulfed me in a hug. 'I love it! And it will make such a difference from Kyle insisting on his board games... and the inevitable cheating. Thank you.'

I stashed my gifts in my bag and bid Todd another 'Merry Christmas' before heading out of the door. I was looking forward to spending some time with my family, but I would miss the calm solace of the books.

My phone buzzed. I was relieved to have an excuse to escape the stuffy living room where I'd been wedged firmly on the sofa with my siblings for countless hours, with only the TV and a buffet of left overs for entertainment. Every time I tried to sneak a book out to read, they booed and walloped me with a scatter cushion.

'Hi Todd.'

'Sorry to disturb you on Boxing Day, but I wanted to say don't rush back for a shift tomorrow.'

'It's okay, I'm looking forward to it.'

'We won't be busy. Have some quality time with your family.'

I scowled down the line. I was really ready for some quality time with some books. 'But-'

'I insist. See you on the twenty-ninth.'

He hung up and I let out a huff. A rich and uninspired Aunt had given me a very nice wodge of cash for Christmas, but I was counting on the overtime to have enough to buy the recipe book from Todd before he sold it to the dilettante with the hat.

'Alright love?' Mum called out from the kitchen.

'Yeah.'

I wandered in and perched at the breakfast bar while she beavered around arranging some cheese, nuts and dried fruit on a board.

'Fancy a snack?'

'I'm stuffed.'

She rolled her eyes at me and muttered about me wasting away.

'I'm fine Mum.'

'I worry about what you feed yourself when you're away studying. You work so hard.'

'I do fine.'

'Hmmm, you never cook anymore. It's such a shame, I couldn't get you out of the kitchen when you were little.'

'Actually, I wanted to ask you about that.' My brain started to scramble excitedly, what if I didn't need to buy the book after all? What if it was still in the family?

Her eyes lit up, just like Mamie's. 'Ask me about cooking?'

'Do you remember that recipe book that Mamie had? The really old one?'

'Of course. She called it her bible.'

Alert, I sat up straighter. 'Do you know where it went?'

'It's been years since I've seen it.' She hugged her arms to her chest and a small curl crept to her lips. 'I'd forgotten all about it.'

'What happened to it?' I urged.

Mum's face fell. 'Probably got chucked out. It's a real shame actually. I'd love to see it again. Mamie used to do the most amazing tarte Tatin from it.'

'I remember that, I think.'

'Such wonderful family meals. It was like Christmas every Sunday.'

'I remember. Her chicken was divine.' A waft of Tarragon drifted through my mind.

'She kept up her cooking right to the end you know, I think it's why she lived as long as she did.' A tear crept in to the corner of Mum's eye. 'This has brought back some lovely memories. Why'd you ask all of a sudden?'

'It's no matter.' Picking at a walnut, I tried to cover up my sadness and disappointment with a smile. 'Just a silly idea.'

Now I coveted the book even more. It was like a long-lost family heirloom. Mum would be thrilled to see it again, plus, I could focus my studies on it and finally get started on my dissertation.

'Are there any chocolates left?' My younger brother called out from his position in the lounge, interrupting my musings.

'No, you lot finished them off yesterday like a hoard of angry seagulls.' Mum shouted back.

'Actually yes.' I suddenly remembered my gift from Todd and Kyle, which I'd stashed in my bag. Nestled at the bottom of the bag, under the truffles was the ribbon tied envelope.

Passing the truffles around, I wriggled myself back in to my spot on the sofa and fingered the silky red bow. Giving it a tug, it unwound with a flutter and I prised open the envelope. Inside was a stack of notes cuffed in a slip of paper.

An advance on your wages and a Christmas bonus. Thank you for all your hard work. T.

Fanning out the notes I was overwhelmed by Todd's gesture. Recently I sensed the bookstore had been struggling. An advance would really stretch the budget, let alone the bonus. Todd would be seeing it all again soon though. Now I could afford the book!

With a happy heart I entered Greenway's, raring to go for my shift. I'd arrived a few minutes early in order to purchase my special book before I started, otherwise I wouldn't be able to concentrate. I'd missed the smell of the place, the feel of the silky-smooth covers and the soft muffled hum that seemed to seep around the shop; the sound of a million hushed conversations trapped between the pages.

The shop floor was deserted, but this wasn't unusual. Bowling into the office, I called out a cheery hello, but it was empty too. My eyes flicked to the shelf where Todd had been keeping Les Trois Poules. It wasn't there. Determined to keep rational, I told myself he'd probably just moved it. I cast my gaze around the room, but nothing stood out.

There must be a completely reasonable explanation.

Moving over to the desk, I flipped over some paperwork. There were some letters emblazoned with black and red lettering and there propped on top was a business card. The card the Bogart impersonator had left. I felt my stomach plunge. He must have sold him the book.

My book.

At that moment, the office door swung open again and Todd walked in.

'Jeez, Gabrielle!'

Startled, I jumped. 'Woah!'

'What are you doing going through my desk?' His brow furrowed.

'What? I was just looking for my book. You sold my book!'

'There's all the finances on there. You can't be just rummaging through it.' Todd marched over.

'Where's the book?' I held out the stack of papers, the business card sliding on top.

He ripped them out of my hands. 'You shouldn't be nosing through all this, it's private paperwork.'

The look in Todd's eye wasn't anger as much as fear. And it stopped me in my tracks. I looked at the sheaf of papers, really looked at it, and saw the bold red print. Payment due. Response required. Final notice. Shit.

'Todd, I had no idea it was this bad.'

He shuffled the papers protectively and failed to meet my eye.

'I feel like a failure.'

'How bad is it?'

'We did okay before Christmas, not great, but okay. Enough to keep the wolf from the door.'

A surge of guilt pulsed through me. There I was, angry about losing a book, when Todd was on the verge of losing his whole livelihood - his whole life.

'For how long though?'

'Another few months. Unless I can turn this place around by April, I think I may need to close.'

'I guess you need every penny you can get.' I indicated to the business card.

'Him and the late-night opening are the reason we're still going. I'm keeping his card in case I can get hold of any more books from his list.'

I sighed. 'Well, if I can't have Les Trois Poules, then at least it's helped to keep this place going.'

Todd looked at me strangely. 'What do you mean?'

'You sold my book to the guy in the fedora, didn't you?'

Todd looked awkward. 'I admit I sold your book. But not to that rich collector.'

'Who did you sell it to?'

'That was a term of the sale. It had to be anonymous.'

A knot of jealousy gripped me inside. I deserved to know my book had gone to a good home. Surely?

'Todd? It's gone now, you can at least tell me.'

His strained face broke into a smile. 'You'll find out.' He cocked his wrist to reveal his watch. 'Let's go, your shift's about to start.'

It was disappointingly quiet. I stationed myself at the till and used the time to surf the Internet and come up with some more money-making events to help support the shop. Starting a new digital folder called 'Greenway's- here to stay!', I saved a host of ideas, such as holding author events and participating in world book day. Just as I was trying to figure out the finer points of holding a 'blind date with a book' event for Valentine's Day, the bell gave its tinkle.

'Hi there.' Neo entered the shop, radiating enticement.

'Hi!' My posture sprung to attention as I jolted upright.

Try not to act like such an eager puppy, Gabrielle.

'I was hoping you'd be in.'

'Oh? Anything I can help you with today?' *Like shoving all the books off the counter and being overwhelmed by a passionate embrace, your lips greedily ensnaring mine, your hand raking through my hair like-*

'Yes, do you sell book marks?'

Well, that's disappointing.

'Yep.' I ran my hand over the collection on the edge of the counter.

After a quick ponder, he selected a pretty one made of card.

'Do you want a bag?'

'No, it's fine. Can I borrow a pen?'

Unclicking the nib from the chamber, I passed him the one I stored in my apron. As he bent over, I caught a waft of aftershave; fragrant like a fresh sea breeze. Straightening up, he handed back the pen and flashed a dazzling smile. He placed a paper bag he was holding on the counter and dropped the bookmark inside.

'Did you have a good Christmas?' he asked.

'Yes thanks, you?'

'It was good thanks. Fun with the kids.'

'How did your niece and nephew like their gifts?'

'They loved them - especially the chocolate.' He grinned at the recollection.

Gosh, that dimple could make me melt.

The bell by the door sung out, as once again the universe conspired against me, and a lady walked in. Perhaps I would have the courage to take this further one day, when I didn't have an audience.

Todd emerged from his office. Now the shop was beginning to feel positively crowded.

'Kyle's on the phone in there. Go and let him know if you want a coffee, he's going to drop by.'

'Actually, yes please. I'm gasping.'

Todd took over my spot at the till and started chatting with Neo as I left.

When I came back. Todd was serving the other customer and Neo was nowhere to be seen.

'Is this your bag?' he asked the lady.

'No, it was already here,' she replied.

'That was Neo's, he must have left it behind.' I stepped up to join them.

'Do you have his number?'

'No.' I almost choked on my laugh. *I wish.*

'We'd better hold on to it for him, I'm sure he'll be back.'

The lady left with her purchase and then it was just me, Todd and the bag. Until Todd went back to the office.

The bag seemed to pulsate, but I fought the urge to look in it. It wasn't mine after all. Knowing my luck, Neo would come back for it just as I was elbow deep going through his stuff.

Must ignore the bag.

Unable to stop my eyes tracking to the door every minute, anticipating the return of Neo, I almost scowled at Kyle when he crossed the threshold.

'That's some thanks for bringing you a coffee.'

'Sorry, I was hoping it would be someone else.'

Kyle waggled his eye brows and passed me the cup.

'Thank you,' I said with sincerity.

'You're welcome. Oh, what's this?' Kyle set the remaining coffees down and picked up Neo's bag.

'Neo left it behind.'

'*Neo* did, did he?'

'What's that supposed to mean?'

'Very convenient,' he said raising the pitch of his voice. 'Todd mentioned you and this Neo to me. What's inside?'

'I don't know!'

'Let's have a look.'

I slapped Kyle's hand down as he reached out for it. 'Surely that's breaking some sort of privacy laws.'

'We need to be sure it's Neo's, don't we?' Kyle persisted in opening up the bag.

With a feeble attempt to try and stop Kyle, my curiosity won out. I watched him closely as he made a big show of looking into the bag and rummaging around, giving some exaggerated grunts of intrigue.

'What is it?'

'Very interesting,' said Kyle, moving the bag in close to his body.

'Show me!'

Kyle giggled and moved it just out of my reach as I grabbed for it.

'Kyle!' I snatched it from him and spun away, pulling it in to my chest.

My heart pounded against the bulky object inside. This is ridiculous, why am I getting worked up over a bit of shopping? Because it's Neo's.

Except it wasn't.

Opening up the bag, I pulled out a gift-wrapped box of some sort with a book mark on top. The book mark Neo had just bought. Turning it over revealed a note. He must have scribbled it when he borrowed the pen.

Merry Christmas, Gabrielle.

It was for me?

The wrapped box in my hand suddenly felt hot and heavy. Either that or my fingers were going funny. I could feel through the paper, it wasn't a box after all. There was a hard spine and pointy corners. It could only be one thing. Holding my breath, I slipped my finger under the tape and tore it apart. The gilded sinuous vines on the cover of *Les Trois Poules* glinted in the shop's light as the wrap fell away. It was my book.

A tear welled into the corner of my eye as I exhaled.

'What's wrong, Gabi?' Kyle was suddenly close, crowding me.

'Nothing. I'm fine.'

'What's the gift? Has it upset you?'

'Not at all.' Smiling made the tear drop onto my cheek and trickle under my chin. 'I'm a bit overcome. It's a really lovely gift.'

'Isn't this the-'

'Yep, it's the book I wanted. I'd been saving up for it.' *How on earth had Neo afforded it?* I paused. 'I owe Todd an apology. I was so mad at him, I thought he'd sold it from under me.'

'My Todd's a bit of a dark horse, isn't he?'

'Did I hear my name?' Todd entered from the office. His hair looked dishevelled like he'd run many a worried hand through it.

'Thanks, Todd.' I held up the book with a grin.

'I'm glad you've got it now. It wasn't from me though!'

'I know, but you only sold it to someone who was going to give it to me.'

'That's true. I'm relieved to find it wasn't an elaborate double bluff in order for someone else to get their hands on that bloody book.' With a clap, Todd rubbed his hands together. 'So, tell me all the gossip, how did he give it to you? Who said what? I want all the details.'

'You're gonna be disappointed, darlin',' said Kyle. 'It was more like a poorly executed Secret Santa.'

'Huh?'

'I haven't actually seen him,' I explained. 'It was in the bag he left behind.'

'And you opened it? What if he comes back looking for it?'

'Well, it was labelled for me.'

'But maybe he wanted to give it to you in person.'

I hadn't thought of that. 'Errr-'

Kyle interrupted. 'Phone him and tell him.'

'I haven't got his number.' I looked at Todd with a hopeful expression.

He shrugged and shook his head. 'No idea.'

'I guess I just need to wait until he next comes in then.'

I looked down at my coveted book.

'Do you want your break now?' asked Todd.

'So, you can go and look at it?'

In reply, I nodded vehemently.

He dipped his head towards the back office. 'Go on then, I'll cover you.'

'But-'

'If Neo comes in I'll be sure to let you know,' said Todd with a smirk. Kyle started bouncing up and down with excitement. 'Or you'll hear Kyle self-combust, one way or the other we'll tell you.'

There was no sign of Neo over the next couple of days. I'd almost given myself whiplash with my constant craning around to look at who was coming in. I tried to look for him on the Internet, but lacking his last name meant my search was a flop. Todd assured me that he'd paid in cash, so even if I did break all the rules and try to track him down through his payment details I wouldn't get anywhere. I wouldn't know where to begin to do that, but it was a dead end before I'd even started.

Kyle entered the shop, setting the bell above the door to do it's tinkling dance.

'Chill your beans, it's just me,' he called out.

'Hi.' My voice sounded flat. Despite having my dream book, I was borderline moping.

'Come on Gabi, he'll come in eventually.' He approached the counter. 'He used to be in all the time, didn't he?'

'Yes, although he rarely bought anything.' I carried on pricing up a stack of new arrivals.

'Perhaps he was just coming to see you then?'

The ridiculous missions he'd set me on flashed through my mind. He'd had me looking for authors from A to Z.

'Maybe. But where is he now?'

'He's given you the book. It's your move.' Kyle raised one questioning eyebrow. 'So, what do you know about him?'

With a huff, I counted off on my fingers. 'He's called Neo. He's a student. He has a sister and a niece and nephew.'

'Go on.'

I clasped the book I was holding to my chest. 'He has the most adorable dimple when he smiles.'

'There must be more. Come on think!'

'He's kind, he's funny. He's thoughtful.'

Kyle looked at me imploringly.

'He has a radio show.' My eyes met Kyle's, who was looking giddy with excitement.

'Let's get it on then. A student one, I presume? Unless we've had a minor celebrity in our midst the whole time and no one thought to tell me?'

'Yes, that's what he said.'

Kyle took out his phone and searched for the University radio's online stream. The sounds of a classic rock song suddenly surrounded us. 'What time is he on?'

'I don't know.'

'I guess the shop has a new sound track then. I'll go and warn Todd, so he doesn't pop a hernia.'

'He's a purist. I don't think he'll like music on in the shop.'

Kyle soon came back with a smug grin. 'I told him we were trialling it, in case it helped boost customer numbers and sales.'

'And that worked?'

'He said we need to try anything and everything.'

'I've got a few ideas stored away about that. I'll try and have a meeting with him about it later.'

A lady's voice chatted out over the airwaves, catching our attention. '...thank you, you wonderful listeners. It's been so much fun with you today. Next on we have Neo Knight. Stay tuned.'

My eyes bulged and I looked to Kyle. Suddenly I felt a churning deep inside.

Kyle clutched his face. 'It's a post-Christmas miracle!'

The rich sound of Otis Redding piped out, singing about a New Year's Resolution with Carla Thomas. Bluesy trumpets and saxophones punctuated the soulful vocals. Kyle grabbed hold of my hands and started swinging and swaying me around the shop floor.

'Kyyyle!' I giggled. Embarrassed.

'What? There's no one here.'

As the song stopped we turned to listen to Neo starting to talk. It was eerie. His soft voice felt like he was right in the room with us; talking to us and only us.

'Good afternoon! New Year is coming. A fresh start. A new leaf. In this crazy crimbo limbo week, let's look towards next year and what we hope to achieve. Have you got any resolutions? Any aims and goals? Any fears you want to master? Call in to let me know. Perhaps our soundtrack today will inspire you. Next up we have Rhianna and Work. I know I need to get on with some work work work.'

'Cheesy, but he's actually pretty good,' exclaimed Kyle.

'This feels wrong. Maybe I shouldn't be listening. It's like I'm a voyeur, but with ears.'

'You're *supposed* to listen to radio shows. And, he's just asked you to ring in. You've got to do it.'

'I can't.' I looked at Kyle. 'Can I?'

With an exuberant nod, Kyle grinned at me.

As the song finished, Neo started chatting again, distracting me from my conversation. 'Here's our first caller. What's your name and your resolution?'

'It's Scarlet and I'm calling to say, *it's really over* to my ex, you know who you are. It's over for good this time. Next year, we are absolutely not getting back together.'

'So, Scarlet, your New Year's resolution is to stay single?'

'Oh no, I'm not writing off my love life for everyone. I'm just not getting back with that cheating douchebag.'

'I've got just the songs for you. How about some Little Mix to keep you strong in your goal? But first, let's start off with some Taylor Swift.'

Speaking out over the pop song, I asked Kyle, 'What am I going to say? I can't talk on the radio!'

'You won't actually be on air. They'll have a call screener. They won't let just anyone on, you never know what people are gonna say. Just tell them you want to give Neo a message and then when you're speaking to him say thanks... or whatever.'

Rolling my eyes at Kyle's mischievous expression, I said. 'Here goes nothing.'

I called the number Neo had read out, while the music continued playing in the background.

Kyle looked on with expectation. I gestured for him to go away, but he shook his head, mischief dancing across his face.

With a sigh, I walked round to the back section of the shop, where all the pre-loved and vintage books were. I could feel the books shimmying with excitement as they listened.

Finally, the call was answered. I explained to the call screener that I wanted to speak to Neo or pass a message on and they said I could chat to him during the next song. I felt my pulse surging as I waited. *What if I'd got it all wrong?*

I looked around my literary fortress and wrought power from the books. *I can do this!*

Suddenly, Neo's voice was in my ear.

'Hi. It's Gabrielle. From the book shop.'

'Gabrielle?' Neo sounded surprised and there was some bumbling around in the background.

The eyes of a thousand book-bound characters were on me. I had to speak before I lost my nerve. 'Thank you for the book. It was really sweet of you.' I hugged my free arm to my chest. 'How come you just left it here?'

'Erm-'

Determined not to lose my nerve, I ploughed on. 'I hope you don't mind that I opened it. I was completely blown away when I saw it.'

'So you really liked it?'

'Absolutely. I can't believe you remembered about it.'

'You seemed pretty fanatical about it. I almost kept it myself, I was so intrigued.'

I chuckled. 'So... will I get to thank you in person anytime soon?'

'I could come to the shop after my show this afternoon. Does that work for you?'

'I'll be here.'

Kyle rounded the corner and started jumping up and down and leaping around in silent hysterics. I turned away from him, staring at the spines on the shelves, my eyes boring in to them in an effort not to become a puddle of embarrassment. I couldn't believe he'd been ear-wigging. Actually, I could.

'I'd better go. Do you want to say anything on-air?'

'My goodness, no! That's one of my worst fears.'

'But today's show is about confronting them!'

'Absolutely not.'

Neo gave a soft laugh. 'Okay, see you later.'

I hung up and rounded on Kyle, ready to lay into him for snooping.

'I can't believe y-'

'Gabi!' He interrupted me. 'You were on the radio!'

'What?'

'Halfway through the song it suddenly cut out and I heard your and Neo's conversation. Like, all of it.'

'No.' Mortification had made me monosyllabic.

'Yes.'

Colour and heat crept up my neck, all the way up to my hair clip.

'I had no idea.' My breath came out in a shudder.

'I don't think Neo did either. Way to score a date though.'

'It's not a date, he's just dropping by to let me thank him.'

Kyle rolled his eyebrows and sashayed off muttering something about telling Todd. He took his phone with him and the book shop felt strangely quiet. I'd normally enjoy the peace, but my brain kept trying to replay what exactly had been said and working out just how embarrassed I needed to be.

Gratitude washed over me when the door gave a tinkle and a customer walked in. Finally, a distraction. They looked about my age, a stu-denty-type, just happy browsing. Then another one came in. And another.

I rang up a few sales as the shop got busier and busier. Suddenly there were lots of students milling around. The hubbub was enough to drag Todd and Kyle from the office.

Confusion and delight creased Todd's expres-sion while Kyle started flapping his hands in ex-citement.

'You know why this is don't you.' Kyle nudged me with his elbow.

'Because my prayers have finally been an-swered?' Quipped Todd.

'Everyone's come to see Gabi's rendez-vous with Neo!'

Pulling on Todd and Kyle's elbows, I ducked us down behind the counter. 'Are you kidding me?' They squatted down next to me.

Snickering, Kyle said, 'Why else would they be here? They want to see how this plays out, first hand.'

While I hid my face in my hands, Todd chun-tered melodramatically, 'And I thought the shop was saved.'

'Can you get rid of everyone? This is humiliat-ing.' I felt sick.

'Hell no,' said Todd. 'Let's try and make the

most out of this as we can. Get out there and sell some books.' He gave me a cheeky wink.

'Thanks boss,' I huffed and stood up.

When I had time to glance up from my work, I could see there were more people loitering outside; peering in through the window. They didn't seem to be laughing at me though and the customers kept me busy enough not to entirely freak out, although I jumped half a foot every time the bell rang.

Having just matched one customer up with *Wuthering Heights*, trying to help her find a new literary boyfriend to help her get over Mr D'arcy, the bell tinkled again. Glancing at the door, I saw Neo enter, looking rather taken aback.

I ran my hand through my hair and smoothed over my clothes. My mouth was suddenly as dry as old parchment.

Neo approached, his shy smile completely beguiling.

He stopped in front of me, his eyes flicking around as the bustle in the shop abruptly vanished. Silence.

'Hi.' *Smooth Gabrielle, very smooth.*

We shared a look of mutual horror as we realised the customers seemed to be giving us all their attention.

'Hi.' He grinned again. 'I'm sorry about the radio, my producer's new. They knocked the switch without realising. Did you hear the rest of the show?'

SARAH-JANE FRASER

I shook my head.

'I only realised we'd been overheard when people started phoning in about it.' He looked over his shoulder. 'I had no idea they'd come out in force to see us.'

'Todd's happy the shop is so busy.'

'I didn't know we had this many listeners,' he replied with a wince. 'I'm sorry, I know you said you'd hate being on the radio.'

I tried to be cool and blasé. It's no problem. But my lips had gone numb with angst so a mumble came out.

Neo swallowed. 'It's only fair that I face my fears too.'

I nodded, racking my brains to think of what he'd said he was scared of.

'So, do you fancy getting away from this audience and perhaps going for a drink?'

'That sounds great, but I'm still working. I can't leave Todd in the lurch with all these customers.'

Kyle popped out of nowhere with my bag and coat. 'I'll cover for you Gabi, have fun.' He ushered us out of the door.

We walked along together, close, almost touching, but not. It was easier being outside and moving; I started to relax. There was a Farmers Market at the end of the road, a picturesque selection of stalls selling tasty produce and artisan foods you didn't know you needed. Our feet found themselves winding through it.

We purchased some hot chocolate from a drinks stall and I wrapped my chilly fingers around it appreciatively. The evening was drawing in and all the Christmas illuminations started to blink into life. Neo's eyes shone in the twinkling lights. We chatted easily and laughter flowed. I felt like I'd known him forever.

My brain tripped into overdrive as I drained the last drops from the paper cup. *Was this the thank you drink? Or was it just a friends' drink? Or a drink drink? Surely we should have a proper drink?*

Either I said something aloud or he read my thoughts but suddenly Neo said, 'The Pig and Rat?' He nodded towards a quirky student bar at the end of the street.

'Sounds good.'

It was quiet when we entered. After placing our order at the bar, we found a free sofa in a peaceful, tucked-away corner. Turning to face him as I sat down, I hooked a leg up, hugging my knee to my chest in a protective curl.

'Thank you so much for my present by the way.'

'You already thanked me.'

'Not in person.'

'It was my pleasure.'

Taking a sip of my wine spritzer, I built up the nerve to say, 'I don't want to sound tacky, but it was such a generous gift. How did you...' My question tapered off; I always felt awkward discussing money.

'Afford it?' Neo gave a shrug. Unperturbed. 'My grandma gave me a pretty hefty inheritance. When you told me about it reminding you of your Mamie, I thought it would put a bit of it to good use. She'd approve.'

I sat up straighter. 'Oh goodness. I'm so sorry for your loss.'

'Huh? Oh no, Grandma's still alive. She keeps giving us chunks of money. She wants to see her grandkids enjoy their "inheritance" while she's still here.'

'That's pretty amazing.'

He smiled fondly. 'She is. And your boss is too. He gave me your staff discount on top.'

Chuckling, I leaned back into the sofa. 'Todd's a good egg.'

Chatting with Neo was so easy. Even uncomfortable conversations were relaxed. Feeling emboldened, I continued my gentle grilling, fascinated to find out more about my mysterious benefactor.

Swirling my drink in the glass, I asked, 'So, what was it that you're so afraid of?' A flirty tone came out in my voice. *Where did that come from?*

He took a deep swig of his beer. 'I've been trying to ask you out for weeks, for most of last term.'

That stopped me in my tracks. 'Really?' I hope

red suited me as I was now coloured from head to toe.

'Yeah, I kept trying to pluck up the courage.'

My heart did some acrobats with my stomach, flip-flopping in tandem.

'I did notice that you popped in a lot.'

He flashed me that gorgeous dimple. 'I couldn't resist.'

Suddenly, I was very conscious that my knee was gently touching his.

'So, when exactly is it that you're going to confront your fears and ask me out?'

Neo's eyes widened. 'I thought we were...'

'Just teasing.'

He chuckled. 'You're not going to make this easy for me.'

'You did broadcast me on live radio without asking!'

'I've had an idea about that. How about facing those fears, but with you in control?'

I gazed at him, intrigued.

'Do you want to come on my show and advertise the shop? Really exorcise your demons and help out Greenway's.'

'Is this another date?'

'Oh god, no. That sounded bad, I-'

I nudged Neo with my elbow. 'I'm messing again.'

'I think I'm struggling to get the hang of this asking you on a date thing.'

'Hmmm, perhaps you need to keep practising.'

'Speaking of which, what are you doing tomorrow night? It's New Year's Eve. Fancy spending it together?'

Taking another sip of my spritzer, I tried to play it cool. 'I was going to have some quality time with my new book...'

'Well, if you come out with me instead, maybe I could ask you on a date for next year too. Really consolidate my new skill?'

'It's worth a try.' I flashed him a coy look.

He placed a hand on my knee and leant in closer. So close I could see how his long eyelashes curled up so thickly that they twisted together. My breath caught in my chest, was he about to-? No.

A glass broke near-by, shattering the moment.

Looking around, Neo waggled his eyebrows. 'They've found us,' he joked.

Our secluded spot was becoming busier as more and more students started filing in to the bar.

Heart racing, I didn't want this evening to end yet, I asked, 'Are you feeling hungry?'

'What are you thinking? Go somewhere for a bite?'

'I've been given this amazing recipe book, maybe you could come back to mine and I could try something out on you?'

'What a wonderful gift.' His dimple peeked out at me and I melted a bit more. 'Let's go.'

He jumped up and held a hand out to me, pulling me up as I took a hold. Wrapping our fingers together, we made our way out of the bar, entwined.

It was much quieter in the street and the cold breeze stung at my ears. We ambled along to the river which reflected the pretty lights from its sparkling surface, and followed its gently winding course.

'While we're cooking perhaps we can work on what you're going to say on the radio.'

'I'm still not a hundred percent sold about being on the radio,' I confessed.

'I've recently found out that confronting your fears is exhilarating.' He gave my fingers a squeeze. 'I promise I'll be there to help you; we can script it all.'

I paused, and leant on the wrought iron safety railing. My heart now pounding for a different reason.

'You'd have it written down for back up.' Neo looked earnest. 'And it would help out Todd and the shop, wouldn't it?'

'How do you know about that?'

'I was in Greenway's a lot, I couldn't help but pick up on it.'

I sighed. 'I guess you're right.' *He just faced his fear, I could too.* 'I've had this idea about an event for 'Dry January', perhaps having some mocktails in the shop and selling self-help books, or cookery and fitness type things. Maybe we could announce that?'

'That's a brilliant idea.' Neo gave me a knee weakening smile.

My eyes were drawn to his mouth and again I wondered what it would feel like on mine. I'm sure he could tell what I was thinking. His tongue flicked out to moisten his lips. His head moved slowly, fractionally towards mine then suddenly he turned away to look over at the river.

I held my breath, tantilised. Frustrated. Nervous.

After a moment, he said, 'I have another deadly fear, I wonder if you could help me with it?'

'I'll do my best,' I whispered, matching his hushed tones.

'There's this beautiful woman who I've been trying to ask out.' He turned back to me. 'Instead, I keep going to her bookshop asking for her help.'

Blinking, I nodded.

'The thing is, I'm petrified of kissing her. What if she pushes me away? Anything you could recommend?'

I moved towards him. 'You know, there's this book called Feel the Fear and Do it Anyway.'

He came closer still, mere centimetres from my face.

'You could try reading that,' I whispered.

He crushed his mouth on to mine, sending fire

from my lips way down deep inside. Mussing my hair with his hand, he pulled me to him and I felt the heat from his body as he pressed against me. The kiss was as passionate as I'd imagined it would be. The heat of our embrace was chased by goose-bumps and a longing for more, as eventually, Neo pulled away.

Glad he was holding me, I felt giddy.

'I knew there was a reason I kept going to you for advice.'

'You should really practice confronting this fear too,' I suggested.

He cupped my face and softly pressed his lips against mine again, it was sweeter this time, calmer and somehow the tingle plunged more deeply to my core.

Tendrils of garlic curled through the air from a waterfront restaurant and my stomach rumbled.

Neo moved his lips to my neck and chuckled at the sound. 'We need to get back to yours for something to eat.'

'I've just realised the flaw in my plan.'

He pulled away slightly. 'Oh?'

I scrunched my nose. 'I haven't translated any recipes yet... and I haven't actually got any food in. Just some left-over turkey curry that my mum packed me off with.'

'That's okay. Do you fancy going out for dinner? There's a lovely Italian in smelling distance from here.'

Relieved, I grinned. 'Sounds amazing.'

He took my hand again and started leading me towards the source of the divine scent.

'You're getting really good at this asking me on a date thing.'

'I'm going to keep practising.' His fingers tightened around mine. 'Make sure I don't lose my knack.'

The End

FOUR CALLING BIRDS

A Christmas Short Story

Am I the only fiancée that's become obsessed with the bathroom? I say I'm just popping in to wash my hands or check my hair, but that's my cover story. It's for the spot lights. I'm addicted. I love the way they hit my diamond and ricochet onto the surfaces, the ceiling, the floor; a thousand tiny sparkles. I'm obsessed. It's my own personal glitter ball. I can't wait to tell the girls.

Kirsty, Annie, Beth and I have been best friends since school days and even if geography keeps us apart we're still very close. Today is Christmas Eve, so I've organised a video call between the four of us. Just because we can't celebrate in person, doesn't mean we can't celebrate together.

'I'm setting up in the bathroom, the Wi-Fi signal's better in here,' I call out as I shut the door behind me. The signal's no different, but the lighting is certainly better.

I put the lid down on the toilet to make a seat and balance my laptop over the sink. It's not too bad; I've been in worse offices.

Opening up the programme, I log on, eager for the other girls to join the meeting. As I wait, I study the patterns of the ring's refraction shimmering over the walls. The bubbles in my glass of chilled prosecco are streaming persistently to the surface, condensation has clouded the outside of the glass. Perfection. The location may leave a little to be desired but, really, this is no

313

different to enjoying a glass of wine in the bath after a long day. Minus the silly shower cap, of course.

A ding sounds out letting me know someone else is logging on.

'Hey Beth!' Her beaming face fills my screen. She's wearing a hair band with large wobbly reindeer antlers attached. 'Happy Christmas!'

'Thanks, Jenny. Merry Christmas! And thanks so much for my gift.'

'I'm glad you opened it.'

Beth holds up her new champagne flute, filled with fizz. I'd been busy shopping on the Internet and sent all the girls a bottle of bubbly and some fancy glassware too. It's been a challenge, but I wanted to make our festive reunion as special as I could from so far away.

'Cheers!' We both call out and I move my glass carefully to the camera as if to clink.

'Where are you?' she asks.

'The bathroom.' I don't want to go into the whys just yet, I want to tell them all at once. He only proposed the other day and I've been itching to shout about it since then, but trying to coordinate us four in the same place at the same time takes quite a bit of organisation, what with time differences and working patterns, so, I decided to wait for our Christmas call and hijack it with my news. Squeeee, I can't wait!

Luckily, the picture goes jerky and the sound cuts out before bursting back on again, saving me from further probing. Annie's chest has muscled onto the display.

'Merry Christmas, girls!'

'Merry Christmas to your girls too, Annie,' I laugh.

'Huh?'

'Have you only sent your boobs along to represent you today?' asked Beth.

'Ha ha! It's my gift for you all - a virtual motorboat!' Annie cackles and then plumps her cleavage for effect, leaving the camera purposefully on her chest.

'You are good to us, thanks Annie,' replies Beth. 'Who invited her?' she stage-whispers.

'Thanks for the Prosecco.' Annie holds up her glass. 'Can't wait until we can do this in person.'

Just then, Kirsty's box nudges its way onto the screen, I have it on gallery mode so I can see all four of us at the same time. We look like a mini version of Celebrity Squares, but with three heads and a pair of boobs. Finally, we're all here.

Kirsty's dark hair's a mess, she looks like hell. Her lips are moving but there's no sound.

'You're on mute!' We all sing out.

I can lip read some swear words, the screen freezes on her rolling her eyes, and then corrects itself as the sound starts. 'Alrigh'?' she croaks.

Annie readjusts her camera position so she can get a better look, suddenly her eyes dance into view. 'Are you? You look awful.'

'Thanks very much. Happy Christmas,' she

says feebly.

'Where's your drink?' I worry. 'Did my parcel not arrive?'

'Yeah... it's in the fridge.' Kirsty looks a bit green around the gills just thinking about it.

'And why is it not in your hand?' Annie demands. 'Where are you? It looks like a prison.'

'I'm in the loo. Just in case. I'm feeling... ropey.'

'Me too!' Annie laughs. 'Although I'm in here to get ready. I've got a *vate*.'

'Huh?' I ask. 'You made that up, right? Is that a video-date or something?'

'Close. A virtual date.' She blushes which is quite irregular for my usually brazen friend.

'On Christmas Eve?' asks Beth.

'Well, you've got to strike while cupid's arrow's hot... or something like that. What do you think? I'm doing full make up. I may have to straighten this mess...' She pulls at a chunk of her tight brown curls.

'No, don't. I love your 'fro,' I reply. 'And surely you want to look like you?'

'Well, I am keeping my joggers and slippers on.' Annie turns away from the screen and primps at her hair in the mirror. 'Hmmm...'

'Are you all in your bathrooms?' Beth is incredulous. 'No one told me.' Her feed lurches around suddenly. 'I'm going in the bathroom too.' As she carries us along with her we get some pixelated, half frozen visions of her house, before the picture settles. A tiled wall crowned by a shower appears on the screen.

'What are you doing?' says Annie, peering at the lens.

'Getting in the bath.'

'Not naked, I hope,' groans Kirsty.

'No, silly! There's a bath tray. It's perfect to balance my tablet on.' Her legs step onto the screen then she wiggles down, places a rolled towel behind her head and lies back in the empty bath, holding her glass, looking smug.

'I miss you guys,' I lament. 'So, why are you feeling so rough, K?'

'Must have had a few too many. Last night.' Kirsty can barely speak in a sentence.

'Hair of the dog, is what you need.' Annie stabs her mascara wand towards her device.

Kirsty shudders.

'Do you want to reschedule?' My friend is ashen. Of course, it'd put the kybosh on my big revelation but, really, I'd prefer her to be healthy and rest up before the big day tomorrow.

'No, no,' she mumbles.

'What on earth were you drinking? It's not like you to get so hungover, you poor thing.'

'I didn't have much. Maybe the wine had corked or something.'

'Corked wine wouldn't do this to you,' says Beth. 'And you'd taste it at the time.'

'Could it be food poisoning? How's Steve?' I knew her husband well. We all hung out a lot when we were younger. I was head bridesmaid at their wedding. 'Is he feeling rough too?'

'He's scoffing at me while drinking beer. It's half the reason I'm in here.'

Looking like she's trying to be diplomatic, Beth starts to ask, 'Kirsty, could you be… pr-'

'I'm not pregnant!' Kirsty's voice screeches and distorts.

'I'm sorry, I was just trying to-' Beth's voice tails off and she looks awkward.

Annie takes over. 'When was your last period?'

'It's due… but I already said. I'm not pregnant. Why does everyone's minds automatically go to this conclusion?'

'Because we're girls. Bad hangovers always equal suspicions of pregnancy. It's a fact.'

'Well, I'm not.'

'There could be a number of perfectly good explanations.' I try to defend Kirsty.

'But are you sure? Have you had unprotected sex recently?' Annie has asked with all the delicacy of a t-rex trying to wrap Christmas presents whilst wearing oven mitts. She's always blundering in, speaking before thinking. The worst thing is she's usually right.

Kirsty pauses and then mumbles, 'There's not been a lot else to do recently.'

'Well, that's it then. Unprotected sex, unusually awful hangover… there's no other explanation.'

'It could just be that I drank too much! I only came off the pill last month, and I was on it for years. It's going to take months to clear my system.'

'Or not. Isn't it risky if you only miss one?' Annie is pulling her no-nonsense face.

'Well, yeah but everything I've read says it can take up to a year when you first stop.'

Annie is persistent. 'But what about the times that people get pregnant when they're actually still taking it?'

Blanching to an even paler shade, Kirsty says, 'But I can't be pregnant, we only just started trying.'

'There is a good chance that you are though.' Beth bites her lip.

'I can't be. I told Steve it'd take at least six months.'

'Ladies!' I try and calm things. Kirsty looks like she's feeling bad enough without us haranguing her. Perhaps if I can change the subject, the others will lay off her. But what do I say? I so want to tell them my news, but I hesitate. I'm not sure how to do it without sounding braggy and inconsiderate.

'Have you done a test?' Annie pipes up again.

Kirsty hesitates. 'No...'

'You should do one.'

Beth nods along in agreement.

To be fair, Annie's right. 'Yes, you should do one...' I agree, recalling Kirsty excitedly telling me she'd bought some when she first decided to come off the pill.

'I'm not...' Kirsty's voice peters out. She stares at us with eyes wide and blood shot, betraying a hint of terror, but also hope.

'K.' I focus on just her face on the screen. 'Why not do one now, we're all here to support you, whatever the result.'

She hesitates, looking torn. 'I can't pee on a stick in front of you.'

'You've peed in front of me many a time.' Annie's words are a bit muffled as she's pouting to apply some gloss, using the webcam as her mirror

'And me,' Beth agrees. 'Half the time there's a free cubicle, but you insist on coming in with me.'

'I'm not usually sober.'

'Yet another reason to be toasting Christmas with us.' Beth holds up her glass meaningfully.

'Think of the times I held your dress up at the wedding. And you don't need to focus the camera on the act,' I add. 'Turn us to the wall or something, in case you get shy kidneys.'

'I couldn't.'

Annie disappears from view and there's a rummaging sound. She comes back into shot. 'I will if you will.'

'What do you mean?' Kirsty looks suspicious, although her interest has clearly been piqued.

Annie holds up a thin, white plastic wrapped

packet. 'My flatmate's paranoid, she's got a stash of these in the cabinet, 'just in case'.'

'Are you suggesting what I think you're suggesting?'

'I'll go first and then you can see how easy it is to pee in front of us, then you do it.'

Kirsty gulps.

'Come on!' Annie unwraps the little stick and holds it up.

'Should I mute you or something?' I ask.

'Nah.' Annie flicks the screen up to focus on the ceiling and there's a muffled sound in the background. 'It says to hold it in the flow for five seconds. Can someone do a timer?'

'Yep.' Beth holds up her wrist with a watch on.

'Okay - go!' Calls out Annie's voice.

'Should we just talk amongst ourselves?' I ask over the sudden tinkling sound.

'It's alright, Beth needs to focus on counting.'

Feeling the need to divert my attention, I study my ring, it looks huge under the lights. A flash of excitement jolts through my stomach at the thought of everything to come. I can't wait to share this with them, but I need to make sure Kirsty is okay first.

'Stop!' Beth announces after a short while.

'I'll just put this on the side for a couple of minutes and then we'll check the result.' The sound of Annie's toilet flushing and a tap running goes off in the background. Then she comes back into shot, readjusting the screen. 'Where were we? Oh yeah, your turn, Kirsty.'

She shakes her head. 'I don't need to go yet.'

'I'm in no rush,' replies Beth.

'My hot vate isn't for another hour or so.' Annie confirms.

'Yep, all the time in the world over here,' I add. I swipe my hair behind an ear and smile at her reassuringly.

'Urgh!'

'Did you get my email, by the way?' Beth asks.

She'd photo-shopped our heads onto a cartoon of some dancing elves and selected our favourite pop song to be played in the background. 'Yes, it was hysterical!' I reply.

'It's just until we can all meet up properly again, and then I'm paying for us all to have a spa day.'

'That sounds amazing,' I reply sincerely. 'Thanks.'

Annie's gone back to sorting her hair in the background. 'Your gifts are all here, wrapped and ready. They won't survive the post, so you'll just have to wait.' She flashes us a cheeky grin.

'I... I kind of forgot,' confesses Kirsty. Her head resting on the sink pedestal. 'Sorry.'

Annie moves back in shot of the camera and pointedly raises an eyebrow. 'Getting forgetful, huh?'

'Oh, bugger off! It would serve you right, if your test is positive.'

Reaching out, off screen, Annie picks up the

stick. She pulls it into the range of the camera. There's just one blue line.

'How do you even read those things?' asks Beth.

Annie holds up the packet next to it to show the meaning of the results. 'Not pregnant!' she sings.

Kirsty sticks her tongue out. 'Fine. I'll show you I'm not either.' She flounces out of the room.

A concerned look crosses Beth's face. 'What are we going to do if she is pregnant?'

'Celebrate!' Annie laughs.

'I can text Steve if she goes into shock.' I wave my phone in the air.

'And if she's not?' Beth continues to worry.

'I'll get Steve on stand-by.'

'Wouldn't he want to be involved?' Beth asks.

'Who? With what?' Kirsty has returned to the bathroom.

'Steve. Shouldn't he be doing this with you?' says Beth.

'Nah, I don't want to freak him out. Especially as I know the result and I'm only doing this to shut you lot up.'

'Delightful,' Annie retorts.

Are you at home? I text Steve.

Are you texting me while on a video call with my wife? Comes his reply. I can picture his face full of bemusement.

Lol. Yep. Nothing to worry about. Just listen out for her in case she feels unwell.

Already on it. I have a bowl, some water and a rehydration sachet at the ready.

I send him a thumbs up emoji. Kirsty's got a good one in Steve. But then again, I've not done too badly myself.

As my attention returns to the conversation, I find Kirsty is talking through how to do her particular test.

'It's a pain they're all a bit different,' comments Beth.

'You could pee in a cup too,' says Annie.

'Ewww, then I'd never be able to drink from it again.'

'You could wash it!'

'Still no. Right. Let's get this over with. Beth, you're on timer duty. Jenny, you're on moral support. Annie, you're practising being quiet.'

Annie salutes to the camera while Beth and I agree. Kirsty directs her device at the mirror so we all see a reflection of ourselves looking back.

'Ready?' Beth holds her watch up.

'Okay, go.' Kirsty's voice is quieter in the background.

I'm not really sure how to be supportive of someone peeing on a stick. 'You can do this!' I call out and then stop, feeling rather obsolete.

'Aaaannd - stop!' Beth announces after a moment.

'So, I'll just put this over here.' I can hear the forced calmness in Kirsty's voice. 'And wait.'

'It'll be okay,' I try and reassure her.

'Annie, you're being too quiet. It's disconcerting. Tell us about this date tonight.' Kirsty is clearly trying to distract herself.

Annie grins. 'We've swapped a few emails, they seem nice. Asks stuff about me, replies to things I've said. We seem to have some stuff in common.'

'Any dick pics?' asks Beth.

'None yet!'

'Sounds promising.' I'm so pleased for Annie. She ended things with her fiancé six months ago and insists she's fine as it was her decision. However, she's always been evasive about why they split and gives a different ridiculous reason each time. The most recent, and my favourite by far, is that it was because he chewed his toenails. It conjured so many vile images, I have to applaud her for immediately putting us off further grilling.

'This is just a drink. If it goes well I might suggest we cook a meal together, virtually of course.'

'Very wise.' Beth nods. 'Then you can find out if he smacks his lips together when he eats or talks with his mouthful.'

Annie looks stricken, probably at the reference to another of her ex's 'flaws' that she'd mentioned.

Trying to put her out of her misery, I say, 'What about you, Beth? Any guys on the horizon?'

'No, I'm enjoying being single for a bit after everything with Craig. Plus work is crazy.' Beth's last boyfriend unceremoniously left her after she got made redundant, prompting a move back to her mum's house. It was a really low point for her, but like a phoenix from the ashes she's risen up, setting up her own legal consultancy firm, which is doing extremely well, even if her office is the spare bedroom.

Annie starts to say, 'What about you, Jenny? How's things with you?' When Beth holds up her watch.

'That's your two minutes. Time to check the result.'

Kirsty looks down the barrel of the camera. 'Time to find out how wrong you all are.' She picks up the stick and looks at it. It's too far away to clearly see the display. She puts it down and picks up the instructions. After a pause, she picks up the stick again. Her head moving between the two. She swallows.

'Wellll?' We all seem to say at the same time.

'It's-'

'Yes?' My god, she's killing me.

'It's... I'm... It's... I'm positive. It's pregnant. I mean, I'm pregnant.' She holds out the white stick, there's one bold blue line and one a lighter, but still very visible, blue line.

There's chaos. Annie, Beth and I start squealing, while Kirsty is staring at the stick, jaw slack. Beth pummels her feet on the bath. Annie's stretched her arms out and is shaking her hair around.

I've moved so close to the screen I'm about an inch away. 'Are you okay?'

Kirsty nods, still stunned. A smile creeps across her face and she looks up. 'I'm okay... I'm great... I'm... I'm pregnant!' She suddenly starts leaping up and down, the stick clutched in her hand. 'Wahoooo-' She calls out.

'Everything alright?' Steve's voice sounds out in the background.

'Shhhhh!' Kirsty comes back into focus and presses a finger to her lips, laughing. Her eyes suddenly brighter. 'All good, just some Christmas fun,' she calls back to him.

'Don't you want him to know?' I whisper.

She looks to the closed door. 'God, I'm desperate to tell him.'

'Go on then, we can reschedule the call for another time.'

Kirsty gives her head a resolute shake. 'I'm going to force myself to wait.'

'How come, surely you're bursting?'

She answers by jumping up and down again, this time silently, fists pumping the air, her mouth wide as if she's screaming.

It's so lovely to see her so happy. After some more leaping, which develops into some crazy dance moves, complete with cheerleading routine and head banging, she sighs loudly and takes hold of her device in both hands, slumping down the wall to the floor. 'Sorry about that. I'm sooo-ooo excited!'

'Please don't stop or apologise on our account.'

'Tired,' Kirsty says, content and breathless.

'Go and tell Steve!' shouts Annie.

She shakes her head stubbornly. 'If I tell him tomorrow, it'll make up for the fact that his Christmas present is crap. I couldn't find anything he'd like, even though I searched everywhere online. Besides, I want a bit of time to get used to the idea. Just me and Em.' She rubs her tummy.

'Em?' Asks Beth.

'Em the embryo.' Kirsty shrugs. 'I think it suits it. Then we could call them Emma or Emmett...' She starts counting names off on her fingers. 'Emmory, Ember, Empress...'

'I think the baby's affected her brain already,' says Annie, pretending she doesn't know that Kirsty can hear her.

Beth suddenly claps. 'Oh, I hope we can all get together properly before too long. Then we can have a party... a baby shower!'

'I love that idea,' says Kirsty.

'You're organising it, right Jenny?' Annie interjects.

'I'd be honoured. You know I love to organise.'

'And you've not had much chance to exercise that talent recently. Good ol' Kirsty giving you an excuse to brush up on your planning skills.'

Annie waggles her eyebrows.

It crosses my mind that soon I'm going to have an awful lot of wonderful things to organise, but they don't know that. A shiver of excitement tingles up my spine and I smile to myself.

How am I going to tell them now though? It feels a bit weird to share my news. I don't want to steal Kirsty's thunder. Although, babies trump rings. So, technically, she'd be stealing my thunder. But if I wait until another day and they find out I didn't tell them straight away, they'd think that was weirder. I don't know what to do! And I'm so happy for Kirsty, this should be all about her.

I really shouldn't say anything.

I won't.

My phone vibrates with a text message, pulling me out of my contemplation. It's probably just Steve wondering what all the fuss is about. I look down at my phone while Beth and Annie are discussing potential baby shower games.

It's from Kirsty.

Don't think I haven't noticed.

I look at the screen, but she's looking off to the side.

What do you mean?

You know! I may be super hungover, distracted and now, apparently, pregnant, but I'm not blind.

She can't know. I send her a head scratching emoji and watch her mouth curl with a smile as she reads the message.

How many carats is it?! She sends a few carrot pictures for good measure.

What? How can she possibly know?

She replies with a diamond ring emoji, and then a series of miniature streamers, popping champagne and heart eyes.

Looking up I can see she's beaming in to the camera.

How did you know?

I'm your bestie. I know you better than you know yourself… and I saw the paragon on your finger

I've been deliberately drinking with my right hand so no one would see!

You played with your hair.

And you managed to see it from that?

You're hosting a videocall from a bathroom! I was on the lookout for it from the get go!

But how did you * know *?

The amount of times you dragged me in to public toilets to look at the rock Steve gave me… I just knew.

She's too bloody observant for her own good. Kirsty always seems to sense what's going on before everyone else. I look up to the screen and she's still grinning at me. There's mascara all over her face, her hair's a wreck but, she's radiant, lit from inside by happiness.

Why haven't you said anything?

I read the text and look up to see Kirsty looking expectantly at the screen.

It's your moment.

I give a little head shake to the screen. Beth and Annie are too absorbed in their discussion to notice our non-verbal communication.

You were going to tell us until I ruined it, weren't you? She immediately sends another message. This is the best day ever. I want us to celebrate together!

Looking mischievous, Kirsty interrupts Beth and Annie's heated debate over the politics of gender reveals. 'Girls, girls, can we wait until I've had a scan before you get too carried away. It's still early days, you know. Can we talk about something else?'

Beth and Annie nod, eyes wide and innocent; looking like kids who've been caught stealing mince pies.

'Speaking of games, hadn't you planned some Christmas fun, Jen?' Kirsty waggles her eyebrows.

I know what she's up to. She's trying to give me an 'in'. The announcement of a baby is a hard act to follow and, honestly, I don't think I should be even trying. I'll just tell them another time. I'm sure they'll understand. I'm sure I can wait.

Trying to put her off, I say, 'Well, there's Pictionary?'

'That's a bit difficult in a bathroom. But I could use my lipstick on the mirror?' offers Annie.

'Charades?' I suggest.

'Nope, my family will have me playing that

solidly between the queen's speech and the Vicar of Dibley reruns tomorrow,' says Beth.

Looking up from texting on her phone, Kirsty says, 'How about two truths and a lie?' In a falsely innocent voice that only I can detect.

'Sounds good,' says Annie. 'Although you know I can't keep secrets, so you'll know mine straight away.'

Beth looks at her phone, distracted and then, zones back in on us. 'Okay.' Her voice sounds timid.

'If you insist.' I roll my eyes. I'm torn. I'm super excited to tell them, my limbs feel all jangly.

'Fab. I'll go first. Which of these is the lie?' She sounds all sing-songy and playful. 'One of my best friends is buying a house.' She counts off on her fingers. 'One of my best friends is engaged… I'm not pregnant.' With a toothy grin she watches all our faces.

Well, that's easy.

Wait.

No way! TWO of those are truths? And the lie must be that she's not pregnant - as we all know she is. Kirsty throws her head back and laughs at all of our responses. You can virtually see the cogs whirring in heads. Our eyes dart suspiciously between each other to see who might be responsible for what.

Annie breaks the impasse. 'So which one of you is buying a house? And which one of you is

ENGAGED?!'

Mystery solved! 'You're buying a house, Beth? That's amazing!' I call out.

Beth's large eyes grow bigger. 'Oh my god! You're engaged!'

'Let's see the ring!'

'Have you set a date?'

'When are you moving?'

'How did he do it?'

'Can you send a link to the estate agents?'

'What's the floor plan like?'

We are all in a tizzy chaos of excitement and intrigue, everyone's shouting and cheering. One of the squares darkens as we are plunged towards Annie's chest again, as she smushes the screen into a hug. There's a muffled sound, so I suspect she's the one now jumping about.

Kirsty, looking significantly better than she did at the start of the call, is grinning from ear to ear. 'Sorry both of you. I know you wanted to share your news today, but you're both too blooming polite to do it. Especially after my bombshell.'

'Give us a looksee then,' says Beth, sitting up straighter.

As I hold my left hand up to the little circle at the top of the screen, the spotlights, dance off it, blinding with a brilliant white gleam. My best friends move in for a better look, their squares all suddenly filled with a close up of their beautiful faces. They 'ooh and ahhh' and my elation spills out with a giggle.

'Jeez, you three! This is the best bloody Christmas ever!' Annie announces.

And it is.

We're more than best friends, we're family. Wherever we are in the world, whatever's going on, we've always got each other. And that's all we need for a happy Christmas.

The End

MORE FROM JENNY AND THE GANG...

If you enjoyed this dalliance into the world of Jenny and friends then try The Spanish Indecision, the first in the Jenny Abroad Series and a finalist in The Wishing Shelf Book Award 2018.

Want to find out more?

Visit here to get your copy of The Spanish Indecision: http://mybook.to/SpanishIndecision

Exciting news:
The sequel is out in 2021!

ACKNOWLEDGEMENTS

This collection of Christmas stories would not have been possible without the help of these wonderful people. Thank you so much for everything you have done.

Hannah Ellis
Alexandra O'Malley
Lisa West
Karen Champion-Patching
Gillian Baxter
Kathryn Fraser
Jenny Kane
Natalie Potts
Faye Cardwell
Andrew Fraser
the wonderfully supportive community
at ChickLitChatHQ
and my Facebook and Twitter followers
who provided me with inspiration
for names, coffee flavours etc.

Thank you to Kirsty McManus for
the beautiful cover design.

BOOKS BY THIS AUTHOR

The Spanish Indecision

Sun, sangria and a scantily clad gladiator- the girly getaway to Spain is just what Jenny George needs to get her head straight. Stuck in a rut at work and fed up with being single, Jenny is desperate to make some changes. The trouble is she's too concerned about everyone else to sort her own life out.

With her best friend's hen-do to orchestrate and other people's problems to solve, the last thing on her mind is romance. Typical Jenny, she keeps missing the hot guy who is staying in their resort. But he's seen her. Is Jenny too distracted to discover who her mystery man is?

Lose yourself in this light-hearted summer romance, and see if Jenny can find herself... and her man.

The Spanish Indecision is a finalist in the Wishing Shelf Book Awards 2018.

Candlelight And Snowball Fights

Grab a hot chocolate, tuck your toes under a loved one and curl up on the sofa with this sweet winter romance…

When Nancy arrives in Denmark to visit her best friend, Tessa, everything seems perfect; the fire is roaring and the snow is gently falling. It's a winter wonderland.

As the snow gets thicker she discovers that things aren't as perfect as they appear. Eager to reconnect with her friend, Nancy is hurt when Tessa is wrapped up with her new beau, leaving her lonely and out in the cold.

Tessa's mysterious colleague, Torben, steps in to keep Nancy company. He could easily be mistaken for a Nordic god but can Nancy melt his icy demeanour?

Will romance kindle as Nancy and Torben get cosy at the fireside? And will Nancy and Tessa's friendship weather the storm? Find out in this warming winter novella… a tale of friendship, love and woolly jumpers.

ABOUT THE AUTHOR

Sarah-Jane Fraser

Sarah-Jane Fraser lives in the West Country with her husband and two daughters.

She's a book worm and loves losing herself in books, both reading and writing. If it's good escapism she loves it, chicklit, fantasy, anything. She knew at the age of six that she wanted to be an author but it took her a little whle to listen to her younger self.

Her debut novel, The Spanish Indecision, was a finalist in the Wishing Shelf Book Award 2018.

KEEP IN TOUCH

I'd love to hear from you!

I love hearing reviews, book recommendations and seeing beautiful cover art, so it would be great to hear from you. For information on forthcoming releases and other bookish things that tickle me then you can follow me here:

Twitter - @S_JFraser
Instagram - sarahjanefraser1
Facebook - www.facebook.com/sjfraserauthor
Goodreads - Sarah-Jane Fraser
Pinterest - @SJFraser

Did you know?

The best thing you can do to help an author is leave a review. I'd be very grateful if you could leave a review on Amazon, Goodreads or anywhere else you fancy. It doesn't have to be long- just a short sentence would be wonderful. Thank you!

Printed in Great Britain
by Amazon